Bliss Jumps the Gun

Bliss Jumps the Gun

A Lenny Bliss Mystery

Bob Sloan

W. W. Norton & Company
New York · London

Copyright © 1999 by Bob Sloan

First published as a Norton paperback 2000

All rights reserved
Printed in the United States of America

For information about permission to reproduce selections from this book,
write to Permissions, W. W. Norton & Company, Inc., 500 Fifth Avenue,
New York, NY 10110.

The text of this book is composed in Waldbaum
with the display set in Matrix Narrow
Composition by A. W. Bennett, Inc.
Manufacturing by Courier Companies
Book design by Chris Welch

Library of Congress Cataloging-in-Publication Data

Sloan, Bob.
Bliss jumps the gun : a Lenny Bliss mystery / Bob Sloan.
p.   cm.
ISBN 0-393-04750-4
I. Title.
PS3569.L5B58   1999
813.54—dc21   99-11662
CIP

ISBN 0-393-32114-2 pbk.

W. W. Norton & Company, Inc., 500 Fifth Avenue, New York, N.Y. 10110
www.wwnorton.com

W. W. Norton & Company Ltd., 10 Coptic Street, London WC1A 1PU

1 2 3 4 5 6 7 8 9 0

For Colonel William Patrick Kennedy

Goin' somewhere I ain't never been before.
　　　　　　　　—Mississippi Fred MacDowell

Act I

Chapter 1

Bliss was wearing the wrong shoes. He should have worn his sneakers, but for some reason at the last second he put on his work shoes, and now instead of darting lithely along the catwalk like the others, he was lumbering.

There were four of them jumping off the Brooklyn Bridge that night, led by an aging hippie who called himself Icarus. Dressed in shorts and sandals, his long black hair flowing past his shoulders, the bungee cord slung casually over his back, the guy looked like he had just strolled in from Venice Beach rather than Flatbush.

They were creeping along on a catwalk under the roadway, the East River hundreds of feet below, black water reflecting the lights of Wall Street where legions of cleaning women worked through the night. Bliss wished he were one of them. Then he wouldn't be where he was on the bridge.

Traffic raced above them, a steady stream of cars even at 2 A.M., oblivious to the panic rising in the throat of the forty-two-year-old cop stumbling just below, trying desperately to prove something, the details of which—like what exactly he was trying to prove and who he wanted to prove it to—were as yet unclear.

Because Bliss had fallen into one of his dark moods. His homicide detective's diet of despair and ugliness was forming a thick barrier between himself and those he loved—his wife, his kids, even his partner, Ward. His own Iron Curtain. The Wall had crumbled in East Berlin, but it was sturdy and intact around Lenny Bliss.

He needed to do something—take some kind of action.

Homicide relied on the whims of the bad guys, waiting for a cascade of rage or jealousy to flood some poor soul, make him go berserk and kill. Then, like scavengers, Bliss and his fellow detectives fed on the remains. He was tired of being at the mercy of the chimeras of evil and death.

So he came up with this plan by following his usual M.O.: Do it all at once. Like the song says, he packed up all his troubles in his old kit bag—and then beat the bag with a stick until it didn't move anymore.

He tripped, banging his knee against one of the girders. The others looked back, and in the darkness Bliss could feel their looks of pity. He hated being in the rear. He wanted to tell them that in high school he was always picked first in gym class. That he wasn't an end-of-the-line kind of guy. He was Lenny Bliss—Homicide. He'd taken guns away from guys who'd rip your ear off your face as easily as pulling petals from a daisy. Easier. There weren't a lot of daisies growing in Manhattan. He decided that if he tripped again, he'd arrest them all, which is what he should have done in the first place— whipped out his badge and cuffs and arrested them before they'd even got started on this eccentric expedition.

But he hadn't. Because he believed that this, The Big Jump, would actually help—one giant leap for Lenny over the grim malaise enveloping him like a shroud. Richard Simmons said a person had to push past the fears and mental limitations he placed on himself. Richard had said that on TV the other morning, and he was looking right at Bliss when he said it. That's where The Big Jump came in. He had to do it for Richard. He wanted to be able to walk right up to him and say, "I did it, I pushed past my fears and limitations!" And then feel the soft brush of Richard's curls on his cheek as he was given a patented Richard Simmons hug.

It was either serendipity or kismet—whichever was the more nefarious—that had led Bliss to overhear two guys talk-

ing about Icarus and his midnight leaps off the Brooklyn
Bridge. He'd been in the bar at the comedy club waiting to
pick up his wife, Rachel, after her last set. "It's the most amazing rush," he heard one guy say. "It makes you look at everything completely different." And Bliss said to himself, *I* want
an amazing rush. *I* want to look at everything differently. The
guy also said Rachel had nice bazooms. Bliss let it go. They
were nice bazooms.

Bliss got the phone number and called Icarus, which was
how he had wound up on the bridge that balmy May night,
about to jump into oblivion. Rachel would no doubt make it
part of her next comedy routine. She'd riff on his panic—
how he was frantically thinking of excuses for turning back,
afraid to confront his fears. Lenny Bliss, who was so needy
that he would even make Richard Simmons depressed, make
Richard gorge on ice cream sundaes and chocolate cake.

They continued in silence. Bliss felt the walkway flatten-
ing out as they neared the center of the bridge. Icarus put up
his hand and they stopped. He dropped to his knees, whipped
out a wrench, and loosened some bolts on the metal grating.
A few seconds later he liberated a three-foot-square piece of
the catwalk and set it down silently. It felt like a scene from
The Dirty Dozen.

The girl was going first, Bliss second. Icarus communicated
all this silently, with hand signals, like they were under water
and he was Lloyd Bridges in *Sea Hunt.* Bliss watched the girl
strap on the harness with cool efficiency. She was all business.
He liked her. She was all of five feet, Chinese or Japanese, with
short hair and a lurid tattoo of a tiger on her shoulder lurking under the strap of her tank top. She casually buckled the
bungee cord into the harness, her face composed, confident,
betraying not the slightest hint of fear. She pulled a white
rabbit's foot out of her pocket and tossed it into the hole. "For
luck," she said. Bliss's stomach did a Luganis. She then kissed

her boyfriend hard on the lips and slipped into the hole like an otter slipping into the sea, disappearing silently into the dark. The cord made a soft twang, like a kid on a kazoo. The girl herself said nothing. Or at least Bliss heard nothing.

He wished he didn't have to go next. He wished he didn't have to go at all. Maybe his precinct would call—a desperate hostage situation had arisen and Bliss had to change places with a group of Swedish tourists. Or there was a jumper (how ironic), and Bliss was needed to talk him down. Anything but this. He wished his nine-year-old daughter Cori would show up in her pajamas, hugging her stuffed animal, tears welling up in her eyes, sniffling, "Daddy, there's a monster in my closet and I'm scared. Daddy, will you come and lie with me?" Then he'd *have* to go back, and what could they say? Even the Asian girl would understand. "My kid needs me," he'd say. So noble. He'd take Cori's hand. "Come on, honey," he'd say, letting his youngest child lead him to safety. . . .

Bliss watched Icarus and the others pull the girl up through the hole. She took off the harness, handed it to Icarus. She shook her head like a young colt. Her face glowed in the moonlight. Now it was his turn.

Icarus attached the harness, and Bliss held the bungee cord, his new umbilicus. It stretched, like a rubber band. But just the other day he had tried wrapping a bundle of last year's checks with a rubber band, and it broke. Because it had come to its last stretch. The bungee cord, too, had only so many stretches. There was a number. Some completely arbitrary number. Not majestic, like with baseball cards—Willie Mays, number 100, Mantle, number 150—but some rookie number, some scrub number, *Bliss's* number, notable only for denoting this moment, his last on earth. A number with no other correlation other than being indelibly etched into every fiber of this bungee cord, fixed like a cancer gene. Number 438, say, and now the mysterious odometer of stretch had reached 437, and the last bit of bungee was about to tick off because the bungee molecules were as tired as he was. They wanted a rest—from stretching, from bearing the load, from the burden of returning everyone safely. Bliss could relate.

"So whattaya say, Lenny? You gotta go now or give up your spot."

He thought about the pancakes he'd had yesterday morning, the John's Pizza he'd eaten last night. Weighing him down. It would only make it happen more quickly.

"It's now or never, Lenny."

Bliss sat with his feet dangling over the side of the hole. The dots of light far below made the water look like some inverted galaxy. Or the glowing pain of the drowned souls suffering in the River Styx. He'd be joining them soon.

"Lenny, it's give-it-up-or-jump time. Go down in a tuck. As soon as you clear the bridge, just lean forward and reach for the water. You ready?"

No, he wasn't nearly ready. But Bliss owed it to Richard Simmons and his partner and his family to push past his limits, to jump through the black hole of his fears.

"What about your gun?" It was the girl, sitting cross-legged on the grating, looking up at him, her face tilted to one side like a cat. He felt the leather holster he wore on his hip. Like his heavy shoes, he should have left it at home. But every other time he'd left the house at midnight it was because he'd been summoned to something bad: a boy dying in a back stairway, blood oozing from a hole in his chest; a woman lying on a dark overpass, bleeding from her womb.

"You might lose it on the way down," she said.

She was right. It could be yanked free from the holster and join the thousands of other guns lying at the bottom of the East River, tossed out of moving cars from the FDR after a robbery or murder. Of course, having his gun wouldn't matter anyway, once his broken body was floating out to sea, the bungee cord trailing after him like limp kite string or the frayed ribbon on a busted birthday balloon.

"Come on, man! We're not going to get our turns!"

And because he'd already gone too far, become Alice in his own private Wonderland, literally about to follow the rabbit (the girl's charm) down the hole, he did what he was never supposed to do: undid his belt and slipped the holster off and handed it to the girl. Like breaking the glass at his wedding, the act seemed to cut him off from everything that had come before it. He was free, without ties, without burdens; light as a feather now, he dropped through the square of missing bridge and fell into the nothingness.

He let go of his knees and reached for the river and that was his last moment of decision before the wind filled his mouth and the water came rushing up and he tried to close his eyes but they were wide with terror and wonder as he plummeted, freely falling as he had done so often in his dreams as a child. He held in his scream and kept his asshole tight and felt the tension in the cord and was starting to slow down as the sound and smell of the water came closer; and then suddenly he stopped and felt the change fall out of his pockets and heard their gentle splash as he started soaring upward and away from the water.

He'd done it.

He wanted to shout. He wanted to phone his family to tell them, "Guess what Daddy just did?" Only, his oldest, Julia, would probably give him the Buster Keaton, and his youngest, Cori, would be upset that he didn't take her with him because *everyone* always does *everything* without her. And his wife? Rachel would sigh deeply and wonder what was next, what horrid creature would surface next from the depths of her husband's existential abyss.

But for now he was beaming as they pulled him up through the hole. They helped him onto the catwalk, and there were pats on the back from Icarus and the others. He was proud of himself and looked for the girl, to see her response, to get her approval and his piece back, but he didn't see her.

"Where'd she go?" he asked.

Icarus put his finger to his lips.

"Never mind that bullshit," Bliss said. "I'm a cop. Where'd the girl go?"

"You're a cop?!"

"Don't get simple on me," Bliss said. "Just tell me where the girl is."

"I don't know," Icarus said. "She must have taken off while I was watching you."

He whipped around to her boyfriend.

"What's her name? Where does she live?"

"I don't know, sir."

"You're her fucking boyfriend and you don't know her name?

"I'm not her boyfriend. I never saw her before tonight."

"But she kissed you."

"It was, like, a total surprise. It could just as easily been you, sir."

"Icarus."

"I only know her first name," Icarus said. "Li-Jung. Or something like that. That's all anyone tells me. I swear."

"Shit."

Bliss stared out into the night, his buoyancy and exhilaration gone. He felt old and stupid, like someone who would wear the wrong shoes to go bungee jumping.

"Um . . . Lenny," Icarus said, his face, plaintive in the moonlight, "do you mind if the others take their turn now? It's going to be morning soon."

DeWayne Reardon knew he shouldn't have picked the guy up, but he'd been driving his taxi for the past twenty minutes

looking for a fare without any luck, so he said what the fuck—
which, if he took two seconds to think about it, was what he
always said right before he did something really stupid.

It was two o'clock in the morning. He'd come up empty
after a few futile tours up Third Avenue. Usually they yielded
a drunken yuppie lurching from one of the bars lining Third
from Seventy-second to Ninety-sixth. Investor boys, still in
their suits, ties undone, jackets slung over their shoulders.
Sometimes a couple who'd just met over beers would make
out in the back seat while they tried to remember each other's
name. But all the yuppies seemed to be walking home that
night, so he headed over to Billy's Topless, and sure enough
there was a guy leaning against a parking sign who looked
like he'd been there all night, summoning his last bit of
strength to signal for a cab. DeWayne hesitated. The guy
might have wedged his last dollar under the garter belt of one
of the dancers, or he might have drunk too much and was
about to toss his cookies in the cab. Or both. But it was such a
slow night, DeWayne decided to risk it.

What the fuck.

"Where to, pal?"

The guy mumbled something that sounded enough like
Seventy-third and Amsterdam for DeWayne to go with it. He
drove up Eighth, just catching the light at Twenty-fourth
Street on the yellow and accelerating to get up to speed with
the staggered greens. He heard the first rumblings at Madison Square Garden and by the time he crossed Thirty-fourth
Street past Macy's, the guy has disappeared from the rearview mirror and was bent over, puking his guts out all over
the back seat.

"Shit!" DeWayne yelled and pulled over. He leaped out of
the cab and ripped the back door open. A puddle of brownish
vomit was flowing slowly but with a glacial inevitability down
the smooth vinyl seat and into the crack, where it would no

doubt remain until the taxi was either junked or driven into the Hudson——which DeWayne was now strongly considering doing, leaving this drunken piece of shit in the back seat.

"You dumb fuck!" DeWayne yelled. He grabbed a handful of the guy's hair and shoved his face into the puke. "Bad dog! Bad fucking dog!"

He made the guy take off his jacket and wipe up what he could, but the cab was already reeking with a vile, fetid smell. DeWayne briefly considered the gun he had stashed in the glove compartment. He could shoot the guy, but that wouldn't make the stink go away.

"You're going to have to pay for this," DeWayne said. "Five hundred bucks."

The guy was now sitting on the curb, holding his head in his hands and moaning.

"Get your wallet out. There's a cash machine across the street."

DeWayne tried to lift the guy to his feet, but he was dead weight. Then he started making retching sounds again, and DeWayne quickly backed up.

"Just give me the card and your PIN number. Do it! Do it now!"

"I haven't got a card," the guy said, too drunk to stand but not to lie. DeWayne kicked him once in the kidney with the point of his shoe. The guy started moaning in earnest now.

"I'm goin' call the pohleesh," he said.

"I *am* the fucking police," DeWayne said.

DeWayne grabbed him by the ear and tried to pull him up. But the guy started yelling like a stuck pig, and DeWayne flashed back to a Puerto Rican kid he'd had once in the back of the patrol car screaming the same way, only in Spanish—*cuño* this and *cuño* that—while DeWayne threatened to wail away at him with his flashlight. But DeWayne had no flashlight now because he wasn't a cop anymore, just a lousy cab driver. So instead, he grabbed one of the guy's fingers and in one quick move bent it back and broke it. The guy instantly curled up like he was on a spring and started moving in a circle like Curly on the *Three Stooges*. That's when DeWayne saw the red and blue lights, and the patrol car pulled up.

DeWayne raised his hands to his shoulders and showed his empty palms, keeping them that way while the cops approached.

"Holy shit, look who's here, Eddie," one of the cops said. "It's Dee-Wayne. Dee-ranged Dee-Wayne. How the hell are you, man?"

DeWayne only vaguely recognized the cop, but obviously the cop knew him.

"Sonofabitch," the other cop—Eddie—said. "Howaya, DeWayne?"

DeWayne just nodded and lowered his hands.

"What happened, Dee-Wayne?" the first cop asked. "The cabby have some kind of epileptic fit while he was driving?"

"*He's* the driver!" the guy on the ground hollered through his tears. "He *kicked* me! He broke my *finger!*"

The first cop feigned astonishment.

"Dee-Wayne was *driving? The* Dee-Wayne Reardon, driving a *taxi?*"

"How the mighty have fallen," Eddie said.

The guy on the ground propped himself up on his elbow. "He tried to rob me, too!" he shouted.

"Well, I should hope so," Eddie said.

"Lookit my finger!" He held it out, blue and swollen and bending the wrong way.

Before the guy could say anything more, the first cop grabbed a hold of it and snapped it back in place. The guy yelped but then quieted down.

"So, DeWayne," Eddie said, "I didn't know you were driving a cab. I heard you were working security at Woolworth's or something."

"What happened?" the first cop asked, "You try to steal some yarn and didn't realize it was hanging out of your pocket?"

"Or maybe he tried to walk out with a canary under his hat, and the bird started talking."

"Canaries don't talk," DeWayne said.

"Yeah, well, if they did, they wouldn't say anything nice about you."

DeWayne felt his face flooding with anger, but he held it together.

"You gotta learn not to take stuff, DeWayne," Eddie said.

"I never took nothing," DeWayne said.

"The problem is," the first cop said, "the higher-ups thought you did. That's why they've got your badge and gun, right Dee-ranged?"

The drunk was looking from the cops to DeWayne.

"Aren't you going to do something?" he asked, eyes wide.

"That you who puked in the back seat?" Eddie asked him. The guy nodded.

"Then shut the fuck up."

"It'll happen to you, too, you self-righteous prick," DeWayne said. "You'll see. You'll reach in your pocket one day for a cigarette and it'll be there. Money, pussy, a Rolex, blow—who knows. But *something* will be there."

"Yeah," the first cop snickered, "well, if anything does wind up in my pocket, Dee-Wayne, I won't be so fucking stupid as to leave it hanging out for half the precinct to see. By the way, who's got the Lexus now? You keep it or'd the bitch get it in the settlement?"

DeWayne hit him with a quick right, but Eddie got between them before he could get off another.

"That's enough, Mike," Eddie said. "You're out of line now. Enough!"

"Get in the cab, motherfucker!" Mike shouted. "Get in and drive away before I write you a ticket for impersonating a human being."

DeWayne got in the cab and tore off. He opened his window and drove with his head leaning out and thought, This is what it's come down to. Six months ago he'd been sitting by his above-ground pool in the backyard of his house in Sunnyside, now he was driving the cab that would lead him to hell. The drunk had obviously been some kind of demon, sent from the netherworld to mark the car with smell so the rest of the devils could sniff him out and torment him further. He wanted to say he'd reached bottom, that it couldn't get any worse. But with a sigh and a shudder, DeWayne Reardon acknowledged that if there was a way to heap more humiliation on himself, he would find it. He was a virtuoso fuckup. That thought mixed with the smell of vomit to make a cocktail of degradation for DeWayne to sip on as he drove off into the night looking for a twenty-four-hour car wash.

Martin Roderick heard the front door to the apartment close and his wife walk in softly in her bare feet. He checked the clock by the bed. It was two in the morning. He stayed motionless as she came into the bedroom and padded into their bathroom, then silently closed the door, not turning on the light until it was completely shut. He heard the water running gently in the sink and, when it was turned off, the snap of her pill bottle, then water again—filling a cup to swallow the pill, no doubt. The gentle click of the light switch was followed by the door opening. In a moment she was next to him, under the sheets.

"Are you all right, Promise?" he asked. He didn't need to know where she'd been. His wife often went out late in the evening, after he'd settled in, usually to see her lover. Tonight she'd been gone a shorter time than usual. Perhaps he'd only played Promise's front nine.

"I took a pill," she said.

"Do you want me to—?"

"No," she said. "Don't do anything, Martin. Please."

"Are you sure . . . ?" He only wanted to rub her back.

"Yes. I'm sure. Please, Martin. Just don't try to do anything."

She turned away from him, and once she did, he didn't dare go near her, touch her. Not tonight. Not *any* night.

He'd get up early, he decided. Before Graciela arrived. Make Promise some scones. Take the butter out of the fridge so it was at room temperature, so his wife could spread it easily and it would melt quickly into the warm, just-baked pastries. Squeeze her some juice, too.

"It's done," Promise said. Silence. "It's over," she added. "Finally, it's over."

She sighed deeply, and the pill carried her off to sleep. Martin wondered what she'd seen, what she'd done, what was now over. A fight with her lover? He wanted no more of her? Or she of him? His wife's secret life was a great source of wonder for Martin, to the point where he realized it was probably much richer in his imagination than in reality. But tonight she seemed especially burdened. How bad it was, he could only guess, but Martin had the feeling there was a better than fifty-fifty chance he'd have to cancel his 11 A.M. tee time tomorrow.

It was two o'clock in the morning, and Bliss's partner, Ward, was heading home to his apartment when he heard the distinctive pops and reached for his gun. He scanned the block and saw only the Korean deli with its lights on. Ward knew the owner, Kim, who stocked the hot sauce he liked so much, bought cases of it just for him. Ward walked down the street, keeping close to the shuttered wall of storefronts, gun now drawn, but in no great hurry. He didn't want to alarm anyone. He was just a regular guy holding four juice glasses with bright-red tomato designs that he'd just bought from a homeless guy. He used to have the same glasses as a kid. He was hoping he'd make it home without them breaking. Now he wasn't so sure.

As Ward passed the open door of the deli, he saw a young man vault over the counter, landing like a cat on the dirty linoleum. The young man looked up, his face childlike, soft with smooth, round cheeks. What Ward didn't know was that the kid had neglected to take his medication that morning, and jolts of maverick chemicals were at that moment careening through his brain, setting off a Rube Goldberg chain of synapses that resulted in the store owner being shot twice in the head, *pop-pop*—the shots Ward had heard from down the street.

The boy smiled at Ward and raised his gun. As he did, Ward dropped the juice glasses, which shattered on the sidewalk at his feet. The boy fired, hitting Ward in the hand. It felt like a bee sting. Ward raised his gun and shot the kid in the eye, then twice more in the chest as he was falling backward into the candy shelf.

Chapter 2

Bliss's plan of telling his family about The Big Jump over breakfast that morning had to be put off. Instead, at 7:30 he was on his way to the hospital.

He had still been in bed when he got the call.

"Ward's been shot," he told his wife as he hung up the phone.

"Bad?" she asked.

"In the hand. I think he's OK."

"Give him my love," Rachel said, taking Bliss by surprise. She was not usually so gracious toward his partner, the person he spent more time with than his family.

"I will."

On the drive over, Bliss wondered how Ward would take to being shot. Cops reacted differently. Sometimes a slug in, say, the leg emboldened them, made them feel invincible—like they were under the wing of a protective angel. For others being shot could be debilitating. Bliss had seen some very rough boys who, once they'd taken a bullet, shattered like glass and that was it—desk jockeys until early retirement.

Ward was sitting up in bed when Bliss arrived, his bandaged hand resting in his lap. He didn't appear to be in great pain. His girlfriend, Malikha, sat next to the bed, holding his good hand.

"Partner," Ward said.

Bliss hugged the man with whom he daily risked his life.

"I caught a bullet," Ward said. "I saw it coming. Saw where he was pointing the gun. Saw his finger pulling the trigger like it was in super slow-mo, and I knew I could do it, that I could reach out and catch the bullet. So I did. I caught the fucking bullet. It was pure reflexes, an Ozzie Smith kind of thing."

Under the bandage a lump rose like an ant hill on the back of Ward's hand just below the knuckles. The bullet was nestled inside, like a crocus bulb getting ready for spring.

"It was a shot off of Mantle's bat, partner. A line drive. A frozen rope. A *bullet!*" Ward said, his voice becoming stronger. "I snagged it right in the pocket like Brooks Robinson." He turned his hand over, pointing to the bandage where the entry wound was on his palm. "A neat little hole," he said. "A stigmata. Three down, one to go. I'll have a halo soon. Latin words in gold leaf flowing from my mouth like the saints in the pictures." Ward closed his eyes. He was sweating. Malikha gently wiped his brow.

"He's talking like this bullet thing has taken him to a higher plane," she said. "Like he's been to the mountain."

"To the *top* of the mountain," Ward said, his deep baritone filling the room. "Just me. Alone. Carrying my own bags. No Sherpas. This is better than mushrooms. I've gone further than Timothy Leary or Ken Kesey. Dennis Hopper in the middle of the desert on primo acid never saw what I did in that moment. That brilliant flash. I was rowing with the Kings. Waltzing with Joan of Arc. Fuck the road less traveled. The bullet caught is what counts."

Ward stroked the bump on his hand like it was something holy.

"He won't let the doctor take it out," Malikha said. "He threatened to shoot her if she tried to touch it. To track down her parents and shoot them, too. The whole time he's hooked up to a monitor and his heart doesn't beat any faster. He's raving about shoving an oatmeal spoon down the throat of the doctor's first born and his pulse is steady as a metronome."

"She was a mousy thing," Ward said.

"She was your *doctor*," Malikha scolded.

"She could hardly see over the bed. Probably has to stand on a phone book to reach the operating table."

My partner, Bliss thought.

"Anyway, no mere doctor can touch this hand," Ward said, his eyes closed. "It's sacred."

The way his partner was sitting in the bed, Bliss could almost see Ward's white hospital sheets as flowing robes, Ward ascendant, taking his place in some aberrant pantheon of saints and sinners.

"Removing my bullet would be like throwing the Shroud of Turin in the laundry," Ward said. "In Italy they've got whole cathedrals built around some saint's bone no bigger than a chicken wing. Just *think* what they could do with the hand that caught the bullet. People will make pilgrimages to the Sacred Basilica of the Hand of Ward. Walk to it with dried peas in their shoes, walk on their *knees*."

Malikha leaned down close to Ward's ear and graced it

with the tip of her tongue. "There's a certain sacred basilica *I* want your hand in," she said, "and I want it there soon."

Ward calmed. He looked long and hard at Malikha, and his eyes gradually came into focus. She rubbed his temple, soothing him with her gentle touch. He gingerly lifted his hand and slowly unwrapped the bandage. He exhaled deeply, pressed his palm up to his mouth, and startled them both with a ferocious sucking sound. A moment later he opened his mouth—and there was the slug between his teeth. He spit it out on the sheet.

"Picked that up sucking tokens from turnstiles when I was a kid," Ward said, sporting a mischievous grin. "Break a toothpick in the slot to keep the token from going in all the way. Then you suck it out and make a run for it. In Kansas they got whippersnappers. In Harlem we've got tokensuckers. Basically the same thing. Except there aren't any white picket fences on Lenox Avenue. No treehouses. No paper routes. Not a whole lot of whippersnapper *zeitgeist* where I grew up."

Ward was back.

Malikha went to look for the doctor to rebandage Ward's now deslugged hand.

"I was worried for a while there, partner," Bliss said.

"Yeah. Well, I did catch a bullet. How many men can claim as much?"

Ward grabbed Bliss's arm and held it tightly.

"He was just a kid," Ward said. "I could see it when I stood over him, lying on the floor of the store, his blood mixing with Kim's, the owner."

"Fifteen, the report said."

"He looked twelve. Even with half his face blown away."

This, Bliss sensed, was the true source of his partner's raving. For all Ward's bravura, he did not like shooting people, especially young black kids.

He was glad Malikha was there. She and Ward had been

together since the murder of the Russian prostitute. She'd been a good influence on his partner as she segued from fine young thang to paramour to now just Malikha.

"The doctor will be back in a minute," she said. "I told her you would be discreet."

"Get her a stepladder," Ward said. "I hope she sat in the first row at med school. Otherwise she couldn't have seen the blackboard. Maybe she missed the lesson on bullet wounds to the hand."

Bliss flashed to another hospital room, he and Ward visiting a fellow detective shot off-duty trying to break up a bar fight. The bullet had gone through the guy's neck, and he'd been all bandaged up, tubes in his nose and arms. Drip bags. Monitors. Ward didn't speak, didn't make a play for the nurse. Instead, he surprised Bliss and held the guy's hand. For an hour they stayed that way, standing by the bed, the injured detective's hand dwarfed in Ward's huge mitt. It was an image Bliss had kept with him, to temper the rough savagery with which his partner held other hands—or throats or testicles—his intention more malicious, like Hippocrates turned inside out: First do harm, then figure out what the hell was going on.

"They're going to give me a new partner now," Bliss said. "Ginkgo. Or worse, Bermudez."

"Yeah. But when I come back, there'll be a divine glow around the two of us. An aura. We'll never sit in traffic again. The bad guys will confess without asking. They'll get on line to give up their grandmothers."

Bliss sighed. "Well, I'm going to *need* some divine help."

"What's up, partner?"

And Bliss told him the story of the bridge and the bungee jump and the girl who had waltzed with his piece.

"Lenny, what were you thinking?"

"I don't know. I wanted to prove something."

"You've survived eighteen years on the force. What's left to prove?"

"I'm not sure."

"Maybe he wanted it on his own terms," Malikha said.

"Something like that."

"The girl's name was Li-Jung?" Ward asked.

"Yeah."

"She Chinese?"

"Yeah."

"We'll pull Icarus's phone records, see where she called from."

"He said she used a pay phone."

"So what are you going to do?"

"I don't know."

"You packing?"

"No."

"You want my throw-down piece?"

"No. I want my gun back."

"Let me work on it," Ward said. "I'll be on light duty, anyway. I'll hold out my hand, and it'll lead me right to it. Don't worry, partner. I've got the Shining."

The guy banging on the window of DeWayne's cab woke him up.

"Wall Street!" the guy shouted. When DeWayne didn't respond quickly enough, the guy flagged another taxi cruising by and grabbed it.

DeWayne checked his watch. It was 7:30. He'd only slept about three hours. He needed coffee. He needed to pee. Easier said than done. It was too light out to piss in Central Park, and he'd have to order a full breakfast to use the bathroom in the diner. He didn't feel like breakfast. So he unscrewed his ginger ale bottle and relieved himself. The taxi driver's best friend. Need to get the two-liter size, he thought.

The donut shop was across the street. As usual, DeWayne was the only white guy among the drivers. The rest were from far-off lands—Indians, Afghanis, Pakistanis—he wasn't exactly sure which. He ordered coffee and a cruller, to help keep the coffee from eating through his stomach. He stood outside the shop. Clear-eyed young men and women in work-out clothes jogged by, on their way to the gym. Some carried squash racquets, their skin glistening, radiating health. DeWayne belched and looked over the row of yellow cabs lining the avenue around the donut shop like bees hovering around the hive, the donuts and coffee their queen.

He was looking for one cab in particular that had sprinted through a red light around two o'clock last night to grab a fare in front of DeWayne. DeWayne wanted to have a talk with the guy. But even if he found the cab, he couldn't be sure it would be the same driver. Drivers traded off, and the day man might already have taken over. Two guys sharing their beds and their cabs, taking half-day shifts in each, one sleeping while the other drove, one driving while the other slept in rooms lined with bunks like the hold of a tramp steamer. Twelve hours driving, twelve hours sleeping. Yet as squalid as their lives might be, they had it all over DeWayne because their lives held a future: They were on their way up, while DeWayne Reardon was very much on his way down.

As usual, Martin Roderick was the first one up. It was 7:30. He quietly got out of bed and put on his silk robe. He loved the feel of his silk robe in the morning. It was an anniversary present, though he'd had to buy it for himself. For their next anniversary he would get himself an ascot. And a tin of foie gras.

Promise breathed deeply and evenly, her blond hair spread out on the pillow, a golden sunrise behind her head. *It's done,* she'd said last night—before taking a pill for the first time in weeks. Something serious must have happened. *It's finally over*.

Martin went to check on James, his stepson, but his room was still empty. James hadn't been home for the past two nights.

Martin folded the shimmering black pants that James had left lying on the floor, the legs of which seemed impossibly narrow.

He put the dirty socks, underwear, and T-shirt in the hamper.

He took the sneakers to the closet and, while there, straightened the rest of the shoes.

Where was he? True, James often wasn't home in the morning, but he usually didn't stay away this long. He at least stopped in for clean socks, fresh boxers.

Martin straightened the bed and fluffed the pillows. Something was wrong.

It's finally over. Maybe Promise had meant that her affair, the late-night trysts with her secret lover, were now a thing of the past. No more long showers before getting into bed, washing away his smell, the lingering scent of their passion. Honestly, he would have preferred the coital aroma, as the sound of the shower invariably woke him up. But Promise had never told him about the beginning of this affair, so Martin doubted she would inform him that it was finished.

Perhaps she meant *James* was over, that her son had finally wised up and left for good. Lately he'd been home merely to bathe and drop off his laundry while he rehearsed *Macbeth*, which Martin knew only because he'd found a script in James's back pocket before sending the pants to the cleaners.

Maybe James had found a Lady Macbeth and was now hatching wicked plots. Weak and impressionable, James had always wanted a mentor—but definitely someone with greater fortitude than Martin, who certainly had never killed anyone or climbed mountains or slept naked in the desert. To James, Martin was a factotum—making sure the laundry was done, arranging travel plans, ordering clothes from catalogues, keeping the larder stocked. For fifteen years Martin had diligently taken care of him, the only father the boy had ever known. But if James passed Martin on the street, he would probably walk by unaware.

It's finally over. It could mean anything, but Martin was inclined to believe Promise had meant James. The curtain had finally come down on *that* depressing saga, the tawdry sideshow that was their family; the decrepit spook house that was James's childhood. Now over, finally over.

Perhaps that's why she was sleeping so soundly.

Chapter 3

Bliss's new partner was a wiry guy with eyebrows of consequence and black hair slicked back into a little pony tail. His name was Artie Barsamian, and he looked like someone who would try to sell you a lot more stereo equipment than you actually needed. Artie had been transferred to Homicide from the Garment Center Task Force, which dealt with impeding the creative ways of ripping off the few clothing manufacturers still left in the city. Extortion. Theft. Racketeering. Artie was telling him about his adventures as they drove to the crime scene.

"Say you own a factory," Artie said, his elbow leaning on the open window of the car. "Bliss Sportswear, call it—which, by the way, has got a nice ring. You get an order, say two hundred dozen Calvin Klein dresses, like the A-line knit number he was showing last spring."

"A-line knit?"

"Yeah. Each one's worth two hundred and eighty bucks retail. So you make the two hundred dozen, but unbeknownst to Calvin—who, by the way, is a real prince, just so you should know—you've still got a hundred labels left over. Savvy you."

"Savvy me."

"So you have the Chinese ladies working for you make a hundred more dresses, and you fold them up and put them into three or four boxes, and now you've got twenty-eight thousand dollars' worth of retail merchandise in the trunk of your car."

"What kind of car do I have?"

"A DeVille."

"Why not a Mercedes?"

"Not enough room in the trunk. Anyway, now you've got to sell the dresses to someone. I mean, how many of these can you unload on your mother-in-law?"

"At least a dozen if they're half price."

"Right. So maybe you call up a guy you know with a store down on Rivington Street who's wise to the scam and is willing to take the goods off your hands. He has a following with the Long Island ladies who can't pass up a bargain, who are willing to make the trip down to the Lower East Side and pay cash, too. So you sell him the dresses cheap—but not *too* cheap because this is *real* Calvin, not imitation—say, fifty bucks each. Then he sells them for a hundred. He makes five grand, you make five grand, and Calvin, he hasn't actually lost a thing because you didn't really steal anything except the labels."

"So how do you stop a scam like that?" Bliss asked.

"You'd think it would be easy, but it's not. It dangerous, too. Mob stuff, the trucking union. Lot of guys think G.C.T.F.'s a walk in the park, but we see our share of action. Definitely, a lot of action."

Bliss could see that it bugged Artie, working around the old timers in the garment center, the schnorrers and tummlers, kibbitzers and kvetchers. Not the most hard-ass assignment. Not very glamorous police work.

"So, anyway," Bliss asked, "how'd you catch them?"

Artie threw himself back into the story.

"Had to go undercover. *Deep* cover." Artie paused ominously to let this sink in. "I gained fifty pounds trying to look the part. Started smoking cigars. Ate kishka. *You* ever eat kishka? It tastes just like it sounds. Say it."

"Kishka."

"That's exactly what it tastes like. We set up a storefront on Delancey Street. I spread the word I was looking for some bargain merchandise. Stuff that fell off a truck."

"That took balls."

"I'll say."

"Catch anybody?"

"Yeah. A couple of kids with a shitload of DKNY. Turns out they were distant relatives of Donna's niece, Karen Karan. We had to let them walk with a warning. Then they transferred me over here. Sorry about your partner. Caught a bullet, right?"

"He'll be OK."

"You think we'll see a body?"

"It's not a sure thing, Artie, but usually there's at least one around when there's a murder."

"That's what I thought," Artie said. He took a B-movie pause, his voice turning foreboding. "I've seen what bullets can do."

"Yeah, they'll shred the lining of a sports jacket pretty bad," Bliss said. "Wreak havoc on the hem of an A-line knit."

"It was outside a social club," Artie said, turning to Bliss, his face hard, obviously wanting to prove something. "Two guys thought they were going with the same girl. Monica Alvarado. Four years ago, and I still remember her name. I was in uniform then. One kid shot the other in the face. Blood everywhere. But I looked. I forced myself to look. It took a lot of effort, but I didn't turn away."

Bliss didn't have the heart to tell Artie that after a while you wished you *could* turn away, you wished death affected you again, that you didn't see the murdered in terms of whether they were easy cases—happy when a likely suspect crouched sobbing in the next room, pissed off when it seemed like the killer had escaped, never to be seen again.

They rode in silence. His new partner was worse than Bliss could have imagined. Worse than the incontinent Ginkgo or the fiery Bermudez. Because Artie Barsamian seemed a patently regular guy—someone who liked to chat, who wanted to impress him, and, worst of all, seemed intent on finding a way to become Bliss's friend.

DeWayne parked his cab in front of his apartment house and turned off the motor. Opening the door, he emptied the ginger ale bottle against the curb. He didn't want any of the drunks or homeless men on the street to find the bottle in the trash and think it *was* ginger ale.

He got out of the cab and immediately saw Henry, one of the local homeless guys, ambling toward him, dressed in rags, pushing his baby carriage full of junk. Two giant garbage bags of deposit bottles and cans were tied together and slung over his shoulder like the leather pouches of a Pony Express rider. DeWayne handed Henry the few coins he hadn't changed into bills at the donut shop. Henry clasped the money tightly, nodding, bobbing up and down, grinning fiercely, talking some kind of gibberish that DeWayne took to be his version of thanks.

It used to be DeWayne's kids greeting him when he came home from work, running out to the driveway to meet him, jumping into his arms, waiting to be carried up the path, up to his wife standing on the front stoop, relieved that he had returned alive from another day as a cop.

Daddy's home!

Henry set down his bags of cans and started wiping DeWayne's cab with a grimy rag he used just for that purpose—a rag far dirtier than the cab and smearing some kind of grease all over the hood. DeWayne grabbed the rag from Henry's hand and shoved it in his face, tried to shove it down Henry's throat so he would stop making those pathetic mumblings and gurglings, so he would choke and not be shuffling over to DeWayne with his travesty of a welcome.

Daddy's home!

He pulled his hand away, and Henry staggered back, gagging and coughing.

"Sorry, Henry. Just get a cleaner rag next time, will you?"

Henry nodded apologetically and limped away, dragging his bags of cans like the goat that the village has tied all its troubles to, all its misery and bad omens. The scapegoat that the villagers would throw stones at to drive the poor beast from their midst so their troubles would never return.

DeWayne Reardon, however, knew better.

Martin poured the cream into the flour-and-butter mixture and stirred. Gradually the dough for the scones started to come together, just as it was supposed to. It was why he enjoyed baking so much. If you were attentive and carefully followed the recipe, it always worked. Martin only wished the rest of his life was so obliging.

Take James, Martin's irascible brat of a stepson. If the boy had really left home, it would upset everything. Because without James around, Promise had little need for him. Martin's sole responsibility in their marriage was to serve as James's father, though in Martin's case he was more like the nanny. And, as so often happened on the Upper East Side, when the children left home, the nanny became dispensable.

Especially if he got so distracted that he overkneaded the scones, as he was doing now. He couldn't remember the last time *that* happened. A few gentle turns was all the dough warranted, and here he was pounding it into the board as if he were making a crusty peasant bread.

You should never bake pastries with a lot on your mind.

Martin didn't want to be dispensable. He had suffered too much humiliation, too many indignities taking care of James, to be cast aside now. If James was gone, then Promise would have to be gone, too. That way Martin would be left alone. He liked the sound of that. Promise and James both out of his life and Martin alone and free to wear his silk robe the whole day if he liked, to play golf whenever he wanted, to call his elegant escorts. He wondered if there was some way of making it happen.

Martin decided to throw out the dough and start over. Scones could be ruined so easily by even the simplest mistake. He started remeasuring the flour, breaking up more butter into tiny pieces. He kept his focus this time, making sure the scones were as light and flaky and golden brown as they were every other morning. If they weren't, Promise might sense something was wrong. And Martin didn't want that. No, there was no need for Promise to be suspicious. Not yet, anyway.

Act II

Chapter 4

Bliss and Artie were looking at James Roderick lying center stage, dead, one arm draped across his chest, the other off to his side, as if with his last breath he had set free a dove.

"Hey Artie," Bliss said, "if an actor dies on stage and no one's in the audience, is he really dead?"

Artie didn't seem to get it. Instead he took out his notebook, clicked his pen.

Ward's absence was starting to weigh heavier.

"He doesn't look dead," Artie finally said. "He looks asleep."

"He's in the sleep of death," Bliss said. "He's shaken off the mortal coil."

Artie clearly wasn't impressed. "If a guy's going to *be* dead, he oughta *look* dead."

He seemed disappointed over the absence of gaping wounds, twisted limbs, pieces of body cut away like the melon a fruit vendor uses to display its ripeness.

"Don't you think, Lenny? A little lasagna spilling out of his stomach, ziti with tomato cream sauce oozing from his head. Jesus. I mean this looks like he's napping before the show."

His new partner may have felt cheated, but for Bliss the absence of savagery was a relief. No open windows displaying the internal workings of the body (better than the exhibits at the science museum), no sunbathing organs, no ravaged torsos looking like pirates had dug for treasure in their bellies, no strategically placed knife wounds (keeping in mind the three Ls of lacerations: location, location, location). James Roderick lay there as if he was waiting for the director to yell

33

"cut" or whatever they said in the theater so he could get up and grab a cappuccino and think about sleeping with the stage manager.

But on closer inspection, you didn't need a program to see that James was playing the part of dead that morning. There were signs of strangulation on his neck, faint red marks, tracings of fingers that were too subtle to be noticed from the back row but from up close were horribly vivid. The back of his head had also suffered serious trauma, perhaps from being hit with a blunt, heavy object.

"What's that?" Artie said, pointing to a crown lying a few yards from James's head.

"Looks like a crown," Bliss said. "Heavy is the head that wears it."

Artie looked at him strangely.

"Must have fallen off when the kid hit the ground," Artie said.

"Unless he abdicated first," Bliss said.

Artie looked at him more strangely.

Now he really missed Ward. If a detective says something funny and his partner's not there to hear it, is he really clever? Or is he just seen as a doddering fool to be met with an incredulous gaze designed to push him closer to retirement. . . .

It was a small space, like most experimental theater spaces. Nothing like the opulent Broadway theaters.

"It probably was an actual warehouse before this," Artie pointed out. "Hence the name: Performance Warehouse." Artie made a note of it in his book.

The uniforms told Bliss that all six members of the theater company had been present when James's body was discovered, so each one would have to be interviewed. For the moment they waited in the audience, attentively watching the stage, which buzzed with activity. The lab boys were hunting around for a possible murder weapon. The police photographer was taking photos. It was kind of like a play, Bliss thought. Only James Roderick wasn't going to be taking a curtain call any time soon.

Cardozo, the medical examiner, was bent over the body, studying it like he had just dropped his keys on the beach. Bliss knew him well. Once an energetic forensic pathologist, Cardozo was now a tired, sardonic jester who always looked like he was in desperate need of a meal. Once, in passing, Cardozo had said, *I really* am *a doctor, but I wish I only played one on TV.*

Cardozo stood up as Bliss and Artie approached.

"Well, if you're going to die," he said, "you might as well do it center stage. Especially if you're an actor."

"Whattaya think, Doc?" an enthusiastic Artie asked him.

"I think he's dead," Cardozo said wearily. "You wanna hold a mirror up to his mouth to check for steam you can, but in the humble opinion of this medical expert, he's definitely dead. He's suffered a blow to the cranium. I could tell because I moved his head slightly to the side and felt the back and there was a big bump there. And it was a little mushy. Big bumps and mushy spots on the back of the head are usually caused by blows. There weren't any anterior lacerations to the scalp, so I would say this particular blow was caused by something dull. A baseball bat, maybe. Better yet, a cricket bat. The kid have any Limeys wanting to kill him?"

"Not that we know of," Artie said, then added portentously, "not *yet*, anyway."

Bliss's new partner was a regular Barney Fife.

"Well, you keep at it, young man," Cardozo said, with the weariness of someone who'd seen too much, like the troops who liberated Dachau or relief workers in Rwanda.

Bliss cleared his throat. "Any chance the thing on his head could have happened when he hit the floor?"

"It's a possibility," Cardozo said. "It appears as if he fell

straight back. Like he was in a trance. Hypnotized. Any homi-
cidal hypnotists on the loose?"

"*I* don't know of any," Artie said. "But Lenny has been
working Homicide longer than me."

"And where have you been working, son?"

"Garment Center Task Force."

"Maybe you met my brother-in-law, Bernie Maslin, Maslin
Fashions—Clothes for Tomorrow Today."

"I heard of him."

"You'd remember if you'd met him. Everything he's ever
eaten is on his tie. Speaking of eating, is it lunch yet?"

"What about his neck?" Bliss asked.

Cardozo got down on one knee. "I feel like Al Jolson," he
muttered. He pulled down the collar of James's shirt. "These
red marks are most definitely fingers. And while I can't say
with impunity until I get back to the lab, I'm pretty sure they
were human fingers. I hope this narrows it down a little bit
for you."

"Anything else?" Bliss asked.

"Possible internal hemorrhaging. I'll know more in a day
or two. I'll give you a call." Cardozo groaned as he got back to
his feet. He picked up his black bag, then took a moment
to cast a melancholy gaze at the corpse. "Good night, sweet
prince," he said in rich, round tones. He looked back at Bliss.
"I once desired to be an actor, Lenny, but my father wouldn't
let me. Wanted me to be a doctor instead. A nobler profession.
But *my* patients are all dead. 'To be or not to be' isn't the
question. For me it's strictly *not to be*. Alas." He stood for a
moment to look wistfully out at the audience, then exited in
search of a breakfast special.

It then occurred to Bliss that he, too, was on stage, where
his wife most wanted to be—standing in front of a crowd,
making them laugh. Maybe he should tell a joke. *You hear the
one about the triple homicide in Red Hook? What did one floater*

say to the other? Comics, like actors, craved adulation. And Bliss, the detective, craved . . . what? Applause? That wasn't it. He imagined the theater's seats filled with the families of murder victims whose killers he had tracked down—the brothers of the raped and stabbed, the sisters of the summarily executed, parents of the sodomized and bludgeoned—all rising in unison and bursting into spontaneous applause, thanking Bliss, praising him, grateful to him. The five-year-old niece of a slain bus driver meets him center stage with a bouquet of flowers like he was a diva, a *star*. No, gratitude, these accolades, they weren't for him. He'd run, he'd flee the stage before he'd let that happen. But then again, maybe if he could force himself to hear the applause, he wouldn't be jumping off of bridges, giving his gun away to total strangers.

"That shirt . . ." Artie said, standing back from the body like it was a painting he might buy, a little something to brighten up the den. "Lenny, look at it."

A clue, perhaps. Bliss scoped the shirt. He saw bupkes.

"It's Hugo Boss," Artie said. "Not the sporty line, either. That's a hundred and sixty dollar shirt. Feel it—later, after you take the rubber gloves off—the thickness of the cotton." Artie was excited, rubbing his hands together like some Long Shot Louie watching his horse widen its lead down the back stretch.

"What about the shoes?" Lenny asked.

"Doc Martens. Casual. Understated. What do we know about James?"

"At this point, very little."

"I can tell you he's loaded. You gotta trust me on this, Lenny."

"OK."

"The jeans cost almost as much as the shirt. They're Diesel."

"Diesel."

"Yeah. And check out the clocking on those socks."

"Some clocking."

"The kid stinks of money. Maybe someone's boosting him. Got something on him. From his past. Porno shots he did in college to make money. Full frontal, wearing a little sailor cap. That kind of thing. They agree to meet here on stage. To make the payoff. The deal goes sour. The kid gets whacked."

"Maybe . . ."

Artie cut him off. "I take it back." He closed his eyes, concentrating. "Someone in this room did it," he said. "I can feel it."

"You mean one of the lab boys?"

"No. I mean one of *them*," he said, referring to the actors sitting in the seats.

His new partner was just full of surprises.

"You can *feel* it?" Bliss asked.

"Yeah."

He couldn't wait to tell Ward. Artie's first day on the job, and already he's having hunches. Like Hercule Poirot. Maybe the lights would suddenly go out, then a gunshot, then a woman's scream.

"So you got a hunch someone in the room did it, is that right Artie?"

"Yeah," he said. "That's right. Someone in this room killed James Roderick."

Then Artie walked to the front of the stage and faced the members of the Performance Warehouse with a fearsome grimace, an avenging angel who, by sheer force of will, would get one or all of them to confess.

DeWayne went to put the key in the padlock on his front door, but someone had jimmied the clasp.

He pushed open the door. The place had been trashed—which actually made it look neater than when he had left.

DeWayne kicked pieces of garbage out of the way as he walked to the couch. He sat down and reached to turn on the lamp only to discover it was gone. He also noticed the toaster was missing. Fuck it. It didn't work anyway.

In all his years on the force, busting down doors in the most sordid neighborhoods, he had never been in such a depressing place. The squalid hovels that squatters had set up in abandoned buildings were somehow homier. His apartment reminded him of a basement shooting gallery—only instead of crack vials and needles and used lighters littering the floor, he had pizza crusts and beer bottles and Chinese food containers. He should pay Henry to clean it up.

But deep down DeWayne knew he didn't want it tidy. The filth was part of the punishment he was inflicting on himself, living in his own vile prison, only a few thin walls and broken windows separating him from the homeless men outside. That's probably where he'd wind up—pushing around a baby carriage filled with junk, scrounging through garbage cans. Maybe he'd find his toaster, after whoever stole it realized it was broken.

DeWayne closed his eyes and tried to sleep. He would be back in the cab soon. He had nothing else to do. The toaster made him think about mornings with his kids, getting up with them before school, making cinnamon toast while his wife was in the shower. Sometimes they'd ask him questions—math, history—and since they were still little, it was stuff he actually knew. It had made him feel good, smart, like he was part of their lives, like all the shit he was into on the job was worth it.

He was glad was toaster was gone—one less link to his past. Besides, word would get around the neighborhood that there was nothing in his apartment worth taking. Except it would be nice if someone stole his refrigerator. Then he wouldn't have to clean it out.

Bliss decided to get the first phase of the investigation
started and interview the six members of the Performance
Warehouse, find out what they knew about James, who
might want to kill him.

They were scattered around the theater. One paced in the
back, mumbling to himself. Another watched like a gargoyle,
her cropped, jet-black hair making her look like a veteran drill
sergeant. Behind her sat a creepy man with perfectly parted
hair and squarish black glasses, like a librarian in a *Twilight
Zone* episode. He wrote feverishly in a notebook resting in
his lap. Another, with a glowing cascade of golden hair, sat
hunched in her seat, knees drawn up, making dark, unrecog-
nizable sounds that only Bliss, the guru of grief, understood.

Someone should comfort her, Bliss thought. One of her fellow actors. But maybe that wasn't part of the script.

The last two actors, a boy and a girl, were in their early
twenties, sitting next to each other, studying the movements
of the detectives and uniformed officers with great intensity.
Bliss couldn't tell if they were in shock or doing some kind of
acting thing, observing the way policemen moved and talked.

The girl spoke up.

"I have an Alexander lesson," she announced. "I have to go
soon." She stood up, one hand resting on her hip, a skinny,
petulant, waiflike girl with lush, pouty lips and a pierced nose.
Bliss wondered if she played all her parts that way. Juliet on
the balcony, diamond nostril stud sparkling: "It is the East /
and Juliet's nose is the sun." But, then, he'd forgotten this was
an avant-garde theater. If they did Shakespeare, they might
leave out every other word or use only women. Or midgets.
And if they needed a dead body in one of the scenes, what
then? Maybe supply a real one for themselves.

"When can we get outta here?" she asked.

"You go when Lenny or I *let* you go," Artie said, making
his presence felt.

Lenny's wife had once dragged him to an avant-garde performance, a benefit for another experimental theater. Rachel's friend was on the board and had hoped the Blisses would donate some money.

The play—if you could call it that—had opened with a little girl standing alone in a spotlight. Done up in pigtails and a pink gingham dress (a symbol of lost innocence?), she held a birthday cake and kept trying to blow out the candles, only they were *trick* candles (our heartless society?) that kept reigniting. Then a muscular young man, dressed in a G-string, limped across the stage lip-synching to Nat King Cole playing out of a giant loudspeaker that he was carrying on his shoulder (a symbol of Atlas or Sisyphus or maybe some kind of exhibitionist moving man?). This went on for about twenty minutes, and all Bliss could think about was how the little girl should be home in bed because it was a *school* night and what kind of parent would allow their six-year-old to hang around these weirdos, anyway?

Then he had heard a car alarm go off and after a few seconds realized it was his. But in order to leave the theater he had to walk across the front of the stage. When he got to the edge of the acting area, the speaker man had turned and looked directly at him, daring him to go past. Bliss remembered thinking, Who the fuck does this guy think he is, wanting to grab the girl, throw her in the back seat, and drive her home. Instead he lowered his eyes and headed for the exit.

He returned at intermission, and several people had come up to him and said how good he was, his *intensity*, his *stylized naturalism*, and asked what other work he'd done, what other plays he'd been in. The second act featured two men in Hawaiian skirts doing a cheesy hula dance, the payoff being their shlongs would occasionally peek through the grass like the heads of bashful snakes. While this was going on, a television ran a silent loop of a 1950s commercial for a washing machine, the woman smiling as she put in the detergent, set the cycle, and then removed the cleanest wash she'd ever had.

"So how about it?" the young actress—intruding into his reverie—now wanted to know, clearly upset, though seemingly not about the death of her cohort. "We've been sitting here for a while. Besides, I have to pay for the lesson even if I don't show up."

"How much they getting for an Alexander class these days?" Artie asked her, like he knew what she was talking about.

"Eighty dollars."

Artie nodded confirmation. Eighty dollars. He wrote it down in his book. Another clue!

"We need to talk to everyone before they leave," Bliss said. "We'll need names and addresses, too."

"So I'll go first," the girl said, leaping up on the stage with incredible ease. She presented herself to Bliss and looked him square in the eye. "My name is Lisa Hormone. Yes, like the joke, How do you make a whore moan? I live on Avenue A and Third Street. There's no number. If you need to question me at home, just ring the bell next to the bodega and I'll throw down the keys. The *top* bell. I saw James dead when everyone else did. And contrary to what you think about an actress in the avant-garde theater, I didn't sleep with him, and I'm not a lesbian, and I work at a law office at night, and I don't have crabs. Can I go now?"

There was brief applause from the guy with the notebook.

"Fabulous monologue, Lisa," he said. "We'll use it in the scene when the murderers come for Lady Macduff."

"Thanks," she said, patently pleased as punch.

"I got most of it," he said, "Just repeat the part after 'not a lesbian.' "

Artie piped in, "She said she works in a law office at night and doesn't have crabs. Do people still get crabs?"

It was turning into vaudeville. Instant theater. Like Tang.

Say anything, these people turn it into a show. Their next play would be all about the investigation: *James Dies*. It was worse than his wife, who based her comedy on Bliss's life as a cop.

And you know, ladies and gentleman, instead of having albums with vacation photos, in our house we gather on the sofa and look at books of mug shots. My kids think we have a large, diverse family. But they wonder why no one's smiling. I say it's because instead of "cheese," the photographer had them say "plea bargain."

Bliss needed his regular partner, Ward, to get these dilettantes in order. He was turning into policeman lite. It was time to investigate, for the detectives to detect.

"So what about it, Mr. Policeman," Lisa Hormone said, "do you need to speak to me anymore, or can I go?"

Bliss walked over, stood above the diminutive actress, and stared at her. At first she met his gaze, like it was a game. But Bliss was funneling all his pain and anger into his face— anger over not seeing his kids enough, over not being able to open up to his wife, over hating his job and being devoted to it, over losing his gun, over seeing his partner hurt. Slowly the young actress withered under the onslaught of such genuine intensity. The sound of the zipper sealing James's body in thick black plastic broke the spell. Lisa sat down solemnly, and Bliss formally began looking for the young man's killer.

Ward had been sitting on the bench all morning, and he didn't know why. A bright orange glow of sunlight surrounded him. He heard children laughing and the lively sing-song of a double-dutch rhyme; in the distance, a harmonica. Birds chirped, and several flew down to join him—brightly colored birds, strange for New York, landing and gathering at his feet. He felt they were the spirits of old friends who'd come to sit with him, men he used to know when he was growing up, kindly, wise old men come to keep him company and enjoy the bright, clear day.

A bag of bread crumbs appeared next to him. He gladly scattered them on the ground and more birds came, joining the ones on the bench, and soon there was quite a crowd. Ward watched the birds organize themselves into letters. E-N-D I-T the birds spelled, like a marching band at halftime. A message. End what? he asked them, but they flew away.

A woman pushing a baby carriage appeared at his bench. Other women gathered around, large black women who reminded him of his momma, with huge breasts full and heavy enough to suckle the world, leaning over the carriage and peering at the baby. Smiling. Making faces.

Suddenly one of the women recoiled in horror, putting her hand up to her face. The others followed, running away as best they could, shrieking, their great udders heaving on their chests.

Something is wrong with this baby, Ward thought. Before he could investigate, a car arrived, slowing to a crawl in front of the carriage. The window lowered, and the muzzles of several guns appeared. Ward tried to get up from the bench, but he couldn't move. He could only watch as the guns turned slowly toward the baby carriage. He wanted to get up and save the baby, but he was stuck to the bench.

He saw the baby's bottle fly out of the carriage. And then the barrel of a shotgun craned up from the blankets and aimed at the car.

End it, Ward thought.

The guns flashed and Ward bolted from the bench. With arms outstretched, he caught it all—the bullets from the pistols, the buckshot from the rifle nabbed before it could scatter.

He saw the faces of the boys in the car, children's faces, kids not nearly old enough to drive, barely big enough to see over the window; the infant in the carriage, struggling to hold up the shotgun, yanking at the trigger with all of his might, feet braced against the side of the carriage, eyes hardened with effort, pulling frantically with both hands to get off a shot. The others were reloading, banging in a new clip, taking aim again, firing.

End it!

Ward reached out, but the bullets went through his hands, through the holes in his palms, hitting the carriage, sending it spinning down the sidewalk, blood spurting from it like a fountain; shotgun blasts connecting with the car, blowing away the faces of the boys at the window, shredding their skin.

End it, please! Ward shouted, staring at his useless hands, their palms riddled with holes.

Then he woke up. Malikha was patting his brow with a cool cloth.

"Some nap," she said.

She put a glass of water to his lips, and Ward took a sip.

"I did the best I could," he said.

"I know you did, baby," she said.

"I didn't mean to shoot him." Ward said. "He was some momma's son."

She patted his forehead some more.

"I'm tired of seeing them die."

"I know, baby, I know."

She held him tightly.

"Help me," he said. "Help me keep my dreams away."

Chapter 5

DeWayne was parked in front of Mimi's Pizza having lunch, but the foul odor lingering in his cab was killing his appetite.

He ordered double pepperoni on his slice, hoping it would overpower the smell, which he now feared would never go away. It would become his signature, his trademark. *Ick, Mommy, we got the vomit cab again.*

"You free?" It was a woman's voice.

"I'm eating lunch," he said, not looking up. If he looked up, he'd have to make a decision. If he made a decision, he'd make the wrong one.

"I'm not going far," the voice said, sounding helpless.

"I'm eating," he said harshly, trying to scare her off.

"Can I sit in the back until you're done? I'll wait. You can start the meter."

This was too much.

"I can't eat with someone in the back."

"Please."

He looked up. It wasn't a woman, but there was lipstick, there was eyeshadow, there were black tracks of mascara-stained tears. There were bruises, too.

"Get in," he said. He was turning into a fucking angel of mercy, the cab his wings.

"Thank you, darling, so very much."

But DeWayne knew he was no angel. It was a ruse that he could be anyone's salvation. He was just a sucker. A rube. This whimpering transvestite was just more punishment being heaped on him by some sour, malevolent demigod. The one that broke zippers, dropped birdshit on heads, broke fan belts, tore condoms, distributed hemorrhoids and root canals. He'd become the pet project of some adolescent demon who had his number, a black-light poster of poor DeWayne on the wall of his pit, who devotedly sent messengers filled with puke and distress to punish him. His pizza now looked like something wounded, something dragged in by an animal, itself sick and dying. He threw the slice out the window and watched it scurry away, slithering to a sewer grate and disappearing down the storm drain. Part of it was in him now.

"Where to?" he asked, though he knew the answer already because there was only one more punishment left for the fiend to inflict on him, one more lash to lay on his already blistered back.

"Brooklyn," the incubus replied. "Way out in Brooklyn."

"Brooklyn," DeWayne sighed. "Well, what the fuck."

And he started the car and turned on the meter and began his long drive to hell.

Bliss gave Artie two of the actors to interview, the grieving blond and the young man. He took the other four himself and spoke to Lisa Hormone first.

"Tell me who discovered the body."

"We all did. The whole company meets at a coffee shop for our morning espresso," Lisa said. "Not *latte*. This is *avant-garde* theater. James never arrived, but that didn't surprise us. Communication, like remembering to show up and making a *date* with someone, or calling someone *back* after they'd left several *messages* on his machine, was not his strong suit. Anyway, after espresso we got to the theater and saw James lying on the stage and thought he was sleeping, probably after partying all night and then going home to fuck some total stranger, like he usually did. We should have known he was dead—only dead could he look so peaceful. But any face of James that was gentle was a lie. With all due respect for the dead, James was a spoiled little prick and brought trouble wherever he went. He was the Johnny Appleseed of bad karma."

She swiveled in her chair and shouted to the guy with the notebook.

"Hey, Algernon! I just said that James was the Johnny Appleseed of bad karma! How's that? Was that a good line?"

"Fabulous!" Algernon adjusted his glasses and wrote it down.

Miss Hormone smiled and stretched purposefully, her shirt

lifting slightly to reveal her smooth, flat stomach and a navel pierced with a gold ring. No doubt just a few years ago she was a little girl putting on plays in her living room, dressing up in mommy's dress and heels, one of daddy's ties around her neck, singing, *The hills are alive....* Now she was Lisa Hormone—avant-garde actress, and Bliss couldn't help but notice *her* hills were very much alive under her shirt. *They* were probably pierced, too.

"Katrina our director—"

"The woman with the bifocals."

"Right. She told us to form a circle around James and begin a Tibetan chant we know to wake him. When he didn't move, someone—I think it was Algernon, our resident playwright—touched his cheek and said he was too cold to be alive."

"So you assumed he must be dead."

"Not right away," she said, looking at Bliss like he was an idiot. "When we're rehearsing one of our avant-garde pieces, when we're *really* in the moment, we transcend the present, radically alter our reality."

"I'll bet."

"Don't patronize me. By the way, I'll see your ass in small claims court when I sue you for the eighty bucks I lost for missing my class."

"I'll write you a note."

"They don't take notes. You just don't *miss* an Alexander class."

"OK. So, anyway, you're all in a circle around James, believing he's traveling somewhere on some kind of internal journey or something and was just *pretending* to be dead."

"That's a pedestrian way of putting it, but basically, yeah. Until Wolf kicked him in the butt a few times and said, 'Looks like pretty boy bought the farm.' Wolf was in Nam."

"That would be *Viet*nam."

"Cute."

It was Wolf's turn now, the guy who had been pacing the back of the theater. Wolf was a taut, wiry man with a two-inch scar on his forehead. But beneath his military bearing, Bliss sensed an inherent kindness. Wolf probably played the bad guy, the despotic king, the evil twin, the dark figure lurking in the alley with a hard-on for anything weak and soft—but always with a twinkle in his eye.

"So, Wolf, what happened after you kicked him?"

"I kicked him again," Wolf said. "To make sure. Charlie used to lie in a ditch with the dead, then, once your back was turned, do a Lazarus and put a bullet in your ass.

"Besides, death is only a state of mind," he continued. "When I worked with Grotowski in Poland, there was an actor who could put himself in a death trance for a couple of hours, then wake up and eat a kielbasa like nothing happened. Good thing he wasn't a Hasid, or he would have been in the ground. Hasids get buried fast. No wakes. Like drive-thru. You're a Hasid, you better snore when you're sleeping, otherwise you could wake up in a pine box."

"Wolf, if I could just ask you—"

"That's why they've got those beards, so their wives can see the whiskers fluttering while they sleep, to know they're still breathing. Hey, lighten up, Detective."

"I'd like to, Mr. Wolf—"

"Just Wolf. No nails, by the way. You know that? A Hasidic casket has to be put together with pegs. We needed a wooden casket once for a piece we did on Verdun. Eight-hundred thousand dead in ten days. That's pizzicato death. *Plink, plink, plink*. One dead every time you touch a string. Pluck through a minuet, that's a thousand corpses right there. Hundreds of thousands more died a few days later from the mustard gas. You know how you die from mustard gas? You cough yourself to death. Three, four days of straight coughing while your lungs slowly fill with fluid until you drown. In Nam, on a *very* bad day, I'd see twelve to fifteen casualties, tops. But in Verdun there were trenches full of dead. *Dead* dead. Around fifty thousand corpses a day on each side. Fucking James. I knew something like this would happen. Crash and burn, man. Crash and burn." Wolf rubbed his head, scratched his ear, and mystically stroked his goatee. "Sorry, but what was the question again?" he asked.

Bliss had almost forgotten himself, he'd been so caught up in the story. This Wolf was good.

"After you ascertained that James was dead by using your patented field-goal method," Bliss said, "did you then call the police, Wolf?"

"Not yet. We were all in a circle—you know, for warm-ups—so Katrina suggested we do the Native American Dance for the Dead from our piece on the destruction of the Nava-jos. They believe in the circle of life. That the spirits of their dead ancestors come back. Not like the Egyptians. They believed that once you're dead, you stay dead, but death is like some kind of bachelor pad. That's the way we did it in our X-rated piece about the Pharaohs, *Tit for Tut.*

"I missed that one."

"Too bad. Tut—that was me—was this swingin' '60s single guy—Haggar slacks, Hawaiian shirts, bamboo shades. Nefer-titi was a stewardess on Air Egypt. Different cultures have different beliefs about death. Take the Viet Cong. They die loud. Screaming. Legs twitching. Shoot one out of a tree, he falls screaming like Louis Prima; then he hits the ground and starts wriggling and twitching, legs whacking the trunk—*bam, bam*—a kind of death rhythm. I still hear it some nights. My dreams are long solos backed by the grim beat of death, the rhythm of dying Charlie twitching against the thick trunks of ancient bamboo. Now I got one more death to haunt me. You must have that, too, I imagine."

"Occupational hazard."

"Right. Hey, sorry again, but what was the question?"

"When did you call the police?"

"After Katrina got her video camera, to capture our re-
sponses to James being dead. Katrina's like Picasso. She sees
everything from all sides at once. And what's inside, too. Like
one of those viewers on the scenic overlook. Drop in a quarter, turn the handle, she's looking directly at the scenic view
of your soul. The locus of your deepest truth. I'll tell you a
story."

Bliss was about to stop him, but at the same time he really
wanted to hear it.

"Some guys bought me a birthday present once in Nam.
We were up near the DMZ. Three of us, in a lookout watching for Charlie, searching the mountains, scanning the sea,
smoking so much dope we couldn't tell the cliffs from the
waves. Eight-hour shifts for five weeks straight. We lost all
sense of time. You'd climb up the tower, blink twice, relief
would be tapping you on the shoulder. Did eight hours pass?
Eight minutes? Eight heartbeats? Time stopped or turned
inside out or spiraled inward. We couldn't tell. Then my
birthday came. I hear my present two clicks away, the whine
of her scooter coming down the dirt road, concupiscence on a
Honda, a little cloud of dust hovering above her, harbinger of
her fecund mystery. The other two guys had split the cost of
my present. Chipped in for my chippy. I was turning eighteen. She was twelve. Or fifteen. Or eleven. They counted the
years differently for Vietnamese girls. Like dogs. So she was
really sixty. Or a hundred and sixty. 'No kissy,' she said. 'Just
fucky.' They took her first. They paid, after all. Eddie, who
was oldest, pointed her head to the mountains. No kissy. Jer-
maine turned her to the China Sea. Just fucky. She was smiling when I came down. Her whole body curled like a smile—
smooth, soft yellow flesh on green jungle floor. 'My birthday,'

I said. 'Happy birthday, G.I. Joe,' she said. 'You give me big one what you got, fucky fucky.' 'No,' I said. 'OK, kissy, too.' 'No,' I said. I couldn't do it. She was just a child. Then she sat up and that little girl looked right through me, just like Katrina does. Her eyes inside me, her gaze in my organs, seeing all. Knowing all. No secrets. 'Fuck you, G.I. Joe faggot,' she said. 'I hope you get one bullet in mouth, one in balls.' Then she got on her scooter and left." Wolf held his head tightly, palms pressed to his temples, eyes open but not seeing.

Then he relaxed and looked at Bliss. "What was the question?"

"The police."

"Right. First we talked to the camera, answering Katrina's questions, helping her make art."

"You're kidding."

"I'm quite serious," Katrina put in.

It was the director's turn now. She had a husky voice, like Mister Ed with a bad cold. A hoarse horse. She sat across from Bliss and rolled herself a cigarette, using tobacco from a leather pouch marked with symbols and hieroglyphs. Bliss was thinking he might need Joseph Campbell to help him crack this case. Or Carl Jung. Katrina licked the paper, lit her cigarette, and inhaled deeply.

"We are surrounded every day by images of death. I was curious to see how people might respond to a *real* dead body."

"But these weren't *people* responding," Bliss said. "These were *actors*."

"There is no excuse for sarcasm," she said. "Irony, yes. But sarcasm is for the intellectually impoverished." She took a deep drag on her cigarette. "The question is, have we become so inured to death that being near an actual corpse would have no effect? The Hopis believe the spirit of the dead hovers in the room for several minutes before joining the spirit world, their last words before dying still on their lips."

"James had been dead for several hours already. The only one who sensed his spirit was the person who killed him."

She held her cigarette in noirish pose and slowly blew out the smoke. "I see," she said.

"Did *you* think James was an asshole, too?"

"James was an extremely difficult individual," she said. "But you have to understand, Detective, our theater embraces the difficult, nourishes it." She cast a glance in Ms. Hormone's direction. "But as I personally made no sexual overtures for James to rebuff, my response to his arrogance might be less vehement than others."

"You must have done well on your SATs," Bliss said. She chose to ignore him. Just like his older daughter. He continued, undaunted. "No one seems to be surprised that James was murdered. What about you?"

"James, like Lisa, is . . . was . . . a relatively new member of the group. They haven't been through what we have—Wolf, Algernon, Constance, and myself. We've done everything, went on pilgrimages to India, Pakistan, Tibet, tripped in the desert, chanted until we passed out, whipped each other, slept with each other, deprived each other of food and water, pretended to kill each other. There's more. Much more. We've taken each other places in this rehearsal space that you only see a glimmer of in your dreams. Found levels of elation and pain that are usually reserved only for the holy, the shamans of the world, the criminals."

"Is it possible that one of you felt the only thing left to experience was murder?"

"Like Leopold and Loeb? We did a piece on them a few years ago. *Compulsion '88*, we called it. I played Leopold, the more aggressive of the two. I can assure you, Detective, that being inside his head was terrifying. I was in no way sympathetic to his design."

"What about the others?"

"They felt the same way. Of course, Wolf killed a number of people in Vietnam. Shot them, grenaded them, even strangled one, so he said. James was strangled, wasn't he? Curious. But war is different. Even Wolf never killed anyone he knew."

"But you've thought about it. All of you. Murdering someone."

"Who hasn't? Taking a life. What the consequences might be. What you would feel like afterward. Haven't you, Detective? Encountering some despicable criminals, haven't you thought, What if I end it now? Terminate this evil. Won't I feel better? Won't I sleep more soundly knowing that dead, this man will never rape another woman? Never kill another child? Hasn't it crossed your mind?"

Bliss wanted to tell her about his jump, about his own search for meaning. If anyone was ever going to understand what he was doing on the Brooklyn Bridge in the middle of the night, it would be Katrina. Who could see into your soul, find your truth. Bliss could see why she was the director. Why, when she said "dervish," they all spun around. Maybe he'd ask her later, after he'd ascertained that she wasn't the murderer.

"In any event," she said, "in answer to your question, was I surprised that James was murdered? I'm not really surprised by anything anymore."

"Neither am I," said Bliss. Which wasn't really true because the members of the Performance Warehouse were surprising the shit out of him. "So who finally called the police?" he asked.

"Algernon did."

"Why?"

"Because I felt it was time for the next scene," Algernon, the one with the squarish glasses, said. He sat across from Bliss now, fingers drumming nervously on his notepad. "The denouement, to see what happens when the cops arrive."

"Enter the police, stage left."

"I saw you all come slogging through and had an epiphany: You're really just handymen—plumbers coming to fix a pipe."

Bliss nodded. "You've got a puddle of dead human on the floor, then we come in to see where it leaked from."

"He started to stink."

"He voided," Bliss said. "That often happens with dead people."

"What was that word?"

"Voided."

"Nice." Algernon wrote it down.

"So you're the writer, Algernon," Bliss said. "Help me out here with the plot. Who killed James?"

"We don't usually worry about plots, but I can assure you it was no one in the group."

"Some of you thought James was a real prick."

"Yeah. But he had an incredible dynamism on stage. That's why he was here."

"Did he audition?"

"No. Constance saw him in a show or something and asked him to come by."

"Constance is the one with the blond hair."

"Yes."

"She knew him before he came here?"

"I don't think she *knew* him. She just saw him perform."

"Did anyone from the theater notify his family?" Bliss asked.

"No. That's the detective's job, isn't it. Actually, if you don't mind, could I be there when you call them? I'd like to hear what you say."

"This is not happening for your benefit, Algernon."

"Are you sure? Hey, maybe we could do a little improv right now. *Ring-ring. Ring-ring.*" He shaped his hand into a telephone, thumb by his ear, pinkie in front of his mouth. "*Ring-ring*. Hello?"

Bliss played along. "Hello, is this the Roderick family?" he asked.

"Yes."

"This is Detective Bliss with the New York Police Department, Homicide Division. Mr. Roderick, I'm afraid I have some bad news for you."

Algernon screwed up his face, attempting fear. But he only managed to look dyspeptic. "It's about James, isn't it. Oh, my God, tell me it isn't about James! Please, tell me it's not about my son, James!"

Bliss could see why Algernon was a writer and not an actor.

"I'm afraid it is, Mr. Roderick. I'm sorry to tell you your son has gotten mixed up with some pretentious, avant-garde assholes who don't have a genuine bone in their bodies. I worry about him being involved with these phony fucks, and I think you should get James away from them before something bad happens to him—though I fear it's already too late."

Algernon had long since put down his pretend phone and was staring incredulously at Bliss.

"Close your mouth, Algy," Bliss said.

Algy did. Then he snapped out of his trance, Wyatt Earped his pencil, and started writing.

"After 'avant-garde assholes,' " he asked eagerly, "what did you say next?"

Li-Jung had to leave for work, but she couldn't take her eyes off the gun that sat on the kitchen table. Her very own weapon—six deaths tucked away, waiting patiently in their shells. Like snails.

She'd held guns before. Lots of boys back home in Iowa had them, under the front seats of their trucks along with empty beer cans and spare lug nuts and tire jacks. This one guy, Bobby, showed her the pistol he'd used to shoot his sister's dog—a dog he said was too goddamn old but hadn't looked all that old to Li-Jung.

But shooting a person, that was different. She'd seen it in the movies lots of times. In *Natural Born Killers* they just walked up to someone and shot them the same way you'd pat them on the back. Casually. Like, Hi, how are you? *Bang*. You going to finish those French fries? *Pop*. Mom, dad, before I go to school, I have a little surprise for you.

Kids who saw that movie were supposed to have gone out and done the same thing. Shooting people for the fun of it, just to hear their last words, to see which way they would fall over. Was that happening to her?

But Li-Jung had been wanting to shoot some people for a while now. She had a few in mind, men who she'd had encounters with back in Iowa. Dimwitted boys who didn't even try to *pretend* they liked her. Who didn't even talk to her as they drove to a secluded spot in the woods. Who acted like she owed *them* something for turning on the heater in the truck while they yanked her panties down to her shins.

These were the ones she wanted to see with a gun pressed to their temples, the ones who refused to make believe. Even if they didn't know her last name or if she was Chinese or Japanese ("chop-chop there, little geisha girl") or even how old she was, if they'd only pretended that they'd cared, it would have been all right. Because there was always some possibility of romance, with the moon shining through the pines and the stars out and the crickets chirping. Even while she was lying on a worn patch of grass, her bare legs rubbing against the dirt as she coupled with a friend of a friend, it was still possible to impersonate something like love.

Yes, there were men who she had thought about killing. Not many, but a few. Shooting them or stabbing them or

knocking them on the head with a tire iron and then setting
a rock on their gas pedal and sending them and their truck
over a cliff. She never did, but the scenarios kept her up late
into the night. Acts of retribution where she was in control,
where the blue-eyed boys who thought they were so slick
crawled on their knees in the dirt and begged her for mercy.
She watched the movies playing nightly on the ceiling above
her bed, her own private solar system revolving in a slow but
determined orbit of retribution and vengeance.

But now it was time for work. She picked up the gun and
made sure that the safety was on and stuffed it in her backpack along with her apron and brushed her teeth and set off
for work. She felt better having it with her.

Artie was in the process of interviewing the young actor when
Bliss approached.

"Where'd the blond woman go?" Bliss asked him.

Artie scanned the theater.

"She must have slipped off," he said.

"Not good, Artie."

"Ezra's still here."

"That's me," Ezra said.

"What gives, Ezra?" He had a pleasant face. His features
got along nicely with each other. He was the kind of kid you
might see folk dancing or collecting for Greenpeace. "How'd
you wind up in this menagerie?" Bliss asked.

"I interned here when I was in college. After graduation, I
was lucky enough to be invited into the company."

"Did you know James well?"

Artie interrupted. "I already asked him that, Lenny."

"Good." Bliss turned back to the kid, expecting an answer.

"He'd only been here a few months," Ezra said. "They
wanted him to play Macbeth. Or at least one aspect of Macbeth's character. Several actors were actually going to play
the role. It's Katrina's concept."

"It's a concept, all right," Bliss said. "Do you know where James lived?

Again Artie jumped in.

"I got it right here, Lenny," he said, holding out his notebook for Bliss to see. "Apartment house on Fifth Avenue."

"With his parents," Ezra added. "Or at least one of them is his parent. I'm not sure if it's the mother or father who's the real one."

"James talk to you much?"

"I wasn't nearly daring enough for James. He was living on the edge. He played the part of the Macbeth who enjoyed killing the king. Katrina said he was conceived in the witches' cauldron. A man after her own heart."

"You know if he had a girlfriend, boyfriend, any special relationships with any of the other actors?"

"I asked him that, too, Lenny," Artie said. "I also asked him if James ever mentioned anything about his life being in danger."

"And what did Ezra say?"

"Not that I recall," Ezra said.

Bliss sensed that for the moment there was nothing more to be gotten from the actors.

"Hey, Ezra, let us know if you think of anything James might have said—or anything at all that might have some bearing on his death. OK?"

"Anything at *all*!" Artie added for emphasis. Bliss had his own Greek chorus.

"Sure," Ezra said and took the card Bliss handed him.

On his way out, Bliss stood at the chalk outline of James's body, the smaller circle of the crown orbiting the body like a moon. Bliss wouldn't be surprised if the Performance Warehouse left it there, using it as part of their set for Macbeth. Blending performance with reality or some such bullshit. Why wasn't anyone upset? Why no tears? And why did Constance, the woman with the blond hair, leave so discreetly?

To answer these and other pressing questions, Bliss needed three witches of his own, to give him a premonition or two about this case, a glimpse into the future. And to tell him where his gun was. And why his older daughter had stopped talking to him. And whether his wife was going to run off with some slick, young mogul when she went out to Hollywood. He could use a whole legion of witches. A battalion, armed to the teeth with newt eyes and frog toes, each with a simmering cauldron conjuring up spells to battle his nemeses—many of which, Bliss feared, resided deep inside his own heart.

Promise finally made her appearance in the kitchen at noon. She looked refreshed, having showered and brushed out her thick blond hair.

"Scone?" Martin asked, offering her the plate. She took two. He poured her some coffee and set the cup down on the table.

"Very nice, Martin," she said biting into the pastry.

"Thank you, dear," he replied. He was looking for a clue, some hint of what had happened the night before. He decided to press the issue, just a bit. He waited until the cup was at her lips.

"James is not in his room," he said.

Not a flicker, not a missed beat.

"He's probably at a friend's," she said.

James didn't have any friends that Martin knew of.

"He's been away two nights," he said.

"He's twenty-two. He's a big boy."

He couldn't remember Promise ever referring to her son as a "big boy." It was always "my poor James—rescue him, Martin, please." And off Martin would go, like Lassie, to retrieve "poor James," now sporting a new tattoo or teeth marks from some rancid hole in the East Village.

"I'm worried about him not having any clean clothes," he said.

"Oh, Martin," she said, looking at him like he was a puppy, "what would we do without you?"

Without me, Martin thought. It was already starting.

Martin dabbed his finger and picked up some crumbs from Promise's scone that had dropped on the counter.

"Where were you last night?" he asked.

"Me?"

"Yes."

"Out."

"I see."

Normally she would have reprimanded him for his queries. Instead, she stood up from the table and looked at him, her face surprisingly vulnerable—something he hadn't seen since they were first married.

"Hold me," she said, reaching her arms out to embrace him, pressing her cheek against his robe.

This was bad.

She pulled her head back and looked at Martin, letting her top teeth seductively graze her bottom lip. "Do you want to go in the bedroom?"

Oh, this was very bad. Sex had never been part of their lives while she needed him. If she wanted sex now, it only stood to reason she no longer needed him. Something had changed. Something was wrong. He wanted James to walk in, the open wound in Promise's side that would never heal, the thing that made Martin indispensable to her.

"Come," she said, taking his hand.

With great trepidation, he let Promise lead him to their bedroom.

"Wait," he said.

"Why?"

"I need to turn off the espresso machine."

"Be quick."

He needed a moment.

"Don't be nervous," she said, laughing gently. "You're my husband."

It wasn't nerves at all. He just wished this didn't feel so much like some kind of good-bye.

Chapter 6

DeWayne couldn't understand why he wasn't still getting it for free.

"Because you ain't a cop no more," Dawn said, chewing her gum next to him in the front seat of his cab.

"So what?" he retorted. "It's two o'clock in the afternoon. Who else is going to want you this time of day?"

"You'd be surprised," she said. "This is New York, baby. Anyway, you drive a taxi now. See? It ain't blue, it's yellow. Am I right?"

"Yeah."

"And something else—it stinks like puke in here. Whatcha been doin', sleepin' in the back seat?"

"It's a long story."

"They always are with you, DeWayne. But when you was a cop, it was different—you scratched my back, I scratched yours. 'Cept it wasn't your back you wanted scratched, was it?" She started laughing, opening her mouth wide enough for DeWayne to see that she was missing most of her molars. "Am I right?"

"What about for old times' sake?" he asked.

"Can't live in the past, baby," Dawn said. "Anyway, what's

twenty dollars to you? One trip to LaGuardia, am I right? You got a Jap tourist in the back seat, you could take him through Brooklyn and turn it into fifty. Am I right? 'Cept they may not tip so big what with the back seat smellin' so bad." She pulled a rubber out of her purse and forced a lopsided smile at DeWayne. "You got the twenty dollars, I'll open this up. Otherwise, drive me back to Tenth Avenue."

DeWayne couldn't believe it. Dawn, this toothless *thing*, who used to *beg* to do him for free so he'd let her work her favorite corner. Dawn, this whore, this purveyor of orifice, this smorgasbord of fuck holes, wanted money from *him*.

"What'll it be, DeWayne?"

He wanted it and he didn't. He wanted *something*. Some kind of release. But he was having a hard time imagining himself in that foul, lopsided swamp of a mouth. He also knew that five minutes after she was done, the same emptiness and longing would be there. And he'd be out twenty bucks. But what difference did *that* make? He was so far behind the eight ball, there was no way he'd ever catch up. He needed to talk to his wife, Antoinette, but he couldn't get near her because of the restraining order. He heard the car door open.

"OK, OK, wait," he said.

"Wait for what? Look, there's *traffic* out there." She pointed outside. "And they can't *see* me when I'm in *here* with you." She pointed at the seat between them. She was talking to him like he was idiot. "I gotta look out for number one," she said. "Am I right?"

"Just shut up for a second!"

"That's it. I'm outta here."

She started opening the door, but he gripped her by the arm and yanked her back in the car.

"*Fuck you!*" she screamed and reached across the dash, and before he knew it she'd hit the horn three times.

"What the fuck are you doing?!" DeWayne shouted, wanting to smash her nose flat on to her face, to grab her throat and squeeze it tight. But she was flailing away, slapping at him, trying to gash his cheek with her nails. He grabbed on to a handful of her hair, which kept her from flying out the door, but he couldn't do anything else unless he could get to the gun in the glove compartment and shoot her. Then there was a loud bang on the window near his head. DeWayne froze.

"You OK, Dawn?"

"*Where the fuck* were *you?*" Dawn screamed at the man. She turned to DeWayne. "Let go of my hair!"

There was another rap on his window.

"Let go of her hair, man. Just let her out of the car and nobody gets hurt."

"I'm a cop," DeWayne said.

"You *were* a cop, you piece of shit cocksucker!" Dawn shouted as she scrambled out the door. "But you were too busy shovin' your needle dick around and takin' what didn't belong to you that you got booted!" She slammed the door and then poked her head through the window. "Face it, DeWayne. Face reality. Dee-ranged Dee-Wayne. That's you."

DeWayne went to open his door, wanting to get out and grab her, throw her down, find some soft place in her belly and ram his foot through it. But the guy standing next to the car slammed the door shut right in his face.

"Be cool, man," he said, like it was some kind of Shaft movie. Then he spoke to Dawn. "The man pay you what he owes you?"

"Let the prick go," she said. "You'd only be doin' him a favor by kickin' the shit outta him." She flashed DeWayne the bird. "Turd of the month." She flipped a quarter through the window onto the front seat. "Here's your tip, cabby. Have a nice day."

She walked off toward the corner, swinging her hips—her way of showing him what he couldn't have.

DeWayne took a moment to cool down, then backed out of the lot and headed east toward midtown. He forced himself to focus on driving, on making some money. Get to a hotel, pick up a fare to one of the airports. Out to LaGuardia and back into the city before rush hour. He was thinking like a cabby. Dawn was right. The two brain cells she had left to rub together had come up with a genuine thought. He had to face reality.

And reality was that DeWayne's life had turned to shit. No more house, no more backyard, no more kids, no more wife. No more being a cop. All the money he made in the taxi went to alimony, but out of guilt he would have sent it to Antionette, anyway. He had no prospects except driving this cab twelve hours a day. And now to top it off, this whore had treated him like he was scum, this woman who was closer to a toad than a human being was walking away from *him*. Wiggling her ass at *him*.

A well-dressed Wall Street type stood at the curb, briefcase at his feet, arm raised. A fare. And farther down the street, two women, arms out, trying to get his attention. And a block past that, a young couple holding hands, waving urgently. All of them with places to go, things they had to do, people who needed to see them, people they needed to see.

As DeWayne waited at the light, he thought about driving the cab right into the Wall Street guy, nailing him as he checked his watch, make him *really* late for that meeting. He wanted to ram the taxi into his briefcase and scatter all his super-important papers all over the street. But DeWayne Reardon didn't do that. Instead, when the light changed, he pulled up and stopped his cab with the passenger-door handle perfectly lined up with the guy's hand and waited for him to get in. Then DeWayne politely asked him where he

was going, and the guy said home and gave the address.
And DeWayne had no choice but to drive the man where he
wanted to go.

He pulled out into the avenue, into the traffic, joining the
yellow micturating stream of taxis flowing through the city.
He started the meter and switched lanes and glared at the
bus driver and cursed another taxi. Because that's what guys
who'd had a life and then pissed it all away did.

When James Roderick was alive, he had lived with his parents
on one of the upper floors of a plush apartment building on
Fifth Avenue with a commanding view of Central Park. It
was two o'clock, and the doorman was sorting the mail into
little cubbies with the names of the tenants, to be handed to
them when they came home from work. Like summer camp,
Bliss thought.

It was one of those apartments where the elevator opened
right into your own front hall. Bliss was impressed. The doorman had phoned up, so Martin Roderick greeted them knowing they were detectives.

"It's about James, isn't it?" he asked.

Eerie. The same words Algernon had used during their pretend conversation, Bliss thought. Everyone who knew this kid
seemed to think he would wind up dead.

"Yes," Bliss said.

"Is he . . . ?"

"He's been killed."

The newspaper Roderick was holding dropped to the floor.

"We're sorry for your loss," Bliss said.

Roderick stared at the ceiling for a moment, biting his lip.

"Where were *you* last night, Mr. Roderick?" Artie asked,
his notebook out, pencil at the ready.

"Here. Home. In bed. Where did it happen?" he asked.

"At the theater."

Roderick nodded, as if in confirmation, as if he already knew.

Artie piped in again. "We'll need to ask you a few questions." He was getting all Jimmy Olson again. Roderick didn't seem to hear him.

"Mr. Roderick, do you need to sit down?" Bliss asked.

"No. I'll . . . I'd better tell my wife."

"Then you'll answer our questions?" Artie said.

"Yes. Of course," Roderick replied. He gestured toward a pair of French doors.

"Wait in there," he said, pointing to a room off the foyer. He turned and disappeared down a long hallway.

"He's hiding something," Artie said. "He's definitely hiding something."

"Artie," Bliss said wearily, "*everyone's* hiding something."

I was right, Martin thought as he closed the hallway door and walked to their bedroom. What Promise had meant when she said it was over. That *James* was over. James was no more.

Martin lingered outside his wife's door. He'd left only moments ago, after their session of lovemaking. She had been wild, reckless, completely overwhelming him, not caring if she received anything in return. He'd gotten up a little before two, thinking he would go shopping for dinner when the doorman rang up and said that police detectives were downstairs.

Martin took a moment to decide what emotion to wear, like he was choosing a tie to go with his jacket. No, choosing a tie was probably more difficult. He was pleased with his response to the police. He thought his reaction was quite authentic. And dropping the newspaper was a nice touch. Eloquent. An action that he hoped spoke louder than any gasp or sob because, for Martin, those would not be easily forthcoming.

How would Promise react when he told her? Pretend, of course. Promise pretended so easily. But pretend what? Remorse? Deep sorrow? Martin would look into her eyes for a clue. Like what the cops did, he thought. To get a read. Would it be genuine? Her tears, would they flow easily? Or would she force them out, jumping back in time to her acting days to summon up the sorrow, paste on the despair like a false nose?

He adjusted a painting that was ever so slightly akilter.

He wiped a bit of dust the cleaning lady had missed along the top of the picture frame.

He pulled a withered leaf from a plant.

He opened the bedroom door. Promise had gotten out of bed and was sitting at her vanity, a huge Art Deco affair with a giant round mirror.

"The police are here," he said. He paused. "James is dead."

She didn't speak, but tears started flowing down her cheeks.

"I know," she said. "I was there."

"Where?"

"At the theater. I went to see James last night." She put her hand to her mouth. "I wanted him to come home."

"Was he already dead?"

"Yes."

"Why didn't you call the police?"

"I don't know, Martin."

"You should have at least told me."

"I'm sorry." She turned to him, more resolute now. "I was afraid she was taking him away from me."

"Constance. Your sister."

"She lured him down there. To be an actor, she told him. But, really, she just wanted him all to herself." She wiped her eyes. "I did love him, Martin. In my own way. You have to believe me."

"I do," he said. What else could he say, under the circumstances?

"Even though we never spent much time together, I did love him."

You loved him, Martin thought, *because James was something you had and Constance didn't.*

"The detectives want to speak with us," he said.

"What did you tell them?"

"I said I would inform you and that we would try to answer their questions."

"I should be in shock."

"It might help."

"Give me a moment," she said. "Shock isn't easy, you know."

"I know, dear," he said.

Shock is never easy, he thought. Even for you.

Bliss was impressed with Roderick's library, though not with the books but rather because of the novelty of having a room— any room—just devoted to one thing. A kitchen that wasn't also a laundry, a den that didn't double as a dining room, a second bathroom that, like in the Bliss apartment, wasn't also storage for the cages and terrariums of deceased animals, the hamster treadmill slowly rusting, the rabbit hutch a barren moonscape of sawdust and pellets, reminding Bliss of Coney Island in winter. He wanted to throw these reliquaries out, but his kids protested. It had become a kind of memorial to past pets, a macabre Forest Lawn. He promised himself that the day they both left for college, the cages were out on the curb.

"Ralph Lauren lives right near here," Artie said. "I was over his place once.

"Tasteful?"

"What would you expect?" Artie held up a finger. "Listen for a second," he said. "What do you hear? Listen good."

Bliss listened. "I don't hear much of anything, Artie," he said. He wasn't sure where this was going.

"Exactly. It's like the rest of the city doesn't exist. I noticed it at Ralph's. These people, they live in a silent world. The street, the sirens, the car horns—they're above it all. Like they've got a pillow pressed down tight over the mouth of the city."

Interesting metaphor, Bliss thought.

Artie opened a window. Outside, someone leaned on his horn. A siren wailed. A cab driver shouted at a bicyclist to get out of the way. Like someone just popped the lid on a jar of New York.

"That's more like it," Artie said. "I gotta go to the can. I'll be right back." He disappeared into the recesses of the apartment. Bliss hoped Artie didn't have any quirks beyond what he'd already displayed. One of Bliss's first partners, an older detective, liked to pull impish pranks when he questioned people in their homes—loosening the top on the salt shaker, putting tiny scratches on their record albums, unscrewing the caps of their soda bottles. He actually carried a burned out lightbulb in his pocket to replace one of their new ones. He retired to Florida not soon after—maybe now he hung around with Bliss's father at the dog track, telling his old man that his son Lenny was the asshole who had once stopped him from putting a pinprick in a lady's diaphragm.

Bliss looked out the window, across Central Park, to the twin spires of the El Dorado apartments and, as he did at least fifty times a year, wished he lived in them. He watched a steady flow of joggers and taxis and bicycles headed uptown on the park drive. He didn't see any horseback riders. He liked seeing horses in the park. Maybe he'd apply for the mounted division. Spend his last days on the force in jodhpurs.

He scoped out the bookshelves. The Rodericks had lots of art books, big ones, mostly about modern painters. Stuck in among them was a yearbook. *The Sentinel—1976.* St. Paul

High School. Seventies yearbooks were always good for a
laugh. Especially the goofy hair on the boys. Roderick seemed
older than that, so it was probably the wife's. Bliss hadn't seen
her yet and didn't know her maiden name, so he wouldn't
know who to look for.

He flipped through. The French Club consisted of kids in
berets and striped shirts, the boys with fake mustaches, a caption read R.M. LIKED GETTING *A LA MODE* WITH THE GIRLS. OO LA
LA. The kids in Home Ec. class wore aprons, the boys looking
embarrassed. FUTURE HOUSE HUSBANDS, the caption read. How
prescient. Whatever happened to Home Ec., anyway? The basketball team all had crew cuts and seemed proud of it. GTOs
and beer and cheerleaders in the back seat. He checked out
the cheerleaders. They were cute. Go Panthers, the St. Paul
High School mascot. How is it that girls in high school look
so good and the boys so odd? There were lots of notes around
the theater page. "Dear Promise," they started. What kind of
name was Promise? "You're a real star! Keep in touch! Luv
Phyllis." Instead of dotting her i's, Phyllis used little happy
faces. Hank wrote "Thank God *you* remembered your lines!"
And then Bliss saw the picture—dressed as Julie in *Our Town*,
the same exquisite features, the same long blond hair, only
fresh, unsullied. Even in the grainy yearbook photo he could
tell. And underneath, the caption: PROMISING PROMISE BENNET
PROMISES TO BE JUST AS BIG A STAR AS HER OLDER SISTER, CON-
STANCE.

Now *that* was a clue. He would have found it out eventually, but it was more gratifying when he did it like a detective.

He put the book away before Artie got back. Clearly it meant
something—that they were sisters—that Constance, the actress who had snuck away from the theater, was James's aunt.
Maybe Constance had enticed James down there and her sister got jealous.

Bliss had worked with a detective several years before

who fancied himself a kind of Zen master. "Remember this, Lenny," he had said, "even fat people have sex. Even ugly people. Dwarves are among the randiest creatures on God's green earth." He had told this to Bliss with an air of deep and profound mystery, like it was going to open up a long series of mystical doors for the fledgling detective. But like most Zen lessons, it was only years later, after working dozens of cases, that it made some kind of sense: Everyone, no matter what their shape or size, had dreams and needs and deep desires, the pursuit of which caused them to act with passion. And wherever there was passion, bad things could happen. Two sisters—one acts, the other wants to. Unrealized hopes? Unfulfilled dreams? A pinch of coveting, perhaps? A smidgen of jealousy? A soupçon of envy? He'd wait to tell Artie. Bliss didn't want him blurting anything out, thinking he was Perry Mason. He'd fill his eager partner in later. Maybe.

Martin Roderick and his wife, Promise, entered the library. She was definitely a younger version of Constance, though if Bliss hadn't known they were related, he might not have put it together. The couple sat down on the soft leather sofa above which hung a large Jackson Pollock. His art-history girlfriend in college had talked about Pollock a lot, how he had put the canvas on the floor and walked around it, assaulting it, torturing it, with paint. To Bliss, the painting was like some weird thought balloon above the Rodericks' heads.

Artie joined them.

"Our condolences," Bliss said.

Promise nodded.

"We just need to ask you a few questions," Bliss said.

She kept her head pressed against her husband's shoulder, almost as if she were hiding her face, so Bliss couldn't see any subtle changes that would give away what she was thinking.

"What do you need to know?" Roderick asked.

"If James ever mentioned that he felt he was in danger," Bliss said. "If someone was threatening him."

"He never said anything."

"Was he in any kind of trouble?" Bliss asked. Like the double, double boil and bubble kind, he thought. Or was it *toil* and *trouble*?

"Not that we knew of," the husband said.

"Some of the actors he worked with told us——"

"Whatever they told you is a lie!" It was the wife now, Promise, her eyes filled with anger.

"Promise, please!" Even Roderick seemed surprised. He tried to pull her close, but she shoved him off.

"James was normal until they got a hold of him! *They're* the crazy ones! Sick! Infectious!"

Her husband tried to hold her hand, but she pushed his hand aside.

"Darling, please don't——"

"They take you over. They call it theater, but it's really mind control. Like a cult. They say, 'Here's a rat—eat it.' You eat it. They corrupt you until you're not yourself anymore. They should be put in an airtight room, all of them——Constance, Wolf, Katrina——and fumigated like locusts. Like vermin. Covered with lye and left in the sun."

She sank back into the couch, her eyes still wide with fury.

"So," Artie said, "you didn't really approve of James working with the theater?"

"I *know* about acting," Promise said. "In *real* theater, you play a part. But in the Warehouse, they change you, twist you around until you fit what they have in mind, and then you play *that,* the *thing* you've become. They're like Dr. Frankenstein, turning people into monsters even a mother can't recognize."

To Bliss, she sounded like someone racked with guilt. It took one to know one, he thought.

"When was the last time you saw your son alive?"

Roderick asked with his eyes if they really had to go on.

"It would help us to know," Bliss said.

"James hadn't been home for the last two nights," Roderick said, his voice remarkably calm. "He often stayed over at a friend's house."

"Any of those friends seem untrustworthy to you? Dangerous? You know, parents sometimes get a bead on those things, even before their kids do."

"He spent most of his time at the theater," Roderick said.

"They killed him," Promise said. "I don't see why you even need to talk to us. It was probably for one of their shows. They do a play about carnivals, they bite the heads off chickens. They're geeks, sodomites. They have sex with each other on stage and videotape it. And because they give it a name, because they get reviews in the *Times,* it's OK. It's *art.* For their play about Vietnam, they cooked a rat on stage. Did any of them tell you about that? The one they call Wolf did it— he slit its throat, gutted it, shoved a skewer through its mouth and cooked it over a little gas stove. They were kind enough to let the audience know with a note in the program: Warning: A live rat will be killed and eaten on stage during the show."

"How do you know all this?" Artie asked.

"I *know* things," she said. "I know it would be a thrill for them to kill someone, an experience they haven't had yet. Then they'll give it a title, write the parts, sell tickets, and put a little note in the program, to ease their conscience: 'No animals were killed creating this piece, though we did strangle one young man, just to see what it was like.'"

There was an uncomfortable pause.

Bliss resumed. "How about girlfriends?"

No answer.

"Boyfriends?"

"*More* lies! Those pretentious, hedonistic . . ." She stopped, then turned to her husband and spoke now with unsettling calm.

"Get rid of them, Martin. Please. They're just cops. Make a phone call. Please. Two feckless cops. Martin, please. Make them gone."

Roderick pulled her close and stroked her hair.

"I think you'd better go now," he said.

"Your kid was murdered!" Artie shouted. "You ain't gonna be combing his hair, tying his shoes, makin' him Maypo in the morning anymore!"

"Please, Detective . . ." Roderick said.

"Look, Mr. Roderick," Bliss said, "this was not a simple robbery, not a random act of violence."

"Now is not a good time to talk. I think you'd better go."

Bliss imagined hundred-dollar-a-minute lawyers bringing up harassment charges for unnecessarily badgering the Rodericks in their time of grief. If the parents weren't interested in helping him find their son's killer, who was he to argue?

There would be more, he knew. The mystery of the sisters had yet to be unraveled. He'd run a pinball off Promise and Constance—But your sister claims . . . But your sister said . . . —See if he racked enough points for a free game. For now, he'd go with the flow and wait a bit to confront them. But he wasn't going to wait long.

"What'd she call us?" Artie asked him on the elevator down.

"Feckless."

"You know what that means?"

"We're without feck," Bliss said.

"Who is this guy Martin, anyway?"

"That's what you're going to find out, Artie."

He left thinking about the painting, how it made sense in a certain way—Pollock trying to get rid of his pain by collecting it on his brush and splattering it on the canvas in the desperate hope that it would stay there. The kind of thing Bliss had tried to do with his Big Jump. But as Pollock dis-

covered, and Bliss already knew, you don't get rid of the pain
that easily—if you ever get rid of it at all.

Chapter 7

Central Park West shouldn't have been so choked at four
o'clock, but a watermain break had turned the whole Upper
West Side into chaos. DeWayne had an old woman in the
back of the cab with her walker and her nurse. And because
of the flooding, he had to cross over to Fifth Avenue at Ninety-
sixth, then back to the West Side at Seventy-ninth—forty-five
minutes to go seventeen blocks, but what could he do? Throw
the lady out on the street? Shoot her? Before that there had
been a group of tourists, shoving addresses in his face written
in ancient tongues for him to decipher—because he was a
taxi driver he was supposed to know Sanskrit, Arabic, Japanese, Gaelic. He couldn't even understand what *borough* they
wanted. And before the tourists, he had waited in front of
an office building for ten minutes while some young woman
manager type in what seemed like a fancy suit ran inside—
just jumped out of the cab before he could say anything, shouting she'd be right back after she picked something up from
her desk, disappearing into the lobby, the meter reaching
twenty dollars before he'd checked the Bloomingdale's bag
she'd left on the back seat and found the shoe box inside filled
only with tissue paper.

But it was the father and the son he picked up that had
really thrown DeWayne for a loop, sending him into McGovern's Bar for a late afternoon drink.

"To the 'Twenty-one' Club," the father says. Very distin-

guished, the both of them. Suits neatly pressed, shiny silk
hankies in their jacket pockets. Not saying anything for a
while, just sitting next to each other in the back seat, both lost
in thought.

Then the father slaps his son on the knee and says, "Goddamn, Dukes, you did it. You pulled it off." And in unison they
break out into these huge smiles, perfect white teeth glistening. And then DeWayne catches the guy looking at his son,
and he's practically bursting with pride. "Let's celebrate," he
says. "We deserve it!" The tab's six-fifty. The old man gives
DeWayne a ten spot and tells him to keep the change. They
walk up the steps to the restaurant, the son puts his arm
around his dad's shoulder, like they're a portable Hallmark
moment.

DeWayne tried to remember the last time he had anything
to celebrate.

"What about you?" he asked the bartender in McGovern's.
"When was the last time you had anything to celebrate."

"This morning," he said. "I didn't wake up dead."

"But if you *were* dead, you wouldn't know it."

"Yes, I would. 'Cause the boss, old man McGovern, would
kill me."

"But you'd already be dead."

"Not dead enough. You want another one?"

DeWayne had once carried a wad of twenties so thick, he
couldn't fold it—had to divvy it up into two pockets. He once
saw the eyes of the car dealer practically pop out of his head
when he put thirty-eight thousand on his desk in fifties and
hundreds. And, further back, a lifetime ago, he went to work
in the morning thinking he was making the world a better
place—that being a cop meant being one of the good guys.
But that was ancient history, a memory now shrouded in a
dark haze of regret.

"That your cab?" the bartender asked.

DeWayne didn't even bother looking. "Yeah."

"The meter maid's writing you a ticket."

"It's worth it," DeWayne said. Because the bartender had given him the answer to why all this bad stuff was happening to him: DeWayne was already dead; he just wasn't dead enough.

On his way home from the Rodericks' apartment, Bliss drove to the hospital to visit Ward.

"He's been watching talk shows all day," Malikha said when Bliss arrived. "Not even the good ones. If it was Oprah, maybe I could understand. He says he wants to be on one of them. He wants to tell his story."

"How I caught the bullet," Ward said. "How I saw it leave the gun."

"Then you can talk about your sex change," Bliss said. "Once you had a hole in your hand, you could see inside that you were really a woman."

Ward shook his head sadly at the nonbeliever, then turned zombielike toward the tube and watched a lady in a flower-print dress proclaim her philosophy of self-help.

"It's up to each of us to discover our own inner celebrity," the lady in the flower-print dress said. "You may not have the legs of Cindy Crawford or the brains of Henry Kissinger or the muscles of Arnold Schwartzenegger, but you have *something special* inside you, and you have to find it." And here the lady in the flower-print dress closed her eyes and raised up her fists for exclamation. "Find it, your *inner celebrity*, and be proud of it! Show it off to the world!"

Ward held his hand out to the television, palm out, like he was directing traffic.

"Here it is!" he shouted. "My inner celebrity! I caught a bullet!"

At which point Malikha punched off the television.

"You're worrying me, baby," she said. She ran her fingers through his soft black curls. "I think you need to talk to someone."

"But this is my inner celebrity," Ward said. "I'm sure of it. The bullet."

Which bullet? Bliss thought. The one that had gone through Ward's hand or the one that his partner had shot through the head of the young boy?

Cases involving young kids, no matter how dirty, how much at fault they were, upset his partner. Ward would take a moment, kneeling next to the body, looking at the limp hands now resting peacefully, the dead face now eased of the creases that moments before defined a meanness, an anger deeply etched in brows and cheeks that should have been smooth. It had happened so often over the past ten years that Ward had a eulogy ready for these fallen children, lines from Langston Hughes:

He was my ace boy, gone away
Wake up and live, he used to say.

"I need you back," Bliss said.

"I know, partner," Ward said. "I'll be there soon."

Bliss left as Malikha played some Aretha softly on the boom box. "Day Dreaming." She danced slowly around the hospital room, her hips moving gently to the sultry rhythm of the music. Maybe her attentions could bring Ward back.

Weakness was not something Bliss had ever associated with his partner. He needed Ward's strength, his will, the way he pursued criminals with a single-minded vengeance. And he needed his partner to get him back his gun.

Li-Jung had been cleaning shrimp for most of the afternoon. Hundreds of shrimp. For the past two hours, she and the Mexican dishwasher had been getting them ready for the big cocktail party that Dave the caterer was preparing for that night. Peeling off the shells but leaving the last little bit of tail in place. That's the way Dave wanted them for his appetizer trays, which the tuxedoed waiters would soon pass among the rich and famous at the party. She wondered what the guests did with the little piece of shrimp tail when they were finished——the fancy ladies, gesturing as demurely as they could with a bit of shellfish in their hand, the self-important men trying to appear suave as they slipped the tail into their jacket pocket or an unsuspecting plant. Maybe it was the caterer's subtle way of getting revenge.

She slit another shrimp down the back and used the tip of the knife to pry out the black ribbon of intestine——shrimp shit. Sometimes it was yellowish brown and sometimes it was greenish gray, depending, she imagined, on what the shrimp had eaten or what time of day it had been caught. One out of every ten had no shit in it at all, just a clear strip of membrane dangling off the tip of the knife like dental floss.

"All cleaned out," she said. "Must have had coffee that morning."

The dishwasher didn't understand much English, but he smiled, anyway.

She was adept at cleaning shrimp. Also at cutting onions, mincing garlic, chopping ginger, making wontons. She'd been doing it in her parents' restaurant since she was a kid. The China Palace it was called, and Li-Jung was the princess—— trapped in the tower by the evil king, her father. As a child, she had spent her days endlessly filling spring rolls, chopping ginger and garlic. Then when she was twelve she started making wontons. She'd start working right after school, sitting at one of the tables in the front of the restaurant until dinner time, then moving to the pantry in the back to work on a cutting board set up on a couple of empty beer cases. She'd stay at it through into the dinner rush, keeping her father supplied with ingredients, pushing herself faster as it got busier, never stopping until the last order was filled. Then she'd start on her homework, and when it was quiet and her father had washed the stove and cleaned out the wok, he would fix her something to eat. Leftovers. Whatever dish had been slow that night.

She never played with friends after school—no swings in the playground, no hopscotch in the parking lot, no bike riding, no dolls. Her world was chopping vegetables and taking the seeds out of green and red peppers. Her hands were full of tiny cuts and always smelled—often from fish, usually from garlic.

Customers had to walk past the China Palace kitchen to get to the bathroom, and sometimes kids from her school would see her working, dressed in an apron, a knife in her hand, a bowl in her lap. They'd look embarrassed and say hi, trying to pretend it was all perfectly natural, that all fifth graders had to spend their evenings with their fingers smelling of fermented black beans and covered with flecks of raw pork. At first she smiled and waved back, but after a while she learned to never look up and stayed bent over the board, trying to disappear into the bowl of chopped meat or ground fish or mushrooms minced with scallions.

After a while she could roll the wontons with her eyes closed, which made it easier to pretend she was somewhere else, that she had long blond hair and bright blue eyes and lived in a *real* palace, a golden palace that sparkled and didn't smell and where so much fruit grew in the garden that if you were hungry you just plucked a piece and ate it and no one ever had to cook. She dreamed that her fingers were slipping pearls on silky gold chains instead of rolling rice dough around balls of diced pork and ginger. With her eyes closed she could pretend that some valiant knight would come on horseback, and, flourishing his sword, he would slay the pitiless ogre who owned the China Palace, the one now standing sweating over the stove, the evil ogre who cursed his daughter, who had given her this yellow, thick-lipped face, who shook and stirred the wok like a demon, sweat dripping into the food, his strings of greasy black hair falling in front of his sad, empty eyes.

And then the stalwart knight would slay the mother ogre, not because she was evil but to put her out of her misery, so she wouldn't have to force a smile onto her heavy mouth and make squeaky sounds of gratitude when the customers walked in. *How many for dinner, prease? Yes, prease. Yes, solly. Light this way.* Hunched over, nodding, bowing, the smile fixed like it was painted on, walking with tiny steps. *Tea? Yes I bling it light away. Duck sauce? Noodles? Yes, is coming.* The knight would put an end to it all and carry Li-Jung away to a clean, white world that didn't reek of fish guts and chicken feet, where the grease didn't soak into her clothes and infuse her skin with the smell that made it seem like she was carrying the restaurant with her. In school they called her Chopsticks or Column A in a mean way, sniffing at her like dogs. *Smells like you had lo mein on the menu last night, eh, Chopsticks?*

And there wasn't one kid who, like in the movies, tried to be her friend, who risked the ridicule of the others to sit with her at lunch, walk to the China Palace after school and make wontons together, Li-Jung teaching her friend the tricks, laughing when the first efforts looked like misshapen blobs, then smiling proudly when her friend did them right. In the movie, the friend would bring the wontons home to her family, saying Li-Jung, the Chinese girl in school, had taught her how and Mommy, when can she come to *our* house?

But it never happened. There had been no loyal best friends, no fairy godmothers, no Jiminy Crickets in her life.

So how ironic was it that here in New York she was doing exactly what she had run away from, what she hated most. At least now she was being paid and got to wear a white chef's coat. And unlike her father, Dave the caterer was actually in awe of how fast she cleaned shrimp, how effortlessly she assembled the wontons.

The waiters were taking notice of her, too. There were some cute ones and she'd gone home with a few of them. The latest was Matt, who had flirted with her heavily at a recent party, making idiotic jokes whenever he came into the kitchen to fill up his tray and smiling in an inane Hugh Grantish way. He was nice enough, but she knew what he wanted. The conquest thing. Chinese pussy, wanting to find out whether it was slanted the other way, like in the jokes. The conquest thing was something she knew well. She just hoped one of her conquerors would turn out to be the gallant knight who would rescue her and take her far away.

But back in Iowa, the only knights she'd had to choose from sported tattoos instead of armor and drove beat up 4X4s instead of valiant steeds. And the lush meadows and castles she'd dreamed of became patches of worn dirt near the turn-around at the end of an old logging road with the sweaty, ill-shaven knight moaning on top of her, breathing whiskey breath that in no way smelled of roses or myrrh.

And then she thought about the gun.

Maybe with a gun you didn't need a gallant knight. With a gun, you, yourself, could become the conqueror. She wondered what Matt the waiter would say if she took him back to her place and showed it to him. *Come to my bed*, she'd whisper, and he'd be all excited but then she'd reach under the mattress and there it would be, right in her hand, pointing at him. The smile would go away then, wouldn't it? And maybe his arms would start flapping at his sides, not knowing what to say, not knowing where to move. That would be interesting.

She'd shot guns before, off in the woods, shooting at cans or knotholes or squirrels but really aiming at her father, who she knew would yell at her when she got home, who even now was yelling at her mother because Li-Jung wasn't at the restaurant. She had tried to get lost in the woods, deep in the woods, far away from the China Palace.

It was a good feeling, having the gun. She could see why the boys in her town were so eager to get their first .22 rifle, why they stayed up late into the night cleaning and polishing it. It gave you a sense of power—that someone was alive because you decided *not* to kill them that day. Maybe she'd let Matt the waiter know that sometime. She'd wait for her chance.

Chapter 8

Bliss didn't expect a rabbi to be sitting in his living room when he got home. But then, who does?

"Lenny," his wife said, "this is Rabbi Zorn. You saw him that time you went to the synagogue."

"You may not recognize me sitting down," the rabbi said, chuckling rabbinically.

Truth was, Bliss wouldn't have recognized him if he had on his robes and was blowing a ram's horn.

"This is about Julia's Bas Mitzvah, right?"

"Relax, Dad," Julia said. "It's not an investigation."

"I'm just here to go over a few details," the rabbi said.

"Isn't it still a few weeks away?" Bliss said, suddenly worried that he had forgotten it was that weekend, that he'd need someone to take over his case.

"That's right, honey," his wife said, "so you still have time to let the bad guys know that in three weeks they'll need to take some time off. Make plans to go fishing. Spend some of their ill-gotten gains."

The rabbi cleared his throat. "We were discussing the ceremony," he said. "Your parents, Lenny, will they be coming?"

Lenny felt the color drain from his face. He looked to Rachel for help.

"Most likely not," she said.

He couldn't imagine his father leaving Florida, even for a weekend. Even for his granddaughter's Bas Mitzvah. There were bets to be placed at the dog track—trifectas, quinellas, exactas—all chosen after visits to the confidantes, grooms and trainers that he kept like his informants when he'd been a cop, nurtured by the periodic sawbucks he slipped them; and then there were waitresses in donut shops to flirt with—forty years his junior, but it didn't matter, he still gave them the routine, calling them darling and sweetheart, showing them his badge with a wink, arching back in his chair so they could see how lean he was—more affection than he gave his family in a decade levied on a complete stranger in the time it took to order a cup of coffee.

"You're sure there's no way to get them here?" the rabbi asked. "It's part of the significance of the event, that the Bas Mitzvah be in the presence of the family."

Julia looked over at Bliss.

"How about just Grandma?" she asked.

Bliss wondered if he could somehow just get his mom on a plane, sneak her out of the condominium in a taxi while his father was at his morning poker game.

"We haven't seen her in so long," Cori said.

She would never do it, never leave her Monty alone. How many times had he heard it? Her man might suffer a fatal stroke in her absence, lying on the bathroom floor, unable to get to the phone.

But he *deserves* a stroke, Ma, he wanted to say. He deserves to die alone on the bathroom floor, the phone just out of reach, his last few moments devoted to the lucid vision of what a profoundly evil person he'd been.

"Even if it were just your mother who could come," the rabbi said, "this would be a mitzvah in itself."

But maybe the reason she never left was because she wanted to be there to watch him suffer. That she didn't dare risk being gone in case she missed the moment when he was struck down, so she could hear him cry out in agony, his every wail of pain freeing an arrow that had once pierced her body, an arrow he'd shot there. His mother the saint. Maybe she'd even kick the old fart a few times while he was down. Bliss wished it were so.

"I'm sorry, Rabbi," Bliss said. "I'm sorry, Julia, but I just don't think it can happen."

"But you'll try," Rachel said.

"Yes." He'd make the call, try to reach through to his father. Maybe he could at least get a present out of him for Julia. Monty would find a greyhound called something like Julia's Luck, then circle it in the program and send it to her along with a two-dollar ticket to show.

"But Annette and Norman will of course be there," the rabbi said, meaning Rachel's parents, who already had their names on several plaques around the synagogue and would no doubt make another generous contribution in honor of their oldest granddaughter.

"Yes," Rachel said. "But Rabbi Zorn, you must promise to remind my father that it's *Julia's* celebration, not his."

The rabbi chuckled knowingly. But, then, how else *would* a rabbi chuckle?

"I'll remind him, Rachel. Don't you worry. Because this is most definitely her moment, the time for Julia to express herself, to emerge as a true person."

"Like finding her inner celebrity," Bliss said. "Right?"

His enthusiasm was greeted with unanimous dismay.

"My *inner celebrity*, Dad? Where'd you come up with *that*? Jenny Jones?" Julia shook her head as if to say maybe it wasn't such a good idea letting her dad up on the *bima* in front of the congregation, that he might have a flashback of some kind, start waving his gun around, telling everyone not to move, that he had them covered, that there would be no more praying until they all had alibis for where their souls had been the night before.

They went over more of the arrangements, including the prayer Lenny was to say.

"I get my own prayer?" Lenny asked.

"It's the tradition, that the father of the Bas Mitzvah announces the opening of the ark."

"My own prayer . . ." Bliss said.

He'd seldom been to synagogue in the last few years. He spoke no Hebrew and had even forgotten that the books opened from the other side. Still, he was suddenly flush with a deep excitement, maybe even pride at his daughter's achievement.

The rabbi got up to leave.

"We appreciate your coming by," Rachel said. "Lenny's schedule doesn't allow him a lot of free time."

"He's a noble warrior," the rabbi said.

"Yes, he is," his wife agreed.

He liked this rabbi. As he walked him to the door, Bliss wanted to talk to him about his bungee jump, ask whether there was something in the Talmud that dealt with men desiring to fall from high places as a form of spiritual enlightenment. Or whether, as Bliss suspected, it was just a childish attempt on his part to get attention.

DeWayne sat low in the seat of his cab like he used to do when he was on a stakeout. In the rearview mirror he could see the Lexus in what used to be his driveway. He still had a key. It was in his pocket, along with the $328 he'd made that day driving. He could tool down to Atlantic City in style, check into a hotel, and put everything he had on 00. Then, in one turn of the wheel, have enough money to either start over or have nothing, which would serve as a good reason to shoot himself in the mouth.

He'd paid for the Lexus in cash, fifties and hundreds he'd found in socks, in coffee cans, stuffed in the toes of fancy Italian shoes, tucked away in the drawers, cupboards, and closets where drug dealers lived. Money that had somehow leaped at him, clung to him like burrs, followed after him like he was a dog in heat. Money that belonged to no one, ill-gotten gains like orphans in a storm, looking for shelter, some warm pocket to snuggle up in. He'd enter a dealer's apartment and some kind of radar would click on and he'd go right to the stash. No ripping apart cushions of couches, pulling the feathers out of pillows, punching holes in drywall to loot secret cubbies. He'd say to himself, If I were a drug dealer and I lived in this house, where would I put my money? And there it would be: take the top off the cocktail shaker, remove the back of the Mr. Potato Head, lift the top of the toilet tank, and *voila!* Like he had put it there himself. Like it was his to begin with. DeWayne had had a knack.

And what a lucrative knack it had been. He'd been generous when he was flush. Lending guys money, taking buddies on fishing trips to Montauk, buying them hookers and Knicks tickets and rounds of drinks. They knew the money was dirty. They had to. One cop handing another a handful of big bills. But no one had asked. No one had told him to be careful. No one had said anything to him like, "DeWayne, you fucking

idiot, you're going to get caught just like the guys in the Thirtieth Precinct, the Dirty Thirty, and you'll lose your badge or
worse." No, no one had given him any advice. They just took
what they needed and thanked him and patted him on the
back, figuring it was just some scumbag that got his stash
ripped off and better the good guys should be spending it,
sponsoring a softball team or underwriting a birthday dinner
of lobsters and steak for one of the veteran cop's retirement
parties out on City Island.

DeWayne dozed off for a second, then woke up. He'd been
driving all day and into the night, when the weirdos and
freaks came out. To a cab driver, every night was Halloween
in New York, and DeWayne was just one of the ghouls. His
costume: a dirty cop, his chariot full of other ghouls. All part
of a sordid pageant. He *felt* dirty. He wouldn't let his kids hug
him, afraid they'd come away coated with the decay. No one
talked to him. He'd given up trying to call his friends on the
force. He'd given up on everyone.

He looked at his house, the windows lit up, the shadows of
his wife and kids moving about. *The shadows of his wife and
kids.* It was his own house, paid for with his real salary. It
looked like paradise now. He closed his eyes, and his mind
took himself up the front path, remembering the many times
he'd shoveled off the snow, trimmed the edge, pulled weeds
from the cracks. In his mind he walked up the steps, six of
them. He put his hand to the railing on the right side and felt
it was loose. The bolt going into the concrete stoop needed
tightening. He pictured the bolt and thought how he'd meant
to do it for the last four years. Antoinette nagging him. *Fix
the railing, already. Before someone breaks their neck and sues
us for everything we've got.* He was ready now. His crescent
wrench was in his toolbox in the basement. He could see that,
too—the baby-food jars filled with screws and nuts, the work
table, the vise. He was ready to tighten the bolt now, to get

out the wrench and fix it once and for all. Honey, please, I'm begging you, let me come back and tighten the bolt on the railing. I want to. I'm *ready* now. Please. I can do it. I *want* to do it. That leak under the sink—it'll be gone in the hour. The cracked linoleum in the hallway—a memory by twilight. Please. Let me in. Let me in my house. Let me stand at the end of my children's beds and watch them sleep, the gentle rise and fall of the covers, the soft mumbles of their dreams.

Someone tapped on his window.

"You on duty?"

It took him a moment; then it all rushed back, his reality, the festering-lump-of-DeWayne reality, his leaking fetid sore of a life.

"Where you going?" DeWayne asked.

"Into the city."

He'd been driving for the last sixteen hours. The ginger ale bottle was full and starting to reek. But it was at least a twenty-dollar trip into the city from where they were in Queens. He turned the key and started the cab.

"Take the bridge or the tunnel?" DeWayne asked as he drove past his house, everything he once owned less than twenty yards away, his whole life now an exhibit in a museum, a diorama he could look at but not touch.

"The bridge is fine," the man said. "Not much traffic this time of night, so why pay the toll?"

"Right," DeWayne said.

He started the meter and kept his head forward so the passenger wouldn't see his face fixed in a mask of bitterness and exhaustion, the tears welling in his eyes that refused to flow.

It was luck that Martin should pick up the phone at exactly the same moment as his wife, but a luck he was cultivating as he tried to find a place where Promise would be vulnerable, something he could use to hold over her, something that would look good to the police. He wasn't sure yet what it was, but he hoped some angle would soon present itself, some thread would emerge from the tapestry of this sordid affair that he could use to wrap around her throat and pull it tight.

It was her sister, Constance, on the line. Her older sister, the actress. They rarely spoke. A condition of their marriage was that Martin never have any contact with Constance. He dismissed it as acute sibling rivalry, but he sensed his wife had some hold over her sister.

"You think I killed him," Promise said.

"Yes," Constance replied, contritely.

Their voices were so similar, it took Martin's utmost concentration to tell them apart.

"But you were the one always looking for danger," his wife said, "for new experiences, pushing past your limitations. Did you push past your limitations with James, Aunt Constance?"

"Fuck you, sister, dear."

"Is that how you feel, or is it a line from one of your plays?"

"You killed him because you wanted him for yourself."

"I *had* him"—Promise's voice was so piercing, Martin had to pull the receiver away from his ear—"and you couldn't bear how close we were, just like a *real* mother and son."

"You weren't close to him," Constance said. "You didn't even know his shoe size. *Martin* was the one who took care of him."

"Denigrate me, like you always have."

"I thought you liked that."

"*We* were a *family*. Something you never had."

"Your family made David Koresh's look like Ozzie and Harriet."

"But you had nothing. Because you are the demon seed."

Martin had to stifle a laugh.

"Grow up."

"The product of some satanic coupling—our mother in

the cold Minnesota night being lured to our pond, which should be frozen but instead is steaming, bubbling warm, and she takes off her clothes and mates with a horrid serpent thing, and then you are born."

"Is this what you talk about—at your cozy family dinners?!"

"It's the only answer I came up with, for why you are what you are."

"Look inside yourself, Promise, and there you'll find the true answer. Because there you'll find me."

Promise slammed down the phone and Martin smiled. There was certainly enough anger and suspicion between the two sisters to help his cause. He would let it simmer and keep his eyes open, wait for the right moment.

He put on his shoes and quietly left the apartment. Promise wouldn't be the slightest bit curious finding him gone. He walked north on Fifth, nodding to doormen he recognized, the tops of the trees across the street in the park silhouetted in the moonlight. He found a pay phone by the Metropolitan Museum. From there he made a call to a man he knew who had helped him out of sticky situations before. A man who, for a fee, would get things done. Martin wasn't exactly sure yet what it was he wanted, but he needed to know the man was around so that when the occasion arose, the man could take care of it, the thing Martin wanted done. Pretty much *whatever* Martin wanted done.

Act III

Chapter 9

The first thing Bliss did the next morning was call Constance. Since she was James's aunt, the kid might have confided something to her about his friends, drugs, money he owed. James must have known, trusted, whoever it was who killed him. What troubled Bliss was the blow to the head coupled with the strangulation marks on his neck. He was trying to fit the two together.

"It bothers me, too, partner," Artie said as he stood over Lenny's shoulder studying the crime-scene photos. "I mean, you either whack a guy in the head or you strangle him. You don't do both."

Bliss put up his hand to silence his partner as Constance's answering machine came on. Her voice was soft and enticing. He left a message to call him at the precinct. He called again several times during the next few hours, getting intimate with her message, while he and Artie checked alibis.

Artie, Bliss discovered, was particularly zealous on the phone, spending over an hour with the law office where Lisa Hormone worked.

"Turns out her real name is Lisa Schwartz," Artie said. "She started at eleven P.M., right around the estimated time of death. If she took a cab, she still could have done it."

"You really think so, Artie?"

"She calls herself Hormone," Artie said. "So anything is possible. I think we should check the taxi records, see if anyone picked up a girl with a nose ring near the law office and drove her to Soho."

"Maybe she rode her bike."

"Does she have a bike?"

"I don't know."

"Hmmm."

Artie picked up the phone and left a message for Lisa to call him with information regarding whether she owned a bike and, if so, how many gears it had. Then he hung up.

"You're a stickler, Artie," Bliss said.

"Fuckin'-a, Lenny," Artie said.

Then Bliss got a call from Cardozo.

"Hey, Lenny, just wanted to tell you, about the Roderick kid, looks like there's evidence that he was on the receiving end of some homosexual activity. Or as my lab assistant Audrey put it, 'Dis bad boy been takin' it in the bee-hind.'"

"Audrey knows about such things."

"She gets around. In terms of wear and tear there's nothing out of the ordinary, so I don't think he was forced into it. No semen deposits, so Roger Ramjet must have worn his raincoat. By the way, I have some Polaroids of the area in question I can sell you if you want to see for yourself."

"No thanks."

"They make a nice stocking stuffer."

"You're in a fine humor this morning, Cardozo."

"I try. Hey, Lenny, before I hang up, whattaya think of this poem Audrey made up? 'Rain, rain, go away / you're washing off my DNA.'"

"Cute."

"Yeah. I'm hoping she comes up with a few more. Then we could put out our own line of greeting cards. Photos of deceased John Does on the outside and a snappy bit of poetry inside."

"The perfect thing for Mother's Day."

"People are into morbid these days. What do you think of Morgue Moods as a title?"

"Catchy."

Cardozo was losing it. But he'd probably say the same thing if he heard about Bliss jumping off the Brooklyn Bridge. They were both losing it. Or maybe finding it, in some kind of weird, roundabout way.

Bliss filled Artie in on the latest development concerning James's sexuality.

"Hey, Lenny, I just want you to know I got no problems with that. I mean, working in the garment district you see a little bit of everything."

"I imagine you did," Bliss said.

"I mean, you reach under a skirt over there, you're never sure what you're gonna discover."

"Life's full of surprises, Artie."

"It sure is, Lenny."

They were starting to sound like an old married couple. Bliss was waiting for Artie to pull a couple of knitting needles from his bottom drawer and hand him a skein of wool.

The phone rang again, mercifully ending the chitchat. Bliss picked it up. It was Katrina, director of the Performance Warehouse.

"I've decided to tell you," she told him decisively.

"What?" Bliss asked.

"I think Wolf did it."

"Did what?"

"Killed James."

"What makes you think so?"

"Lately, all this Nam shit has been coming back to him, and Wolf's been acting incredibly volatile and scary."

"He's not always like that?"

"What Wolf does best is tell stories. He spent part of his life living, and now he talks about it. You never saw any of his performances?"

"Sorry."

"Just Wolf and a microphone—completely alone—reconstructing his life in vivid detail. You're reliving it with him. It's better than Chekov."

"Seems he was always living in the past. What's different now?"

"Lately, it's like he can't keep them separate. His past and present."

Who can? Bliss wanted to say.

"Has he threatened anyone?" he asked.

"Not in so many words."

"So he hasn't said anything like, 'Watch out or I'll strangle you like I did James'?"

"Why aren't you taking me seriously, Detective?"

"I'm not sure."

And he wasn't. This case was like a watching a foreign movie with bad subtitles. He could see what was going on, but he knew he wasn't getting most of it. Then again, he'd never worked on a murder case involving an actor before. Maybe this is what they all were like.

"I apologize," he said.

Then Bliss had an impulse and went with it. Isn't that what you were supposed to do in the theater?

"Did Wolf and James have a relationship?" he asked.

She hesitated. "Yes," she said.

"They were having sex."

"I suppose you could call it that. But having *had* sex with Wolf, I would say it's something that bears only a slight resemblance to what you and I think of as making love."

"So Wolf likes girls, too?"

"*Devours* might be a better word."

"Well, thank you for the information, Katrina. I'll look into it."

"I should hope so," she said.

"By the way, have you seen Constance?"

"Did you call her?"

"Many times."

"She's probably home. You may have to knock on her door."

"Thanks."

Bliss recapped the conversation for Artie. Then he told his new partner to call the Rodericks and inform them of this latest development. Maybe James had said something to them about Wolf. Maybe Bliss just wanted to shake things up over at the Rodericks'. See if anything jarred loose.

Artie was excited. "It's starting to fit together," he said.

"We could still use a motive, Artie."

"Yeah, but the pieces of the puzzle are falling into place."

Which was true. If you thought of a murder as a puzzle, then, yes, it could seem as if the pieces were fitting together. But if, like Bliss, you thought of it as digging a hole in sand, knowing that for every shovelful you dug out, at least that much slipped back in, then you weren't so hopeful. His art-history girlfriend in college once took him to see *Waiting for Godot*, very little of which he understood except when one of the guys in the bowlers said that "the tears of the world are always constant—as soon as one stops crying, another starts." Or something like that. It could have been the motto of a detective. He should get it emblazoned on his gun.

His gun.

He called Ward at the hospital. They said he'd left and gone home. Bliss would try him there later.

Because he needed to start looking for his gun, to track down Li-Jung, if that really was her name. He wasn't sure where to begin. It had been more than a day already. The trail was getting cold. He'd driven around the Brooklyn Bridge for hours that night and couldn't find her. He'd spoken to the subway clerks; no Asian girls had come by that they remembered. He was beginning to fear that the only way he was going to find his gun was to get everyone in the city of New York to be absolutely quiet and still, and then Bliss would close his eyes and listen very carefully, so he could hear it when it went off.

———————————

It was the other detective on the phone. Artie, the eager one, the one with something to prove. He informed Martin, in what Martin felt was rather a smug tone of voice, that his "son," James, had been having a homosexual affair with one of the actors at the theater, a certain Wolf. He then asked Martin if he thought this might have some bearing on James's murder.

"Not that I know of, Detective."

"You're absolutely sure."

"As sure as I can be."

"I'd like to come by some time and examine James's room."

"Is that really necessary?"

"You never know what we may turn up. Something that seems very innocent to you might turn out to be a crucial piece of evidence."

"I suppose so."

"Anything you want to confess at this juncture, Mr. Roderick?"

"No, Detective."

"Anything else come to mind you want to tell me about?"

"Not that I can think of."

"You'll let me know if something does."

"I have your number."

"Good."

As Martin hung up the phone, a plan was already forming in his mind. The first part entailed finding Wolf's address. The next part centered around Promise's anger, which the police had already seen. An anger that could easily turn to rage when she found out that her son had been brutalized not only mentally but physically by the members of the Performance Warehouse. One member in particular. One member's member.

He left the apartment and walked downtown this time, thinking it might be wise not to call from the same pay phone twice. He hadn't been to the Frick Collection for a while. He could see the Vermeers, then sit in the courtyard and contemplate his next move. He didn't want to let this opportunity slip away. This chance to escape his ignominious life, more porter than husband, more lackey than lover.

He'd slipped a pair of gloves in his pocket, so he wouldn't leave any prints on the receiver. From now on, he couldn't be too careful.

The woman was already talking on her cellular phone when she got into the cab, holding it with her fingertips pointing out, so as not to ruin her freshly polished nails. DeWayne started the meter and waited for her to tell him where to go.

"I could just take it," she said into the phone. "I could take the four million he's offering and walk away, or I could go for half of everything, which would be about five point seven. But that would mean going to court, and by the time we're through paying the lawyers, it'll wind up being four million, anyway. Besides, it'll be hard on the kids and . . . You're right, Doris, we could . . . we *could* send them to boarding school for a year during the trial, but that means—Wait a second." She put the call on hold and spoke curtly to DeWayne. "*Why* aren't we moving, may I ask?"

"You never told me where you wanted to go."

"Excuse me, but this is *not* my first time in a taxi. Seventy-third and Park," she said. "Your license," she added, craning her neck to see around the partition, "it's blue."

"Yeah."

"That means it's temporary. You're in training. A trainee. You sure you know what you're doing?"

"I was a cop for twelve years."

"As I said, do you *know* what you're doing?"

"Your friend . . ." he said.

"What?"

"On the phone."

"She's not my friend." The woman clicked back on. "Doris, I'll speak to you later." She clicked off.

"You want me to get started now?" DeWayne asked.

The woman didn't say anything.

"Well?"

"What do you think, Mr."—she looked at his license again—"Mr. Reardon? Should I settle for four million or take him to court for five point seven? Or have him killed and get everything?"

"Either settle or kill him," DeWayne said, "but avoid court at all costs." Like most cops, he'd spent far too many hours sitting on hard courtroom benches waiting to testify, usually being told at the last minute that the defendant had copped a plea.

"I think you're right," she said. "Settle or kill him. Good plan. So, did you quit, or did they throw you off the force? Come on, you can tell me. I'll give you a good tip."

"I retired."

"I see. How would you like to kill my husband for me?"

"Sure," DeWayne said, wanting to see where this was going. He threw out a crazy number. "A hundred thousand dollars and he's dead."

"OK."

"Fifty thousand now and fifty thousand before you leave for the funeral home."

"I assume you'll want cash."

"Yeah. Twenties and fifties."

"That shouldn't be a problem," she said. "I'll just tell the bank I'm buying a painting directly from the artist—you know, without the dealer knowing."

"Sure."

"That's a good plan, isn't it?"

"Very good," DeWayne said. He suddenly had images of

New Zealand. South America. Someplace warm, lying in the sun, drinking tropical potions out of coconut shells adorned with those little umbrellas. This was just what he needed.

"It's just that a hundred thousand seems like a lot," she said.

"That's true. If you want, I can find you a crackhead on Avenue B who will do it for sixty bucks, and if you want *two* people whacked, he'll do both for a hundred." DeWayne was enjoying himself, the idea growing on him. He wanted to make it sound good. "The thing you're paying for with me is not the hit. The hit itself, that's a cinch. It's the afterwards. It's easy to find someone to take you to the dance, but there's no guarantee they're going to act like a gentleman on the way home. Those crackhead scumbags will never leave you alone."

"What do you mean?"

"I mean they'll always be knocking at your door asking for more money, or else they'll sell you out next time they're arrested and need something to trade in order to lighten their sentence. I should know. I'm the one they traded with. But with me, once the job's done, you'll never see or hear from me again."

Because he'd be lying in a hammock under the shade of a palm tree, being fanned by a young island maiden in a grass skirt and nothing on top who would employ her native intuition to satisfy his every need. With that image fixed in his head, DeWayne shifted into drive and headed out into the traffic on Madison.

She was interested. He could feel it. Mulling it over. Yeah, he could pocket the first fifty grand and walk away. No harm done. Shit, maybe he'd even pop the guy after all and go for the whole hundred yards. They drove in silence for a few blocks.

"How would you do it?" she asked.

"I'd shoot him and then take him out to this spot I know in the Jersey Pine Barrens. They'd never find the body. Unless you wanted them to. In that case I would leave him in the trunk of a stolen car out in the long-term lot at LaGuardia. Dealer's choice." DeWayne laughed, thinking it would impress her, get her to trust him more.

"What if we did it together?" she said.

"Well . . ."

"I think that's the ticket. The two of us, taking turns. How divine." She was leaning forward, her hands resting on the partition rail, her chin resting on her hands, but her voice was starting to sound a little distant. "I was thinking maybe we could use a knife. For a hundred thousand I should be able to say how we do it. I think that's only fair. We use a knife and cut off parts of him. While he sleeps. I could let you in one night—"

"But then the doorman would—"

"—and you could have a knife. A big knife. A machete. We could tie him down and gag him and then show him the parts we cut off. Fingers, toes, ears, his cock, his nuts. Oh, it's too delicious. Dangle them in front of him, then leave them on his chest, like a buffet. My husband, Herman, loves buffets. They always lose money on him when it's all-you-can-eat. What do you say, Mr. Reardon? This scrumptious little deal interest you? A hundred thousand, and if you bring me a receipt, I'll even reimburse you for the machete."

He turned quickly to get a glimpse of her. Her face was transfixed, like she was in a trance. He turned back and had to swerve to avoid a delivery truck.

"We'll be doing him a favor, Mr. Reardon. Herman's always saying he wants to lose weight, but he doesn't have the mental toughness to go on a diet. So we'll *help* him lose weight. You and me."

Her phone rang. She clicked it on.

"Doris, I'm *so* glad you called back. Guess what? The cabby is going to help me kill Herman. His name's Mr. Reardon. He's an ex-cop, and he knows all about killing people . . . No . . . no, not *handsome*, more like scruffy, I'd say. Manly, but scruffy."

Seventy-third and Park was just around the corner.

"We're here, lady."

"Oh, wait, Doris." She put the phone on hold again. "How much is it?"

"Eleven-sixty."

"I only have ten dollars," she said. "Put the balance on your first installment. Fifty thousand plus one dollar and sixty cents. Add a tip, too. You *will* help me, won't you Mr. Reardon? I *need* you." She clicked the phone on. "I'm home now, Doris. Call me back in a few on my regular number."

The doorman came and opened her door.

"Hello, Pablo," she said. "Guess what, I found someone to do it, to kill Herman."

"Yes, Miss Davis."

She pointed to DeWayne. "He's an ex-cop, so he *knows* about such matters." She took the doorman's hand, and he guided her out. She poked her head back in the cab. "The hardware store on the corner will sharpen the machete for you if it needs it. Just give them my name. Say it's for Gladys. Say, 'Please sharpen this for Gladys.' They'll know who you mean. Oh, and DeWayne, do you think I could have the receipt?"

The door shut, and his grass-skirted maiden and the soft white sand and the cool drinks and the palm trees blowing gently in the breeze went poof and vanished, and in its place was a guy in his early twenties in a thousand-dollar suit smoking a fat cigar and in a huge rush to get to a meeting and who was going to make more money in interest just during this cab ride than DeWayne was going to make for the rest of his life.

And all he could do was push the button on the meter and head back to midtown.

Because poor pathetic shmucks who drove cabs, that's what they did.

Chapter 10

It was noon, and Bliss hadn't made any progress. He called Constance but got her machine again, only this time there was a message just for him, delivered in a sultry purr. "And if this is Detective Bliss, I will call you back soon. I really will." And as if her voice wasn't seductive enough already, she paused and softened her voice until it was just a whisper. "I promise." This one was trouble, he could feel it. The kind of trouble that seemed to follow him around—or maybe he followed *it*. He hoped he'd find the murderer soon, so he wouldn't have to go down there and talk to her in person.

He decided to try Wolf. Wolf liked to tell stories. Maybe he had one about the death of a young actor. A firsthand account. Then they could match the marks on James's neck with Wolf's fingers. That would be good. Juries like it when you could place someone's hands around the dead person's throat. Anyway, Bliss liked listening to Wolf talk.

He dialed Wolf's number and got him on the phone. The actor sounded groggy.

"I'm sorry if I woke you," Bliss said.

"I haven't been to sleep yet," he said.

"Two days?"

"It's James being dead. Bringing back all kinds of memories."

Everything *brings back memories for you, Wolf,* Bliss wanted to say. But he stuck to business.

"I just want to go over where you were the night James was killed."

"I was here. Reading Ikkuyu. The Japanese poet."

"Did anyone call you, so they could verify you were home?"

"The phone rang; it seemed miles away."

"Did you order any food, groceries, beer—anything so someone could confirm you were at home?"

"There was hunger but in someone else's stomach."

"Look, *I* believe you were home," Bliss said, "but the lieutenant, he likes me to verify this kind of stuff."

"I was meditating. Through the night. Focusing. A lion tamer."

"A lion tamer."

"Each lion is capable of swiping the guy's face off at any moment. It's what lions do. It's their nature. But they refrain. Do you know why?"

"They're trained."

"Exactly. Last night, I was training my lions, keeping them on their stands, making them roar at the right time. If I don't keep them in line, they'll try to claw through my body to find a way out."

"Yes, but what I need to know is—"

"Let me tell you about my lions. I'm by myself, on the edge of the jungle, digging the shithole for the platoon. Why am I, the platoon leader, digging the shithole? Because everyone else is tired. Because I want to be alone. Because I never stop. So I'm digging and I hear a noise and I look up and one of the enemy has emerged silently like a ghost from the jungle and is standing above me, some fragment, some shard from the comet Charlie floating free and now coming to kill me. And the noise I hear, what makes me turn, is him pulling on the trigger of his gun, only nothing is happening. He's yanking

the trigger of his AK-47 and it won't go off. Because somewhere in the Ukraine, years ago, some worker had too much
vodka for lunch and came back to the factory, and when this
particular rifle came down the line he did something wrong,
put in some incredibly tiny part the wrong way, just a mil-
limeter askew, but it was enough to keep my head from being
blown off."

Bliss felt himself getting swept up in Wolf's stories again.

"I took my entrenching tool and swung it straight into his
belly, and then I just dodged the puke and blood that gushed
out of his mouth. I buried him in the shithole and then
started digging a new one. This is just one of my lions, Detective. A vicious one. Up until now he always did what he was
told. But after James died, he got ornery, his limbs poking
through the soft earth, trying to pull the trigger again."

"Wolf," Bliss said, his tone like he was speaking to a little
kid, "I want to know what you did the night James was murdered."

"Jump!" Wolf shouted. "Jump through the fucking hoop!"

Bliss felt lucky. People paid twenty-five dollars a ticket for
this, and here he was getting it for free. But suddenly he was
tiring of the monologues. Wolf may have been the darling of
the downtown theater scene, but now he was a murder suspect. And Bliss wanted answers.

"When James died," Wolf said, "the lions started missing
their marks, fucking up the routine. So I had to crack the whip,
get them back in order."

"Wednesday night, Wolf, the night James died, did you
speak to him? Did you see him? Did you sleep with him?"

No response. Only Wolf's breathing, directly in Bliss's ear,
as if the man was getting closer, burrowing through the
phone line.

"Once we landed right outside this village and it was hot.
Charlie was everywhere, and we had about ten yards of open

space between the chopper and the tree line. The first eight men sprinted to safety. But the last guy wouldn't leave the chopper."

"Wolf, I appreciate your bravery, your heroism, but right now I—"

"He's screaming, *I don't wanna die! I don't wanna die!* And I'm shouting at him to—"

"I need to know, Wolf, if—"

"—to get the fuck out of the chopper. *I'm short!* he yells. *Charlie knows I'm short, and they want to get me!* He's grabbing on to the metal leg of the bench in the chopper. *I only got two more weeks! I'm short! Please, Sergeant, please!*"

"Wolf!" Bliss shouted. But to no avail. The guy was lost in memories, either by design or desperation or both. Unreachable. Like Katrina said. Bliss could either listen or hang up the phone. He figured he might as well get his money's worth.

"I'm kicking at his fingers with my boot," Wolf said, "shouting that he's *not* going to die and to get the fuck out of the Hewey before the pilot shoots us both himself because mortar rounds are coming in. I'm hammering the kid's fingers with the heel of my boot and they're bloody and raw and finally he lets go and staggers out of the chopper and is instantly hit in the leg. He buckles and looks up at me for what could only have been a second but seemed like an eternity and then he's hit by like six other rounds and he's bouncing around like one of those punching dolls you have as a kid."

Wolf paused again. Bliss still couldn't tell if these pauses were improvised or rehearsed. Probably both.

"And then one day I'm sitting in the theater—it was during *The Book of Job* piece—and James walks in and I see in him the boy I kicked out of the chopper."

This might be interesting, Bliss thought.

"I thought, Now I have another chance, and I'm not going

to screw it up. I've been cross-legged on stage for three days drinking only water, trying to will boils on my back and face, *being* Job, feeling the pain and agony of his life crumbling around him, and then I see James walk in the theater and I say to myself, I'm *not* going to screw it up this time. God gave me a second chance."

"And did you make the most of it?"

"No. I fucked up again."

Was that a confession? Bliss wondered. It sounded sort of like a confession; admission of some kind of guilt. But to what?

"Did you kill him, Wolf?"

"I don't know," he replied.

And then Wolf stopped talking.

"Wolf?"

Bliss could hear him breathing—deep, raspy breaths, moving further away now. Retreating. Bliss sensed there would be no more from Wolf for a while. He quietly hung up the phone.

"What'd Wolf say?" Artie asked.

"I'm not sure."

"He still on the list?"

"I think Wolf needs his own list."

He wanted somebody to start saying something that made sense.

It was then that Bliss realized he was in a race—that he had to solve the case before the Performance Warehouse turned it into a play. He had to get some arrest warrants issued before they printed up the programs and sent out the invitations to opening night. Art merging with reality. He should quit the force and take a part in the show. Play himself. He could have a long monologue about the bungee jump, losing his gun. Maybe Algernon could even write Bliss some lines, something that would help him make sense out of his life.

"I'm going to talk to that kid Ezra," Bliss said to Artie. "Get clued in on these actors. Meanwhile, try to find out Wolf's real name and see if his prints are on file somewhere."

"Good idea, Lenny."

"Thanks. Also, see if you can find out how Roderick made all his money."

"Definitely. I'm on it."

"Good. And if Constance calls, beep me right away."

"OK," Artie said. "You want to go to the shooting range later?"

"Maybe."

"Squeeze off a few rounds."

"I'll see."

"Guy with the lowest score buys the beers."

"I said I'll see."

"The Rangers are playing tonight, we could—"

"I have to go." Bliss said.

Artie was just excited to be a detective. Why should Bliss hold that against him? Why should he be jealous just because Artie didn't need to be jumping from high places to find some meaning in his life?

Give him time, Bliss thought. Give him time.

Once again, it was noon before Promise stirred. She must have taken an extra pill last night, Martin thought as he carried the scones to her on a silver tray. These had currants in them. Lately the humidity had been ruining the dough, turning everything he baked leaden and soggy. He'd added buttermilk to these, and they had come out light and flaky. The scones were flanked by jam, freshly squeezed juice, and Kona coffee in the French press pot that Martin preferred above all others.

"Breakfast is ready," he announced.

She sat up in the bed and let him rest the tray on her lap. They hadn't spoken about James since the policemen left.

"I've begun making the funeral arrangements," he told her.

"Thank you, Martin."

"Should I let your sister know?"

"Only if she agrees to crawl in the coffin and let herself be buried along with him."

"I'm not sure she'd agree to that."

"Tell her she can take a video camera along. With lights. She can record the whole thing for their next play, the experience of burial. My sister's always been big on experiences."

Martin pushed the plunger down and poured her coffee, adding the cream just the way she liked it. He watched as she took a sip and smiled. He was glad she was comfortable, but he was sure it wouldn't last; she would soon tire of him without James around.

James had already been attending boarding school when Martin arrived on the scene, so his initial parental duties basically involved showing up for visiting days. He'd drive James into town, buy him a new sports jacket, a slew of CDs, a fancy dinner, and then whisk him back to school. Martin's biggest burden in those days was the week between boarding school ending and the start of summer camp. Trips to Disney World had solved that well enough.

But as James grew, so had their worries. Schools couldn't abide his teenage recklessness. Even with significant contributions to several capital campaigns, eliciting promises that James would be treated like the headmaster's own son, the boy always found a way to get himself kicked out.

Promise had wanted nothing to do with it. James became entirely Martin's responsibility. It was Martin who had to solicit the next school, doctor the transcripts, arrange for packing up James's belongings. He had felt more like a travel agent than a father. It was when he needed assistance with some of the more delicate aspects of these arrangements that Martin had first employed the special skills and services of the man he had called on the pay phone.

Over the years he had tried to get close to James, but the boy found him repellent. It was as if he could see right through him. Martin wasn't surprised. Most everyone could see right through him. Or at least they thought they could.

He broke off a piece of scone and smeared it with some jam. "What happened the other night?" he asked Promise.

"Where?"

"At the theater. When you went to see James."

"The door was open. I walked in and saw him lying on the stage. I called to him. He didn't move. I wanted to believe he was asleep."

She started crying, very gently.

"What were you going to say to him?" he asked.

"I wanted to make up for everything. But it was too much, I know." She put her hands to her face. "Too many lost years."

Martin wanted to feel sorry for her, but the decade of disdain he had been subjected to prevented him from being swayed by her momentary weakness.

"How are the scones?" he asked.

She wiped her eyes, took a tiny bite.

"Very light. You've outdone yourself, Martin."

"So, you go to the scene of the crime. You return home and say, *It's finally over.* The next morning James is dead. . . . I think it's important that the police not find out about it. Don't you?"

"Yes."

"They could construe it in a very malicious way."

She took another sip of coffee and closed her eyes. He knew she was thinking: *Martin will take care of this. He'll find a way.* But after it was taken care of, after James was buried and the flowers had dried and wilted on his grave, what then? What would Martin be needed for then?

"I like the currants," she said, "but I prefer blueberries."

"I'll go to the Vinegar Factory this afternoon and pick some up."

"Thank you Martin. You are my prince."

He kissed her hand to conceal his smile of satisfaction as he thought about the wheels he had already set in motion.

It was one o'clock, and Li-Jung had to get ready for work. Matt, the waiter from last night, lay next to her, still asleep. She couldn't believe she had wound up back at her place. The whole point of going home with these boys was that she would go to *their* apartments. In exchange for sex she could have a real shower, listen to their music, maybe borrow some clothes. But she hadn't found out until it was too late that Matt still lived at home. He'd assured her that his parents were going away next weekend, and she could come over, use their Jacuzzi, drink some of his father's fancy wine, cook up some humongous steaks that were in the freezer. Big deal.

She reached underneath the mattress and pulled out Lenny's gun, then placed it gently on the bed next to her. It wasn't a revolver, like she was used to. The bullets were tucked away somewhere in the handle. The clip. It was released by sliding the small lever located above and to the left of the trigger. She'd worked on it yesterday until she was able to pop it in and out with authority, thinking that would get Matt's attention, let him know she was serious.

She sat up in bed and leaned against the wall. Matt had managed to corral all the pillows. She picked up the gun and held it out at arm's length. Each time she did, she was surprised at how heavy it was. She aimed it at the box of cereal on top of the fridge. *Bang*. Tony the Tiger just lost a piece of his tail.

She used the muzzle to push the sheet down off Matt's shoulder. He smacked his lips and rolled onto his back and said, "Mmmmnaanghh." She pushed the sheet down farther, revealing Matt's abs, of which he was so proud. She had to admit they were impressive, each muscle well defined— which was a good thing in case he ever had to count past twenty. Those stomach muscles were what got him the jobs modeling underwear in the mail-order fashion catalogues. His body was the vehicle that transported his abs from one potential viewing sight to another. His brain was the guidance system that maneuvered him to the gym where he could maintain his abs. He was an ab ecosystem. Ab-sessed. He showed her the modeling pictures, which he just happened to carry around with him. In one he wore glasses and briefs and was holding a book, as if he knew how to read. Another had him with boxing gloves in a boxing ring wearing nothing but boxers, looking tough, as if he knew how to hit someone. She knew a guy Clyde back home who had hit another guy so hard, it put him in the hospital for six months. One punch. The guy was drunk, but Clyde was drunker. Clyde's dick was too big to fit inside her, but they were still friends.

But Matt surely didn't know how to read or how to hit any-one. Despite the ripples on his stomach, Matt was soft. He'd grown up on the Upper East Side, in the same neighborhoods where they catered parties. They'd passed his home earlier that night in the cab on their way to her sublet in the East Village. His apartment had three floors—the fiftieth, fifty-first, and fifty-second. A triplex. Their view was the best in the city, he said. *Better* than the Empire State Building because from their apartment you could *see* the Empire State Building and from the Empire State Building you couldn't. Because you were on it. Get it? Yes, Matt, I get it. He'd told her he'd played football in high school and was in a recent issue of *Seventeen* magazine in a spread entitled "New Bods on the Block." Laughing, he sounded more like a hick than the farm boys she'd grown up with.

Matt wasn't able to earn his living yet as a model, so he had to work part-time with Dave the caterer. All night he had made what he thought were witty comments about the way she cut the vegetables and skewered the kebobs. He wanted to get to know her, he'd said. Li-Jung didn't want to be alone, but she definitely didn't want to get to know anyone, to have to talk about her past or about her future. Her past was nobody's business, and her future was too cloudy to discuss.

It only mattered that she was far away from Iowa and her father and the China Palace. That she wasn't a freak anymore. In New York, Chinese women didn't shuffle along, burdened with shopping bags because the supermarket had a sale on scallions, walking two miles to save forty cents a bunch. No. Instead they strutted down the streets of Soho, glamorous in their high heels and fancy clothes, acting like they owned the city. They rushed across midtown in power suits, carrying briefcases, talking into their cellulars, on their way to important meetings. Li-Jung had seen them, and had felt both pride and panic, a deep dread that she could never achieve what they had, would never reach that high. Not long after that, she got her tattoo.

Matt mumbled in his sleep and stretched like he was posing. She knew that the waiters talked about her while they stood behind the buffet, comparing notes. Making stupid waiter jokes (does she do French service?), saying how she was easy.

She pointed the gun at him, at his head, at his abs, at his sex under the sheets. "Bang," she said softly.

Then she put the put the gun away and got up to take a fast rinse in the tub in her kitchen, after which there wouldn't be any more hot water for Matt. She might tell him—or then again she might just let him shiver.

Chapter II

Bliss met Ezra at an old-time Italian pastry shop on Second Avenue where the cannolis were light and the espresso tasted like Florence. The walls were covered in white tiles like the ones in the subway, possibly put in place by the same workmen from Calabria who had tiled the stations, still one of the great architectural accomplishments in New York. At four in the afternoon just some old neighborhood guys were nursing their coffees and talking together.

Bliss hated the cappuccino bars that were springing up everywhere. The last time he'd gone in one, they handed him his coffee in two paper cups nestled together——for insurance reasons, said the goateed, ersatz beatnik, Maynard G. Krebs with a trust fund, behind the counter. And after paying more than a buck for a regular coffee (so expensive because it's *"superior"* coffee——the beans picked off the left side of the tree and only on Wednesdays by smiling South American virgins, joyous in the knowledge that their coffee would not wind up in just *any* pot but in a chic coffee bar), you *still* have to clean up after yourself. Ridiculous.

Ezra was a handsome young man with a softness about him that Bliss liked. He wouldn't have minded a boy like him showing up at the front door to take Julia on a date——a foreign film, or maybe to the Village Vanguard to hear some jazz. The kind of kid who wouldn't balk if Bliss tagged along, especially if someone he liked was playing——Joe Lovano, James Moody, Charlie Haden. And if Bliss didn't go along with them, Ezra looked like the kind of kid he could scare the shit out of before they left, threaten to shoot Ezra's gonads into oblivion if he so much as laid a hand on his daughter, his most prized treasure. Of course, the only snag was that he would need to have his gun in his possession to do that.

Ezra seemed a little nervous when he sat down. Bliss assured him he wasn't a suspect.

"Your alibi checked out," Bliss said. "Your girlfriend confirmed you waited for her to get off work from nine-thirty on."

Ezra looked relieved.

"Were you worried she wouldn't vouch for you?" Bliss asked.

"No. But it's odd to think about the normal stuff you do as being an alibi," Ezra said. "I mean, you're just sitting at the bar in Fanelli's, watching a bunch of pretentious asshole painters flirt with your girlfriend—who's working her ass off for lousy tips like she does every Thursday night—and the bartender serves you a beer just when Bernie Williams hits a home run, and the next day it turns out that because you toasted the Yankees tying the game, it's one of the most significant things you've ever done because your whereabouts can be accounted for."

Bliss was thinking maybe Ezra should be the writer in the group.

"So tell me about the Performance Warehouse."

"Sure." His face lit up. "It was started in the midseventies by Katrina, Constance, and Algernon. They met in an acting class and discovered afterward that they all hated it and were looking for a different kind of theater experience."

"More avant-garde, as Algernon likes to say."

"You have to be careful with Algernon, by the way. He acts a lot goofier than he really is. He lulls you into revealing stuff about yourself, and then he puts it in his next play."

"He'd make a good detective."

"True. So anyway, the three of them created their own

company. Everything was based on ideas and images—what the cutting-edge theaters were doing in the sixties and seventies—breaking away from the kitchen-sink dramas that most American plays are like. Even Edward Albee—you know, *Who's Afraid of Virginia Woolf?*—was pretty much stuck in a classic mold. Characters talking to each other, listening to each other, a logical sequence of time. But the Warehouse was moving in another direction. They borrowed a lot from the Polish guys—Grotowski and Kantor. And everything originally came from Brecht."

"The *Threepenny Opera* guy?"

"Yeah. He wanted to create plays that weren't cathartic experiences for the audience."

"No crying."

"No crying, no joy. He didn't necessarily want the audience to feel. He wanted them to *think*. He kept reminding them that they were watching a play."

"Did he turn the house lights on during the show?"

"No, that was Meyerhold."

"Who was he?"

"A Russian director. After Stanislavsky. The true father of experimental theater. But Brecht felt that if you let the audience use the theater to work through their emotions, as a catharsis, you were actually doing them a favor. You made them feel better. They became complacent. That wasn't what Brecht wanted theater to do. Neither did the Performance Warehouse. They didn't make nice theater, plays that were easy to sit through. They weren't really even plays. They'd take a classic piece of theater and deconstruct it, make something new out of it."

"And take off their clothes?"

"So you heard about their Nursery Rhyme Project."

"No."

"*Mother Goosed*, it was called. It's kind of legendary now,

I guess. It was mostly about how the Old Woman in the Shoe got so many kids."

"In the precinct we have a saying: Jack and Jill went up the hill, Jill came down with a ten dollar bill."

"So you get the idea."

"Tell me about Wolf," Bliss said.

"He brought something unique to the group because *he* was so unique. He stayed after one of their shows. *Broken Eggs*, it was called. Constance made omelets for the audience while Katrina and Algernon recited the names of every soldier who died in the battle of Fort Sumter. 'Jason Livingston, born Augusta, Maine, 1846, died Fort Sumter, 1861.' And then Constance would smile at someone in the audience and ask very sweetly, 'And what do you want in *your* omelet?' It's amazing. I've seen a tape of it. Anyway, after the show was over, Wolf remained in his seat. Then, as the story goes, he took off his shoes and socks and curled up on the stage and went to sleep. For the next two years he swept the floors, took tickets, handed out programs. To eat, he'd arm wrestle guys in the local bars or make bets that he could walk on his hands around the block. He hardly ever spoke. But once he started, the Performance Warehouse—and, really, all of American theater—changed forever.

"Wolf's life, his stories, became the essence of all the Warehouse's productions. His two tours in Nam, his years living on a Hopi reservation, the characters he met hitchhiking around the country, mushrooms in the dessert, gang rapes in cornfields, screwing heiresses on their husband's snooker tables . . . We studied their work in college. Also Joseph Chaikin, Richard Foreman, Mabou Mines. Most likely you've never heard of them."

"Sorry."

"Hardly anyone has. In Europe they'd be titans. Here they drift on and off of unemployment, hoping for a grant or to be supported by a few rich patrons. Angels, they call them."

"Did the Performance Warehouse have their own angels?"

"Constance pretty much kept the theater going."

"Where'd her money come from?"

"Potatoes."

"Yeah?"

"Her father is some kind of potato baron. She lives off the trust fund. Or so I've heard. Don't tell her I was the one who told you."

"I won't. What about Wolf. You think he could have killed James?"

Ezra weighed his words carefully.

"There's a darkness about Wolf," he said. "It's like he glows darkness. Katrina told me he once came into rehearsal, both eyes black, a red welt on his cheek. He'd been beaten up in a bar, he said. Some guy thought he was cheating at arm wrestling. He didn't fight back. Because if he did, he said, because if he fought back, he would've had to kill the guy. He's seen things that would cause lesser men to jump off a bridge. But then, you've probably seen a bit in your time, too, I imagine."

Bliss put the espresso cup to his lips, drained it, and replaced it gently on the saucer. "You have no idea," he said.

At four o'clock, after walking for several hours, Ward found the park bench from his dream, or at least one very much like it. It was in a small park just on the edge of the projects on 105th and Lexington. He sat down and waited, cautious, wary of the hidden dangers, of knives in socks, pistols tucked into the back of pants, of shotguns in baby carriages.

He watched for the car, the one that would cruise slowly past, Uzis perched in its window, spraying bullets.

But it was a peaceful afternoon. Cars drove by like in the dream—hundreds of them—without incident. Then one stopped. The back door opened ominously. Ward unzipped his jacket to access his holster. A man got out, carrying a shop-

ping bag and a casserole covered in aluminum foil. He walked
into the building. He was bringing someone food. His mama,
maybe. Or his old auntie.

It's the calm before the storm, thought Ward. He knew they
were out there—snipers on the roofs, angry young black men
hiding in the garbage cans, pushing loaded clips into Gloks,
releasing safeties off 9mm Targases, waiting for the signal to
show themselves in unison and join the dance, a pernicious
Busby Berkeley extravaganza of rage and random death.

A woman approached, pushing a stroller. The baby from
his dream. It was starting.

Ward reached for his pistol, expecting to see the ancient
face from his dream, a face already contorted with hatred
before the baby fat was even gone. A shotgun instead of a doll,
extra shells instead of a rattle. The woman passed and nodded politely. Then the baby dropped his toy at Ward's feet. *It's
a trick*, he thought. A grenade, a pipe bomb disguised as a blue
plastic telephone. The baby dials a number and primes the
charge. Because there are no more innocent babies uptown.
His dream had told him that. Ward, frozen, saw the baby trying to grab his toy, saw the woman waiting for Ward to pick
it up for him, for the nice man to help. Waiting for the cloud
of dread to clear. So he did, handing the saliva-damp rattle
back to the little child. The woman thanked him and continued on her way.

"I sat for an hour," he told Malikha later, "and no guns. No
shots were fired. No rage that day. Just people. Our people. So
where did my nightmare come from?"

Malikha held his hand with the hole in it and stroked it
gently.

"It's the dreams," she said.

"What do you mean?" Ward was the disciple now, listening to the wisdom of his ravishing oracle.

"The dreams take the boys too far. Wanting everything at

once, they steal the wings and strap them on. Icarus's impulsive children, dreaming beyond what they can achieve. So they fall. They fly too close to the sun and their wings melt away and they fall headlong out of the sky and as they do they think only of taking someone with them as they tumble down and die."

Ward looked at his hand.

"I guess I was lucky," he said. "Say, what's a smart, beautiful young girl like you doing with a funky old man like me, anyway?"

"Learning all the time," she said.

DeWayne was trying to talk some sense into his wife, but she wouldn't listen.

"Antoinette, please . . ."

"Fourteen years I've waited for 'please,' but now it's too late."

"I . . ."

The recorded voice came on, alerting him that he had to put more change into the phone.

"You should have put more change into your *life*, DeWayne," Antoinette said.

"What does *that* mean?"

"That means if you weren't so damn stupid, maybe we wouldn't be in this mess."

"You could have said something when we bought the car, when I put that stack of bills on the salesman's desk, you coulda said, 'Honey, I think there's something not right about this.' Instead you got a vanity plate. 'NETTE,' it said."

"Yeah. What I was trapped in."

As usual, he understood only half of what she was saying.

"So basically you think it's my fault, is that it, DeWayne?"

"No."

"That *I* was the one who took the money."

"I'm not saying that."

"You're the one who always wanted to be *somebody*. Something important. You always wanted to fly. How many times did you—"

"Antoinette."

"—did you say—"

"An—"

"—did you *say* you were tired of being stuck here on the ground. Stuck in the mud of your life. That's what we were to you—your family—just so much mud on your shoes."

"That's not true."

"Fine. True, not true—if you stand far enough away, you can't tell the difference. And that's how far away I want to be from you. I sold the pool to Jimmy Corcoran down the street. Forty-eight hundred bucks, which is generous, since it's going to cost him a grand to move it."

"You sold the *pool?*"

"I *had* to sell the pool. Unless some sheik you had in the cab tipped you an oil well and you forgot to tell me."

"No."

"Jimmy said he's gonna let the kids swim in it three afternoons a week and Saturday mornings. He also fixed the crack in the cement on the foundation out back."

"You boffing him, Antoinette?"

She didn't answer. He heard only the sound of her chewing gum. Juicy Fruit. One and a half sticks. Exactly. She taught the kids. Chew the first for forty-five seconds; then add the half stick, for an additional charge of flavor.

"Do me a favor, DeWayne," she said at last. "When the recording comes on again, don't put in any more money. Just let the time run out. You can see the kids Sunday afternoon. But as regards to this specific call in particular, just let the time run out."

Chapter 12

It was 5:30 and Bliss was tired. The Performance Warehouse was exhausting him. He wanted to go home, but he had made the mistake of calling in for messages. Artie told him that Algernon Mann, playwright and all-around avant-gardist, wanted Bliss to call him back.

"I tried, Lenny, but he would only speak to you."

"OK. Thanks, Artie."

"Oh, and by the way, I found out a little about our boy Martin Roderick. Seems like he's just a kind of overgrown gigolo. Doesn't really have any money of his own. He lives off his wife. Hey, guess where her fortune comes from."

"Potatoes."

"How'd you know?"

Bliss could feel Artie deflating. "I get around. Any word from Constance?"

"No."

"Shit. Hey, I think you can call it a day, Artie."

"Sure. You decide if you're interested in watching the Rangers?"

"Not tonight. I want to get home."

"OK. Then maybe I'll just stay here a little longer, make a few more calls."

"See you tomorrow, Artie."

"Yeah."

Reluctantly, Bliss called Algernon, hoping the writer would simply spew out a few more twisted metaphors and be done with it, so Bliss could get home in time for dinner.

"At last," Algernon said.

"What's up, Algy?" Appropriate moniker for the guy, Bliss thought: green scum on a murky pond.

"Don't be flippant."

"Sorry. I get that way sometimes when murder is in the air. Hey, you guys ever think of doing *The Mousetrap*? Now that's a *real* play. I could do the part of the inspector." He put on his best English accent, which contained equal parts Yiddish and Southern. "Someone in this room is a murderer."

Silence greeted him.

"I guess I didn't get the part."

"Act like a detective for a moment, please. What I have to say isn't easy."

"Go ahead, Algernon. Whatever it is, get it off your chest."

"I want to confess," he said. "I want to confess to the murder of James Roderick."

It was 5:30. The party was starting in less than an hour, and the hostess was getting nervous. Usually they stayed in the living room, but this particular hostess was fluttering around the kitchen, hovering over Li-Jung as she made her wontons.

"You think you have enough?" the woman asked, panic in her voice.

"Dave always has enough," Li-Jung said.

"And those are served hot?"

"Room temp."

"That's okay? No one's going to get sick?"

"I hope not," Li-Jung replied.

Now clearly even more worried, the hostess darted over to Dave. Li-Jung watched him gently pat her on the back and lead her out to the bar.

The hostess's kitchen—done in white marble, like a mausoleum—was bigger than Li-Jung's whole sublet apartment. But it was all for show. The pots and pans still had the tags on them, the broiler tray in the oven was still wrapped in the plastic it had been shipped in, the refrigerator was full of take-out containers. This kitchen wasn't for cooking, except when the caterer came.

Li-Jung was in a corner working at the breakfast table, removed from the chaos, quietly folding her wontons. One hundred and sixty of them. A rice wrapper nestled in her left palm, a bit of filling scooped from the bowl with two fingers of her right hand, place the filling in the center of the wrapper, fold in half, then a twist, and there it was. One of the reasons Dave had hired her was because she knew the deceptively simple folds that turned squares of pastry into something curved and sublime. It had taken her father a week to teach her, and then it took her about six weeks to master the technique. Dave's filling was quite different from her father's. It had wild mushrooms and a bit of ground veal. It was lighter, he said. The fancy ladies liked it.

The hostess returned with one of her friends, conducting a preparty tour of the kitchen, a glass of wine in her hand. She seemed more at ease.

"I *love* what you've done to it!" the friend gushed.

"Oh, I know," said the hostess.

They stood over Li-Jung, oblivious to what she was doing, as if she was just a piece of furniture.

"And you made a little breakfast nook," the friend said.

"Of course. I've wanted a nook here ever since we moved in."

"Oh, I couldn't *live* without my nook," the friend concurred.

They walked away to admire further renovations. These women would make lousy witnesses, Li-Jung thought. If she were to hide in the house and emerge later with her gun, neither would recognize her. She could bag the jewels, watches, the little soaps shaped like fish and shells that they had in the bathroom. She could pick up some new clothes, too. She and

the hostess were about the same size, and she needed pajamas. Li-Jung had once waited in the truck while a guy she
barely knew burgled a house. He told her he needed to run in
and get some beer. She thought he lived there. He came out
twenty minutes later without any beer but with a pillowcase
slung over his shoulder like Santa Claus, filled with stuff that
clanked in the back when they drove down the dirt road to
the place where he liked to park. He wanted to give her a silver teapot when they were done, but she had no use for it. So
he pissed in it and then tossed it into the woods, laughing,
thinking it was kind of political statement, the masses revolting. He was revolting, all right. Later the police matched him
up to the urine and sent him off to jail.

"Hey, babe, how are ya?"

It was Matt, looking all scrubbed and dapper in his tuxedo
uniform.

"Hi, Matt," Li-Jung said.

"Working on those wontons?" he said.

"Yeah."

"You're fast," he said.

Not as fast as you were last night, she thought. Instead she
just nodded.

"You busy after work?"

"I don't think so," she said. She wasn't sure she wanted to
see him again, but she also didn't want to be alone.

"I'll talk to you later," he said.

He flashed his million-dollar smile that, to Matt's chagrin,
had not yet liberated him from passing out hors d'oeuvres for
a living.

"OK," she said.

He patted her on the head. *Like I'm a puppy,* she thought.
Then he made a growling sound as he walked away. This was
a reference to her tattoo of a tiger, which had infatuated him,
got him sucking and slobbering over it as if it weren't just a

picture of a tiger but was actually dangerous. He wanted to know if it meant something in Japan. She said the first thing that came into her head—that it was the symbol of eternal life. She didn't bother telling him she was Chinese. The tattoo was where his mouth spent most of the evening, but sadly her shoulder was not the most sensitive part of her body, and his constant licking of the tiger's tail did little to stimulate or satisfy her. Her real tiger lay in another lair, which she found for herself after he was asleep, when she could slowly take herself down a dark, winding trail and become one with the secret mystical power of the jungle.

Dave the caterer breezed by.

"I'll need those in five minutes," he said, then rushed back to the stove.

She picked up her pace. She remembered an afternoon when she had risked her father's wrath to linger after school, helping the teacher put stuff away in the classroom. When she arrived at the restaurant a half hour late, her father went ballistic. Ungrateful pig, he called her. Screaming about how he wished he'd had a son who would *know* how to work, who he could teach to use the cleaver, the wok, to make sauces, someone who he could pass on his knowledge to. Then he hit her on the back and shoulders with one of the wooden spoons, and she just covered her head while her mother stood by helplessly, eyes cast down, wringing her hands and mumbling something that could have been a plea to stop but was too pathetic to do any good.

Afterward she had sat on her milk crates in the kitchen and, through her tears, flew through the wontons while her father stood silent silently in front of the stove and cooked until the last dinner order was filled. Then he cleaned up and shut the light and never offered her anything to eat or even a ride home. Her mother must have sneaked out of the house, coming back later to get her. They walked home in silence, and Li-Jung remembered how, seen in the fading red neon glow of the China Palace sign, their steps seemed to be exactly the same.

Now, the last wonton finished, she sat back in her chair and thought about Matt. She had chosen to spare him last night, but maybe later, when they were alone, she'd bring out the gun when he wasn't asleep. See how he would respond if she pretended she was dangerous, out of control, that his little Chinese sex-toy puppy was really a mad killer. She remembered the dog that Bobby shot. He had walked right up to it, pulled out the gun, cocked it, and placed it right by the dog's ear. The dog never moved. Matt wouldn't be like that. Matt would be worried, try to talk her out of it. Maybe beg. That would be nice for a change, not to be the one begging.

She could maybe get used to this feeling.

The tiger was starting to roar.

Chapter 13

At 7:30, instead of being at home finishing dinner, being regaled with stories of how dorky the seventh grade boys were or putting lettuce in the plastic box where Cori's snail from science class resided, Bliss rang the bell to Malikha's apartment. He wanted to share Algernon's confession with Ward. He also wanted a drink. He was beginning to feel like the bungee cord hadn't sprung back at all, that he was still just dangling head down above the murky waters of the East River, something to be stared at pitifully as people drove by.

He was holding the cassette in his hand when Ward opened the door.

"What's shakin', partner?"

It was comforting to see Ward returning to form. Bliss needed him desperately.

Malikha lay on the couch, one leg draped over the back, a book in her hand, Nina Simone on the stereo, her sultry voice over snare and brushes: "My baby just cares for me. . . ."

"Want a beer?" Malikha asked.

Bliss nodded.

"I got a confession," Bliss said.

"Well, you came to the right place, partner," Ward said. "Sit down and tell us all about it."

"It's the confession of a guy says he killed James Roderick."

"The actor?" Malikha asked.

"Yeah."

"And you got a Stevie Wonder?" Ward asked. " 'Signed, sealed, delivered—I'm yours'?"

"It's on tape. I sat across from him at a table on the stage, and he made his confession. I got it all." Bliss took the beer Ward offered him and took a long, deep drink.

"My," Ward said, "a little consternation on the job, partner?"

Bliss sank into Ward's recliner and closed his eyes. The theater had been dark when he arrived, lit only by a bare bulb hanging above the stage. A tape recorder and microphone were set up on the table where Algernon had sat.

"Thank you for coming," he had said.

"I wouldn't have missed it."

Algernon had jumped up. "If you're going to be sarcastic, I'm leaving."

"Sorry," Bliss had said.

"I don't have to do this, you know. I don't *have* to make your job easier for you."

"It was your idea."

At which point, Algernon turned on the recorder and proceeded to tell his story.

Bliss hauled himself out of the recliner and slipped the cassette of the confession in Ward's stereo. He hit play, and Algernon's whiny, nasally voice replaced Nina Simone. Bliss sat on the couch. Malikha joined him. Ward took the recliner. They listened together.

"May 12, 1996. My name is Algernon Mann, and I'm here with Officer Bliss—[Bliss, heard off mike: Detective.] Sorry, *Detective* Bliss. I want everything as accurate as possible because this is, after all, my confession. Strange how suddenly everything in my life has led up to this moment. It's the dividing line—things will have happened either before or afterwards. B.C. or A.C. Before Confession or After Confession. When I'm in the big house, reminiscing with friends at visiting hours, it'll be, *Hey, did we do that before the confession or after?*"

"No one says 'the big house' anymore, by the way," Bliss said on the tape.

Algernon ignored him. "This is a huge moment. Very big. Boffo. Mind if I smoke?"

"No," came Bliss's reply.

The sound of cellophane, paper ripping, a match being lit, a deep drag, a slow exhale, then the distinctive sound of a slap.

"Christ! That wasn't necessary, Detective, slapping the cigarette out of my mouth. You playing the good cop and bad cop both? What will you do when I bend over to pick it up? Kick me in the nuts?"

A pause, the sound of the chair scraping against the floor, silence, the chair again, then another deep drag of the cigarette.

"You hit the guy, partner?" Ward asked him.

Bliss stared straight ahead, sipping his beer. "Just listen," he finally said.

Algernon continued, edgier now. His voice wary.

"Like I said, I don't have to do this. You could rely on prints and fibers, DNA if you've got it. But then I could always O.J. my way out of it in court. With a confession, though, it's open and shut, isn't it? So sit back, uncurl your fist, let me make your life easier. You need me, Detective. Don't go fucking it up."

More smoking. He cleared his throat.

"We're talking about the death of a handsome and rich young man, so naturally everyone's interested. The *News* and the *Post* couldn't be more excited if they'd found the original Ten Commandments. Young man dies center stage. Must be putting pressure on your superiors."

The sound of Algernon smoking again.

"I've been thinking about my motive," he continued. "Pre-meditation makes it murder one, right?"

"And was your murdering James Roderick premeditated?"

"If you're asking was there a plan, no, there was no specific plan for murdering James. But there was a general plan for murder I'd been formulating ever since the *Job* piece. Wolf played Job. I was the voice of God. I denied him food for three days, gave him nothing but water. Because of our dedication to verisimilitude—excuse me, that word had six syllables—because of its *realism*, our work tests a person's will and endurance, pushing the line between theater and reality. As God, I understood how murder blurs that line completely. If I could commit a murder, I thought, I could transcend the barriers between art and—"

There was a loud thud, what could have been Algernon falling, then a cry of pain.

"Leave me alone!"

More groans, the dull thud of someone being kicked. Bliss felt his partner's eyes on him, felt Ward thinking that without him there, Bliss had completely wigged out.

Algernon was screaming.

"You son of a bitch! You can't take it, can you?! Being in the presence of someone superior, someone willing to risk everything for their art, to push past the bourgeois restraints that—Agghh!"

Again the sound of someone being slapped.

"Hit me all you want, Detective Bliss! Go ahead. Kick me, now that I'm on the floor. It's where you put all of us artists who show you up for what you are: slaves to your own fears, simpletons whose sole purpose is to keep the few of us who have the courage to lead mankind into the future locked in a deathgrip of—"

Then another thud and a groan and a crash from what might have been the table falling over.

"Look at yourself, Bliss! You've become an animal! You're panicked! You flee from me like you would from lighting. Agghh! No! *No!!*"

And then the sound of the microphone falling and the tape ended. Bliss got up and switched off the tape player.

"I never moved," Bliss said. "I never got up from my chair, never uncrossed my legs." He finished his beer. "It was radio theater. Like *War of the Worlds* and he was Orson Welles. When it was done, he jumped up and spoke to Katrina, the director, who'd been in the audience videotaping the performance. 'Did you get it all?' he asked. It's for their next show. About James's murder. He's already written half of it. They're asking the family for permission to video the funeral. It's sick."

"So you got nothing," Ward said.

"Less than nothing. I need to talk to this woman Constance. I think she actually knows something. Instead, I get this avant-garde screwball."

"What kind of case *is* this?"

"It's a weird nightmare of a play, and I got caught in the middle."

"Can't you book the guy on suspicion? Make him spend a few nights in the Tombs?"

"I'd be doing him a favor. He lives for experience. Thrives on it. The more extreme, the better. Put him in jail, he'd be up until dawn, rapping with the brothers, listening to their life stories. By morning he'd have his next play. Something kinky would only excite him more. Algernon Mann could have a hard-core con's Hebrew National shoved up his ass, and with one hand he'd be stroking the guy's balls and with the other he'd be writing a monologue in his notebook."

"I hope the N.E.A. takes away his grant. Any other leads?"

"Nothing. They're all a little crazy, partner. Everything to them is some kind of performance, a game, theater du jour. And the weird thing is, no one is all that upset about this kid being dead. Even his parents don't seem to want me to try very hard to find his killer."

"Maybe they don't want you following the bread crumbs back to their own cabin in the woods."

"You got it mixed up," Malikha said. "The bread crumbs were Hansel and Gretel, and they led from the gingerbread house."

"Someone was close to him," Ward said. "Have you ever in all our years of dealing with scumbags, the unevolved, guys who would have made Dr. Leakey's all-star team, have you ever met anyone who didn't have someone who was close to them? A mother. A wife. The paraplegic kid on the corner whose wheelchair the killer pushes to the basketball court— lifting him up so he can dunk the ball. There's always somebody out there.

"This woman Constance."

"Find her."

"I need to find my gun."

"I'm on it tomorrow. Meantime, I think you should call it a day, partner. Call it a day and go home."

Martin had been trying to reach his man by phone all afternoon. Since he couldn't have his man calling him at home, Martin had to keep checking in. He'd been to Bergdorf's and bought himself a suit that was being altered. He'd called Tiffany for a quick tryst, but she was busy with someone. He'd called Cassandra, wanting her to meet him for a drink, but she was leaving town to visit her sister—or so she said. Out of ideas, he had taken a cab down to the Chelsea Piers sports complex (a gypsy cab that wouldn't keep a record) to hit some golf balls, calling his man between each bucket—to no avail.

After practicing with all his clubs, he retired to the crab house and ordered a dozen oysters. He found a place by the window and looked out over the water. The sun was setting over New Jersey, and the harbor was lit with a lovely orange glow. You forget there are sunsets in New York, Martin thought.

He watched a cruise ship slowly sail off into the distance. That might be a nice thing to do. Cruise to the Caribbean. Take Tiffany with him. Or Cassandra, maybe. Buy whomever came along a skimpy bikini and watch her wander around the deck.

He called a few more times, and at 7:30 he finally got through. The package had been picked up, the man said, and tomorrow it would be delivered.

That sounded fine, Martin replied. The man hung up. He never wasted words.

Martin returned to his seat. He patted his pocket, feeling the wad of cash he had for payment, withdrawn from the account that he had set up specifically to deal with James-related expenses. And in a way this had to do with James, so it was only fitting that that's where he should get the money. He ordered himself a cognac, the best they had, which wasn't very good and was too cold, besides, but he sipped it slowly and savored it. The ship was long out of sight; by tomorrow it would be in the tropics. A cruise might be just the thing. Maybe he'd take Tiffany and Cassandra both—unless someone else struck his fancy before he sailed.

Chapter 14

It was almost nine o'clock when Bliss finally got home. His family had already finished dinner, but they joined him at the table while he ate. Meatloaf. How can you go wrong with meatloaf? Except Rachel had been making it lately with ground turkey to cut down on the fat, and it tasted a little dry. For Bliss that meant using more ketchup.

Rachel was on the portable phone as she dished out the mashed potatoes. She smiled as he sat down, then gave him a look that said, You forgot to wash your hands, you big lug, and how do you expect to teach your kids anything or be any kind of decent father if you can't remember the *simple* things, like washing your hands before you *eat*, especially after spending the day dragging corpses around and doing God knows what else. She was encyclopedic with her looks. This first one was followed by the one-two combination of eyes rolling upward and four slow sideways shakes of the head. Home two minutes and already he was taking a standing eight count.

So Bliss washed his hands and came back in and showed them to his wife. Both sides, even though Bliss knew that under his fingernails still lay traces of his day's journey—a bit of talc the rubber gloves he wore at the crime scene, fibers from the armchair in the Rodericks' living room, prob-

ably a few flecks of cannoli filling. Chocolate. Still, most of
the spots were wiped clean. Lady Macbeth should have it so
easy. That was probably the part Constance played for the Performance Warehouse. He could see someone killing the king
after falling under her spell. What about killing James? He
filed that away in the unlikely drawer, then picked up his
knife and fork and dug into the meatloaf.

Rachel clicked off the phone.

"Sorry. It's six o'clock on the Coast."

"We're on the coast, too, aren't we, Mom?" Cori said.

"When Mom says 'the Coast,'" Julia said, a distinct older-
sister edge to her voice, "she means California. Hollywood.
Where they make movies."

"Oh." At which point Cori looked like she was about to cry
because once again her older, smarter, and patently perfect
sister was right, and she was unbelievably, stupidly wrong.

"It's not as dry as it usually is," Bliss said, holding a piece
of the meatloaf on his fork in a transparent attempt to not
deal with either Cori's hurt feelings or who on the Coast
Rachel had been chatting with.

"I added an extra egg," Rachel said. But her culinary tri-
umph didn't quite explain the glow Rachel could barely con-
tain. "Um . . . that was Clint's people on the phone. They're
interested. They want to fly me out for a meet next week."

"You mean a 'meeting,' don't you, Mom?" Cori asked.

"A 'meet' is what they *call* a meeting on the Coast," Julia
said.

"Oh."

Bliss knew he should say something. It had been coming
for the last few months. First Rachel had gotten the big-time
agent, then the succession of nibbles from small production
companies wanting to option her life (Bliss wondered if he
and the kids would then be optioned, too). Demi had showed
some interest, Goldie had actually caught Rachel's act when

she was in New York taping Letterman, and Barbra's people were curious about Rachel's mom, if she had show biz aspirations herself, because that would be the part Barbra could play—"a contemporary *Gypsy*" was what Barbra's people had said. But now Clint was serious enough to want to fly her out.

"That's great, honey," he said, like he was reading it off a cue card. But isn't that what they *did* in Hollywood?

"Are they going to make a movie out of your life, Mom?" Julia asked.

"I don't know, sweetie. Maybe."

"Who do you want to play you, Cori?" Julia said. "I want Clare Danes to play me."

"She's too old," Cori said.

"No, she's not. She looks a little young for her age and I look a little older, so it works out perfect."

"I want Vanessa Redgrave," Cori said.

"Who's she?" Julia asked, priming her face for the avalanche of derision she could release as soon as her younger sister once again made an ignorant fool of herself.

"She's the best actress in the world," Cori said. "My teacher told us. She plays in Shakespeare and stuff. And she was in *Mission Impossible*."

"She's *way* too old," Julia chided.

"But she's the best actress in the world. So she can play any part." Cori was proud of her rare victory.

"Who do you want to play you, Dad?" Julia asked.

"Montgomery Clift," Bliss said. "But he's dead."

"How about Brad Pitt?" Julia asked.

"He could play me as a young man. When your mom and I first met."

"What about you, Mom?"

"Oh I don't know. Maybe Elle McPherson."

"Way to go, Mom," Julia said.

"Everything's still a long way off," Rachel said.

"Still, it's pretty exciting," Bliss said.

"Yes, it is," she answered, her voice already a little different, the voice of someone touched by success. "More meatloaf, honey?"

In the taxi on their way to Li-Jung's house, Matt actually took out his magazine spread and showed it to her. Two pages in *Seventeen,* starring "The New Bods on the Block," where he stood with his shirt off, arms clasped behind his head. Matt joked about how his picture was now being pasted inside the lockers of fourteen-year-old girls all across America. He laughed, but then his face became almost wistful, as if he were actually proud of this.

"It's only the beginning, babe," he said. "Soon I'll be doing catalogues—J. Crew, Tommy Hilfiger, all of them. Then beer commercials, and after that, who knows—a sitcom or *Baywatch* or even a guest boyfriend on *Melrose Place.*"

He assured her that they could always use someone with a sculpted set of abs on *Melrose Place.*

"The sky's the limit," he told Li-Jung as he put an arm around her shoulder and pulled her close. "Soon you'll be saying you knew me when."

Yeah, Matt, she wanted to say, *I knew you when you were alive.*

Then he wanted her to go down on him right there in the taxi, like he deserved some kind of reward for his success, her lips on his organ an acknowledgment of his New Bod on the Block-ness. His way of suggesting that Li-Jung do this was by placing his hand on the back of her neck and gently but firmly trying to shove her head toward his lap. She twisted from his grip and moved away.

"Matt, please," she said, "I don't feel like giving you a blow job in the back of this cab." She spoke loudly enough for the driver to hear. Clearly shocked, Matt's hand retreated. Probably other girls that Matt knew didn't talk that way.

But sex in cars had been a way of life for Li-Jung. Her domain. Without it she would have disappeared, become a tiny mouse creeping around the high school, taunted and teased, her thin, waiflike body something you'd see in a magazine ad to save the children—especially next to the big, blond, blue-eyed cows that grazed the halls of her high school.

She became the girl who was willing, the one with the rep, who fit so neatly in the back seat of a car. Not in just *any* car, though. She knew how to say no to guys she thought were *total* creeps, being quite direct if she had to, like she had just been with Matt. Still, she had been in enough cars to know that after she rebuked him, Matt would get all morose and sullen—but only until she forgave him.

"Let me see your abs," she said.

He lifted up his shirt, and she went "Ooohh" while he counted the ridges to make sure they were all there. Then she tweaked his nipple, and he smiled his toothy grin and was back to his New Bod on the Block self again, just as she knew he would be.

Matt laughed and kissed her.

"You're really something," he said.

"Thanks."

She looked out the window and thought about how she couldn't wait to get home to her gun, like it was a new puppy. Couldn't wait until Matt was asleep so she could take it out and see what kinds of tricks she could teach it. Roll over. Sit. Beg. Play dead.

Martin sipped his pear brandy in his study and thought gleefully about how well things were going. Ordering up his scheme like he did his *poussin* from the butcher. All it took was a little initiative and knowing the right person. *The pack-*

age will be delivered tomorrow. It was time, Martin's time to make things happen on his own terms. By tomorrow the detectives would see his wife as the vengeful mother, taking the law in her own hands. Promise would be in so deep that even *she* couldn't lie and cajole her way out of it. Once the package was delivered, Promise would need him more than ever.

He had put up with so much over the last twelve years. Nothing had been easy, but he'd had no choice. The stipend his first wife had given him—because she felt guilty about running off with her gynecologist—was just about gone when he met Promise, as beautiful and haughty as any of the rich, single woman who hung out at The Sign of the Dove. Martin saw her often—men, married or not, swarming around her, vying for her attention, offering their yachts, apartments in Paris and Venice, houses in the Hamptons, islands in the Aegean. Seats in private jets were saved for her, in case she had an urge for a dinner of fresh halibut in Puget Sound or breakfast as the sun rose in the white city of Lisbon.

But only Martin had sensed that she needed something else, something that the rich men overlooked. The father thing. To be taken care of, for everything to be made all right. Unfortunately, he discovered too late that she wasn't looking for a father for herself but for her delinquent rogue of a son.

He poured a touch more brandy into his glass, quite delighted with the way things were falling into place so naturally. What comfort there was in having someone he could call on. *The package will be delivered tomorrow.* Martin didn't know the man's name. Well, he knew *a* name, but he was sure it wasn't *the* name. It was all a kind of kid's game—false identities, talking in code, leaving money in a brown-paper bag. It was remarkable what you could get done for a few thousand dollars. For a stack of hundreds less than a half inch thick,

Martin could rewrite his fate, change his part in the play, make himself a happy ending.

The *package* was one of a pair of earrings that Martin had chosen with great care. Its principal attribute was that once found, it could be easily be linked to Promise. He had found the earrings in the back of her jewelry case. Two interlocking gold hoops, each inlaid with tiny sapphires. Quite elegant. But what made them so perfectly suited to Martin's purpose was that they were a gift from Constance, sent several years ago as a kind of peace offering. Promise had perfunctorily dismissed any thought of reconciliation, but the earrings were too nice to throw away. If his man did his job, the police would find one of the earrings by the body and show it to Constance. And she, with malicious glee, would direct them to her younger sister, Promise. This time Martin's expression, a mixture of disbelief and sorrow, would be well crafted. *Oh, Promise, darling, how could you?*

A half-inch stack of hundreds was all he had needed to buy himself a new future.

The brandy was exquisite. Not too sweet, just a hint of pear. He had two cases sitting in the library closet. He would take a bottle on the cruise to sip in the cabin with whomever he brought along with him—and with whomever else he happened to meet on the ship.

Chapter 15

The ringing phone woke Bliss up. He checked the time—10:30. He must have conked out right after dinner in his clothes, exhausted from his search for justice and worrying about his missing gun. Rachel was sitting up in bed next to him, reading. The ring was the same as always, the click making the connection nothing special, nothing to warn Bliss of what was coming when he picked up the receiver.

"Rachel Davis, please."

He instantly recognized the voice. It was Clint. He was sure of it. Calling, no doubt, from his patio in Carmel overlooking the Pacific. A call just like any other, making the journey through tiny glass tubes stretching across thousands of miles of American soil and history and Clint Eastwood roles, past the graves of silent gunslingers, Civil War veterans, rodeo stars, widowed photographers, Arizona sheriffs, maniacal New York cops—Eastwood calling eastward and into the Bliss bedroom.

"Oh. Yeah. Hold on. And who should I say is calling?"

"Tell her Clint is on the line."

Clint. Not his people, but Clint himself. Calling his wife.

"Clint who?" Bliss asked.

Rachel was reaching for the receiver now, but Bliss wasn't losing her to Hollywood without a fight.

"Eastwood," Clint said. "Clint Eastwood."

Bliss turned his back to her as she pummeled him, trying to grab the phone.

"If this is really Clint Eastwood, tell me who played at the Jazz at Massey Hall Concert?"

"Bird, Diz, Bud Powell, Mingus, and Max Roach," Clint the jazz fan replied without missing a beat.

Rachel stopped and stared at him in complete disbelief.

"OK, that was easy," Bliss said. "Now name the All-American Rhythm Section."

Clint needed a moment here.

"Oh . . . um . . . Count Basie, Jo Jones, and Walter . . . um, Walter Page."

"Wrong. You forgot Freddie Greene. The guitarist. Hah!" Bliss handed the receiver to Rachel, telling her, "He says he's Clint Eastwood, but I'm not so sure."

Grabbing the receiver, Rachel gave him one of her most sacred looks, the one that expressed the feeling that marrying him was the second worst decision of her life——the first being that she had slept with him the night they met at her cousin's wedding. Then she composed herself and put on her best high-school graduation smile and said hi to Clint.

Bliss left the room as Rachel began the conversation that might change their lives forever and went to check on his kids.

Her voice rang out behind him down the hall, full of enthusiasm and——dare he say it?——hope. "Mr. Eastwood . . . of course I will. *Clint* . . . Why that's so kind of you. . . ."

Rachel had been doing her comedy routine steadily the past year, playing clubs in New York, Boston, Philadelphia, and D.C. Now Dirty Harry was calling. The Man with No Name. Bliss wished it was someone he despised, some spineless Hollywood impostor. But it had to be Clint, who he admired, who was no doubt telling his wife right now how much he loved her material, how clever it was. How they wanted to develop it into a script——the life of a cop from the wife's perspective. *It's unique. It's fresh. It's boffo!* Of course, Clint would want her to come out to the Coast. Get the deal together. Meet some stars. Start working on the script.

Bliss opened Cori's door and found her asleep, her Burl Ives tape still playing quietly. *I know an old lady who swallowed a cow. . . .* Please don't ask me how, sweetie, Bliss thought, I've got enough to worry about right now. He pulled the blankets up over her shoulders and kissed her goodnight, just like softhearted cops are supposed to do. He closed the door gently and went to check on his oldest.

Julia slept in what used to be the maid's room, a tiny space just big enough for a bed, dresser, and computer, but that's what she wanted. Julia was almost thirteen now and eager to be as far apart from her parents as she could get. Perhaps the maid's room still had an aura of maidness about it that gave Julia the feeling she was only there in the house temporarily, until a better job came along.

Bliss opened the door to a shrill chorus of "*Dad!*" and immediately closed it. He'd caught a glimpse of Julia and a girlfriend huddled together on the bed. Sharing secrets. Female mysteries. He didn't remember the other girl coming in. Maybe Julia had told Bob the doorman not to buzz. "My dad falls asleep early, especially when he's working on a case like he is now, so don't buzz up to our apartment when my friend arrives. He'll be wearing a leather jacket and carrying a plastic bag of pot in his back pocket. Oh, by the way, Bob, do you have any matches we could borrow?"

He returned to his room as Rachel was hanging up.

"He wants to meet you."

"Who?"

"Clint."

"Oh."

"He didn't know you were a jazz fan."

"I imagine there's a lot about me he doesn't know."

"It's typical of you. To steal my thunder. To barge right in. Clint wants to know if you can come out to the Coast with me."

"I'm in the middle of an investigation."

"That's what I told him. He wants to hear all about it. As usual, in your own quiet way you've become the center of attention."

"I guess Clint and I are a lot alike."

"Fuck you."

But she was smiling now, waving her arms like a little girl and emitting a kind of squeal. "Clint Eastwood called me! He did! He dialed my number with his very own hand!"

"I wonder if he used his trigger finger."

"I should call my dad."

"Yeah. They could be partners on that condo conversion in Flushing."

"Clint liked you," she said.

"Of course he liked me. Everyone likes me. I'm the cop with the heart of gold." Then he remembered: He was the postbungee Bliss, he could push past his mental limits. "Don't call your dad right now," he said. "Instead, take off your shirt."

"But . . ."

"Cori's asleep, and Julia's in her room with a friend trying to convince each other they don't even *have* parents. We're alone. We're safe. Take off your pants, too."

They made love tenderly, with a gentle passion. And Cori didn't wake up and Julia stayed in her room and the bed began to creak but they didn't care. And Bliss's mother didn't call in tears because of his father's abuses and Rachel's father didn't call for further confirmation of his daughter's degradation at having married a cop and they moved together with increased abandon because it was just the two of them tonight, climaxing together and then nestling into each other, not worrying about whether Cori needed covering up or how Julia's friend was getting home but instead sinking into a deep, dreamless sleep.

After having his way with her earlier in the night, which was pretty much the same way he'd had with her the night before, Matt fell asleep. Sex for him was like an alarm clock in reverse. Li-Jung decided that this would be the last time with the New Bod. He just wasn't getting the hang of it. He made love like a tourist, jumping out of the bus for a quick snapshot, then rushing back in. He didn't linger anywhere long enough to understand the customs, so it was really hard for the locals to open up to him.

The exception was his fascination with her tattoo, on which he once again focused his most ardent amorous attentions.

Li-Jung reached under the mattress and brought out the gun, resting it in her lap, the metal cold even through the sheet. The muzzle was pointing right toward Matt's face. She could blow a hole through his head. A *real* blow job. A tiny hole through his forehead, a gaping crater in the back. But Matt wouldn't know what had hit him, so what would be the fun of that? She could wake him up, and he'd start smiling thinking about the tiger and wanting to put his lips to it and make love again, but then he'd see the gun and his eyes would bug out. She'd talk to him, tell him not to stir, not to scream. And she'd have to watch him closely, to make sure he didn't do any fast football moves and take the gun away from her or, worse, start crying and begging. Maybe it was better not to wake him up. Just shoot him. Put a pillow over his head, put the gun in the pillow.

Bang!

She wondered if the cops could find her. She sublet the apartment from an actor named Victor who had gotten a job out of town. Victor's friend had closed the deal. She hadn't given any references and paid the rent in cash. The electricity and phone weren't in her name, and she wasn't supposed to make any long-distance calls, which was fine with her because who was she going to call, anyway? Bobby, to see if he'd shot any more dogs lately? Clyde, to find out what happened at the last parole hearing? Her parents, to see if her mother was bent over any closer to the ground?

Dave the caterer paid her in cash. She had no bank account, no credit cards. She could just drift away to another city, find a new job. Doing what? she wondered. Worry about it later.

Put the pillow over his head, put the gun in the pillow.

Bang!

She knew something like this would happen to her in New

York. Something big. It had started with the tattoo, then came the bungee jump off the bridge. This jump had been different from the one she'd done at the state fair back in high school, the boys then daring her to jump, which she did most casually, showing them she wasn't scared of anything. That's when she got the nickname Kamikaze. Because she was daring and Asian, so what else could they call her. No hesitation. Unlike Lenny, who even in the yellowish glow of the streetlights looked pale, like he was going have a stroke. But Li-Jung hadn't faltered, never broke stride, acted with supreme confidence—unlike her life back in Iowa.

She'd tried one year of college but then dropped out after discovering it wasn't such a good idea to go to school in the same town as where you lived, where your mother still padded around with her shopping bags, where the guys you knew in high school could shout nasty things as they drove by in their trucks.

She hadn't been ready to be a student. She'd felt used up, lost, unworthy of college. When a familiar face dropped by her dorm unannounced, it had been so much easier to jump into the front seat than to study for exams. Get some pizza, go to the movies, swig some beers.

But then one night it all came apart. A local boy, a friend of someone she liked, had wanted to go out. On the phone he'd sounded like a regular guy. She eagerly shoved her history essay in a drawer and waited for him outside her dorm. When his truck pulled up, she got in.

As soon as she had looked at him, she sensed it was wrong. Something about his eyes. He rammed the shifter into first and took off.

He'd been drinking. She could smell it. He was silent, didn't even smile, driving with an intensity that scared her. "Where are we going?" she'd asked. He wouldn't say. "Maybe we could get something to eat. You feel like a burger or something?"

He took her to an open field she'd never been to before, turned off the engine, turned off the lights. He sat, drinking silently from a bottle until the booze was almost gone. She thought of running, but knew she wouldn't get far. "You want to listen to the radio?" she'd asked. Anything to break the silence, to lighten things up. He didn't answer. She reached for the knob, he grabbed her hand, threw it back in her lap. He still hadn't said a word.

Then something apparently clicked inside him, making him decide it was time. "Don't think I'm going to fuck you," he'd said. "I'm saving that for my girlfriend, until after we're married." But there were other things he had wanted done. When he was finished, he shoved her across the seat.

"Whore," he said.

He drove her back to her dorm and dropped her off without a word.

Lying in bed after this, feeling worn and dirty, she had watched as her roommate in her pink fuzzy slippers and pink satiny nightgown finished talking with her parents. *Love you, Mom*, she'd said. She hung up the phone and got into bed and cuddled up with her teddy bear. *Sweet dreams, Li-Jung*, she'd said.

That's when Li-Jung had started to cry.

Great, heaving sobs emerged from deep inside her, and she couldn't stop them. Her roommate had bolted out of bed and rushed to her side; then she ran to get the dorm counselor. They called her parents, but the counselor couldn't make them understand that Li-Jung needed help, that she was having a kind of breakdown. She had pulled herself together enough to go to the infirmary for the next two days. It was there that she decided she had to get away, somewhere where no one would know her, where she could start over, where she wouldn't stick out.

But lately she had been falling into her old pattern. True,

Matt showered more frequently than the men she was used to, but he treated her basically the same. Like the little stunt in the taxi he'd tried to pull.

But now she had the gun. And now it was going to be about someone *else* taking the punishment for a change.

Put the pillow over his head, gently, so as not to wake him. Place another pillow over that pillow. Delicately push the gun in deep, to muffle the sound.

She forced herself to keep her eyes open, like when she bungee jumped, so she could see everything as she fell, face it and not hide, not bow down—*Table for four? Light this way*—not spend her life taking tiny steps in her slippers—*You want tea? I bling you tea*—a smile stuck on her face, pretending she didn't care that everyone else got to eat and enjoy and live the one life they were given.

Bang.

The gun went off. Her lips were suddenly dry, her hand was shaking. She stayed frozen there until a trickle of blood appeared from under the pillow. Then she got out of bed.

Act IV

Chapter 16

Bliss woke up late, around 9:30. He showered and brushed his teeth and reheated some coffee in the microwave and felt a little better. It was too early to call Ward on a Saturday. He heard the TV in Cori's room and found her there alone watching cartoons.

"Mom had to take Julia to a soccer game," she said. "Then they're going shopping for a dress for Julia's Bas Mitzvah. Just looking, today. Mom said I could come, too, when they actually buy it."

"So what do you want to do?"

"I don't know."

"You have breakfast?"

"Yeah."

"You want a donut or a bagel or something?"

"Um . . . OK."

"So get dressed. I'll race you."

"Do buttons count?"

"Yeah. That's my handicap. I have to finish all the buttons."

"Readysetgo!"

He sprinted down the hall into his room, searched through his drawers for fresh underwear and socks. He slipped on his weekend olive khakis and was just digging out a maroon sports shirt when Cori marched in victoriously in jeans and a turtleneck.

Riding that exuberance, they headed to Zabar's for some bagels and Cori's favorite, the chocolate rugelah, and then to

Riverside Park, where they would find a bench and have a little picnic and then go to the playground for a little R&R.

It was rare for Bliss to be alone with just one of his kids
with no agenda, not rushing them to a lesson or a game or
picking them up and dashing home in time for dinner and
homework. It was one of those moments to take notice of, to
remember. Once, back in college, he was escorting his art-
history girlfriend back to her dorm when she suddenly stopped
and pointed to the moon, which was full that night. "Think
about it," she had said. "How many times is there a full moon
to begin with? And how many times when you're outside on
a clear night with a full moon do you actually look up and see
it? And even when you *do* see it, how often do you have the
time to really take it in?" That morning was a rare full moon
with his kid that Bliss actually had time to savor.

He treated himself to smoked sable on an onion roll and
could barely keep from eating it as they headed into Riverside Park to look for a place to sit. Cori wanted to be by the
river, so they walked down the steps and followed the path to
the Hudson and found a bench with all its slats intact and free
of bird poop. They opened their sandwiches and started to
eat. The sable was perfect—oily and slightly smoky, practically melting in his mouth.

"Look at that boat," Cori said.

It actually wasn't a boat but a huge cement barge being
pushed by a tug out toward the harbor. He explained this to
Cori.

"That tugboat must be powerful," she said.

"Yes, sweetie." Bliss said, trying not to think about the case
he had worked involving that same cement company—a mob
hit. He tried to force himself to taste the sable and not think
about the severed fingers, the dimes on the guy's eyes. He was
like that tug, he thought, pushing along the mammoth barge
of his life. Or maybe he was like the barge itself, not in con-

trol, a huge dead weight being pushed out to sea. Or maybe he was the cement on the barge. Or the river. Or the smell of the river. Or the seagull coasting gracefully above the river, effortlessly riding the wind across the water to Hoboken. No, definitely not the seagull. He took his daughter's hand and held it tightly.

"How's that rugelah?" he asked Cori.

"Good," she said, smiling.

Why didn't he know that smile better? he thought. His kid's smile. It should be etched in his brain. In permanent residence. In the penthouse, a whole orchestra of synapses on the verandah playing that tune over and over—My Daughter's Smile—his theme song. How bad was it that if she were smiling, he might not be able to pick his own kid out of a lineup. No wonder he'd given away his gun.

"You want one, Dad?" she asked.

"What?"

"A rugelah.

"OK."

He told her about her great aunt, his mother's sister, who would make her own rugelah, rolling it out on the kitchen table.

"First it would be in a circle. Then she let me sprinkle on the cinnamon and sugar and nuts. Then she cut it into wedges, which we rolled up into rugelah."

"That sounds like fun," Cori said.

"You would have liked her."

"If you liked her, I bet I would have, too," she said.

They sat for a while, just watching the water. Bliss hoped his daughter was OK, that she didn't have little pockets of Lenny-ness buried inside her, waiting to show up without warning, like cicadas, invading her calm with a shrill, deafening whine.

"I jumped off a bridge the other night," he said. Just like

that, blurted it out without thinking, without any drumroll or
fanfare. "A big bridge. The Brooklyn Bridge, in fact."

"What do you mean?"

"I snuck onto the bridge late at night and bungee jumped
through a little hole in the center."

"Why didn't you take me?"

"You were asleep."

"So?"

"I couldn't. No kids allowed. Anyway, I did it."

"Really?"

"Yeah."

"Awesome!"

"Thanks."

"Can I tell the kids in school?"

"Actually, no. I wasn't supposed to be up there."

"But you're a policeman."

"I know. But even still. It has to be our secret."

"Can I tell Mom and Julia?"

Bliss thought for a moment. There was probably a ten-foot
stack of books and magazines counseling against exactly what
he was about to do, but he did it anyway.

"No," he said. "Let this be just between you and me."

"OK," she said, beaming, her eyes wide and bright and, for
the moment, without even the slightest hint of melancholy.

DeWayne couldn't believe it was morning already. The night
before he'd driven until 3 A.M., shuttling a steady parade of
Friday-night revelers from one raucous bar to another. Just to
break up the monotony, he'd headed over to Carnegie Hall,
looking for more sedate passengers, but it turned out to be
Gay Men's Chorus night, and the two men he picked up were
anything but the matronly classical-music doyennes he'd
hoped to find. At least not yet they weren't.

He'd dropped them off in Greenwich Village. There he

picked up a waitress on her way to her boyfriend's in Brooklyn Heights. On the way back, he picked up a girl breaking up with her boyfriend in Brooklyn Heights and who needed to go to the Upper East Side, which started him on the cycle of bars again. Then Fate graced him with two businessmen staying at hotels out by Kennedy because they had to catch early flights. The airport wasn't far from his apartment, so he'd decided to call it a night.

He was hoping to sleep later, but for some reason the guy who robbed him had taken his window shades—which he hadn't noticed until the sun poured in and found his head at the end of the couch like a spotlight. He tried turning away, but he had a lot on his mind. His big mission for the day was to buy some presents for his kids, who he was seeing the following afternoon. He wondered what to get them. He wanted it to be special, so they'd have some good thoughts about him. Antoinette said that some of the kids at school had been mean, saying their dad was a bad man. At one time it seemed like a good thing to move into a neighborhood full of cops and their families. But that was back when he was a cop.

He'd go to the toy store later and look around. Maybe something would catch his eye.

He got up and headed for the shower, feeling that maybe today wasn't going to be as painful. But it was early yet.

The waiter at the Veselka Coffee Shop woke Li-Jung up, her cheek resting on the table. She'd been there for several hours and must have conked out after her second cup of borscht. She remembered asking herself just before falling asleep if she felt better now that she'd fired the gun, but she didn't have an answer.

She asked the waiter to watch her bags. He scowled but said OK in a heavy Eastern European accent. *I'm a murderer*, she wanted to say. But she was sure the waiter wouldn't have looked at her twice—he'd probably seen everything, working the graveyard shift in the East Village.

She went to the bathroom and splashed some water on her face. Why did she still feel so empty inside? Why no rush, no thrill of revenge, just the same sick clammy sadness she'd felt so many other times? It was as if he had still won. Matt dead still somehow made her feel just as lost and dumb and worthless as he had when he was shuttling his abs around. The gun hadn't done anything. She should have woken him up, told him he was about to die for all the assholes who had ever laid a hand on her. She might have felt better then, letting him know he was being sacrificed to ease her pain. Maybe. It probably wasn't Matt she'd wanted to shoot at all, but some ugly satyr that lurked deep inside her, that wasn't going to be gotten rid of with something as easy as a bullet.

Afterward she remembered sitting at the kitchen table, the gun in front of her, the barrel still hot at least a minute after the shot. It made an odd still life: the teapot, the cup, the gun. A yin/yang thing, maybe. She was feeling all jumbled up inside. She wasn't quite sure what to think. She wanted pink fuzzy slippers and a teddy bear. She wanted to be cozy. She wanted lollipops and lullabies. She wanted a mom to tuck her in at night and tell her stories and turn off the light so she could sleep for a long time. The gun hadn't brought her any of that.

Without looking at Matt, she had packed her suitcase and left. It was still several hours until dawn. She'd walked through the East Village, getting a tea at an all-night deli, sipping it as she wandered. When she could walk no farther, she had settled in at the Veselka and grabbed a few minutes of sleep. She looked at herself now in the mirror—the face of a killer. Not sure where she was going. Not sure of anything.

Chapter 17

Just as Bliss was getting back from the park with Cori, the phone rang. It was Artie, with news of an attempted homicide. He was ecstatic.

"One shot. Right in the head. Execution style. Didn't think I'd be seeing one of *these* right away."

"You said *attempted* homicide, Artie."

"Yeah. Bullet only grazed him."

"Sorry, can't make it today, Artie," Bliss said. He was alone with Cori.

"What're you up to?" Artie asked.

Bliss wasn't ready for this. He and Ward never questioned each other about taking a day. They understood it was something important.

"Try Benitez," Bliss said.

"What's wrong?"

The guy was worse than his mother. He should have been a junior-high vice principal. *Admit it, young man, you were smoking in the bathroom.*

"Nothing's wrong." How could he explain that he was feeling good, almost happy, and that he didn't want to deal with any dead people that day? "I'm alone with my kid now. I can't exactly take her with me."

He patted Cori gently on the head. She smiled. She was cradled in his lap, and they were watching cartoons.

"What are you working on?" Bliss asked. He shouldn't have, but he wanted to play the wise veteran advising the eager rookie.

"It seems this guy is helping out a friend who sublet his

apartment to this girl. The guy goes to the apartment to pick
up some stuff for his friend. You with me so far?"

"Yeah." But barely. He was more interested in *Rocky and
Bullwinkle*, the show Cori was watching.

"He knocks on the door, no answer, he lets himself in. He
goes into the bedroom, sees the bed full of blood, and sitting
there is a kid in his twenties, naked, a gash across his forehead
like someone's smeared him with lipstick. The kid's in shock.
E.M.S. arrives, they say he's been shot at close range, but the
bullet just grazed his scalp. They're worried because he's lost
some blood. You still with me?"

"Mmm-hmm." Bliss watched the nefarious Boris and
Natasha give Moose and Squirrel a radio filled with dynamite.

"There are powder marks on the pillowcase," Artie said,
his voice full of pluck, "like someone used it as a silencer. One
bullet to the head. Looks to me like a drug hit."

"Yeah, Artie." But Bullwinkle innocently turned off the
radio before it exploded, making Boris mad.

"This should be fun, huh Lenny? A big-time drug hit?"

No, Boris! Natasha says, but Boris impulsively turns the
radio back on and it blows up. Cori laughed.

"Anyway, the shooter didn't do a good job or else the kid
has a very hard head. Right now we're looking for the chick
subletting the apartment. Oriental girl named Li-Jung."

Bliss grabbed the remote out of Cori's hand and turned off
the TV. "What's her name?"

"Li-Jung. Either she ran or they shot her, too."

"Give me the address. I'll be right over."

"But I thought—"

"Give me the fucking address. And get a woman uniform
there. Tell her she's going to have to do a little baby-sitting."

Martin waited until Promise left. Then he took out the suitcase and laid it on the bed for the next step in his plan: packing her clothes for her imaginary getaway, fleeing after com-

mitting her crime. He folded her bathing suit, her robe, her tennis outfit, the dresses she would wear at night, for sipping drinks by the pool, flirting with the young men.

He slipped her passport into the outside zippered pocket. The ticket he had booked for her to St. Croix would be waiting at the airport. She'd protest when the detectives discovered it, but Martin was prepared, his lines rehearsed: *But you asked me to, Promise. You specifically asked me to book you first class. I've always made her travel arrangements, Detective. In fact, it's all I do.* The suitcase was full and included a single hoop earring, the match to which would be left discreetly at the crime scene. All that remained was the gun, which his man would bring back after the job was done— after he *took out the garbage.*

He closed the bag and slipped it in the back of her closet, hidden behind her gowns.

While he was there, he folded a few of her sweaters.

He fixed a jacket that was half falling off a hanger.

He removed a cashmere turtleneck from a hook where it was developing a protrusion and put it in the hamper for dry-cleaning.

Then he went into the kitchen to turn over the leg of lamb he was marinating.

A young man in khakis and a white T-shirt was standing on the front stoop talking to Artie when Bliss pulled up to the curb. He was clearly agitated, repeatedly making a kind of chopping gesture with his arm, like he was desperate to cut something loose. Bliss could feel Cori's apprehension.

"Can't I wait in the car, Daddy?"

"No," Bliss said, not thinking it through. He was focused only on getting in the apartment and looking for his gun. He got out of the car, went around to Cori's door, and opened it. Taking her hand he pulled her from the car.

"Let's go," Bliss said and led her up the front stoop.

"I *found* him that way!" the young man was shouting.
"Honest! It's my friend's apartment. I was just coming by to
pick up some clothes to send him. I was at the movies last
night. The Film Forum. Seeing *La Strada*. The Fellini film.
I bought popcorn. I'm sure the counter girl remembers me. I
paid with quarters. I'm a waiter. I can tell you how the movie
ends. Anthony Quinn eats an ice cream in one bite. Then he's
crying on the beach. I went to my friend's house afterward.
Honest!"

Artie turned to Bliss with a shit-eating grin. "We got our-
selves quite a little situation here, dontcha think, Lenny?"

Bliss ignored his partner. "Tell me about the girl," he said
to the young man. He felt his grip tighten around Cori's
hand. He forced himself to relax.

Artie looked puzzled.

"Don't you want to—"

"The girl," Bliss said, staring straight into the frightened
eyes of the young man until by force of will he calmed him
down. "Tell me about her."

"Her name was Li-Jung," he said. "She's been subletting
three months now."

"Where'd she come from?" Bliss asked.

"I don't know."

"You didn't ask for references?"

"She said she just arrived in town. She had cash. The apartment's a dump. The bathtub's in the kitchen. This is the place
you start from and work your way up."

"The kid inside almost worked his way dead," Artie said,
clearly proud of his bon mot.

"Where is she?!" Bliss asked, his heart racing. "Where can
I find her?"

"Honest. I don't know. She said she was a cook—she was
going to get a job with a caterer. She didn't like restaurants,
she said. That's all I remember."

Bliss would have the phone records checked. Immediately. Then he'd go over the apartment himself, all afternoon if he had to, until he found something to locate the girl. A return address. A clothing label. A prescription bottle. A sweatshirt with a logo. Something. Meanwhile there'd be an A.P.B. out for her.

"She have any distinguishing features?" Bliss asked the kid.

"Not that I remember."

"No tattoos?"

"I don't—"

"On her shoulder?"

"I didn't—"

"A tiger?"

"I mean, there could have been, I didn't really . . ."

Bliss turned to Artie. "Put it down. As part of the description. A tattoo of a tiger on her shoulder."

Bliss had bought some candy on the way over. He handed it to the uniformed woman officer and introduced her to Cori. Then he kissed his daughter on the forehead and headed up to the apartment to look for his gun.

Li-Jung saw the police from down the street. If she hadn't, she might have walked right into their arms and been on her way to jail now. But luckily she spotted the blue car and the unmarked brown one with the bubble light on the roof. She turned and walked in the opposite direction, casually so as not to attract attention.

She was supposed to have been on the bus to Boston with the $1,200 she'd saved. But a few minutes ago she made the mistake of calling her mother and heard the stunning news.

"Did you get the retter I lote you?" her mother asked.

"You sent me a letter?" Li-Jung felt her mouth go dry.

"On Tuesday."

She panicked. What's today? she thought. Saturday? Did she pick up the mail yesterday? Yes. Something from Actor's Equity for Victor and some catalogues. That was it.

"Li-Jung?"

"Yeah. Great letter. Thanks. Gotta go. I'll call you back. Bye."

Three months in New York and now *she decides to write.* Her mother was some kind of curse on Li-Jung's head.

So instead of going to Port Authority, Li-Jung had lugged her suitcase back to her building to wait for the mail. Sit on the steps. Sip some coffee, enjoy her last day in New York.

Except now it was obvious that Matt's body had been discovered and Lenny was at her doorstep. And if *he* found the letter, he'd know all about her.

If it came in today's mail, she had to intercept it. If it *didn't* come today, the police would certainly be holding her mail, and she would just have to make a run for it. As Li-Jung walked away, she started thinking about the best way to destroy the shit out of her mother's letter.

Chapter 18

It was a half hour later, and Bliss was out of luck. The apartment was full of showbiz crap, all of which seemed to belong to Victor, the owner. Old playbills, Public Theater posters, scripts, a three-foot stack of *Backstage* newspapers. There were *Miss Saigon* coffee mugs on the counter, *Cats* ashtrays, a *Phantom* bath towel draped over the tub, Jekyll-and-Hyde wine glasses rested on a shelf above the sink. They were dusty. It seemed like the girl had never really settled in. No letters, bills, paycheck stubs. Nothing with a postmark. The dresser was empty. No labels from small boutiques they could trace. No clothes for Artie to muse over. Bliss was thinking that the phone records might be his only hope.

"We should talk to the boy's parents," Artie said. "See if they knew if he was into drugs or not."

"Yeah?"

"I was pondering it while you were on your way over. This definitely looks like some kind of retaliation thing. The kid must have had a bad debt with the wrong people. Dontcha think, Lenny?"

"I don't know."

"They tail him, follow him home from some bar with the girl, jimmy the lock, and whack him in his sleep."

Bliss felt like he was stuck in a *Mod Squad* episode. He didn't feel like explaining to Artie that drug dealers don't usually kill people who owe them money if there's a chance of getting it back. The kid looked rich. Threaten him enough, he'd find a way into his father's account. But Bliss was doubtful such wisdom would have slowed Artie down any.

"Or maybe the girl was working *for* them. She meets the kid at the club on purpose, seduces him, tantalizes him with all kinds of Oriental sex tricks—*Kama Sutra*—takes him home, does him until he passes out, and then *she* lets the bad guys in."

"A real hit man doesn't just graze someone," Bliss said. "He shoots them until they're dead."

Artie shrugged. "It could have been his first time. There's a first time for everything. Even shooting people in the head."

"Artie, you talk to the boy's parents," Bliss said. "See if they know anything. Then go to the hospital and speak to the kid. Maybe he can tell us who did this to him."

"Dontcha think I should go to the hospital first?"

"Sure, whatever you decide."

"OK, partner," Artie said. "Sounds good."

Artie was excited, flushed with pride. All this action. Bliss could almost read his mind: It beat selling sportswear all day.

Bliss leaned his head out the window. Cori and the police-woman were playing patty-cake. Ice cream wrappers were at their feet. His daughter was probably having more fun with the policewoman than she did with him.

Li-Jung walked as fast as she could to the Strand Bookstore. She checked her suitcase at the front, pocketed her number, walked around inside for a minute, and then left. She'd return for the suitcase later. She didn't want to have to lug it around while she made her getaway preparations.

She found the lighter fluid at the Gristedes near her building. On sale. It was summer—barbecue season. She got some other things, too, so she wouldn't attract attention—bananas and a bottle of spring water. She ate two of the bananas. The others she put in her backpack for later. She drank what she could of the water, then dumped out the rest. She found a secluded stoop and carefully transferred the lighter fluid into the water bottle, which she had chosen specifically because it was the kind with the sport top that allowed you to squirt the water into your mouth. It sprayed out much faster than the lighter fluid container, which only had a tiny hole.

As she walked back, she went over her plan to intercept the postman and incinerate the letter. She'd do it at number 386. That building was at the far end of the street and had a lot of apartments, so the mailman would be inside a long time. She'd casually approach the cart, spray the fluid, light it, and walk around the corner. At which point she would sprint to the West Fourth Street subway, wait in the center platform for the first train to come (there were four to choose from), and take it in whatever direction it was headed. Later she'd double back to the Strand and pick up her suitcase, then head to Port Authority and grab the first bus to Boston.

She waited down the street, watching the little girl playing with a woman police officer and wondering how Lenny was doing inside. He was probably rummaging through her drawers, emptying her wastebasket, looking for clues—clues that would lead to her. She'd gone through it all herself, trying to imagine anything that could link her to her past. She'd arrived in New York with one suitcase, and now she was leaving with the same. Nothing more, nothing less. No credit cards, no checks, no long-distance calls. That was key, she thought.

Lenny would no doubt track down Dave the caterer, who would try to remember if Li-Jung had ever said anything about where she came from. Dave would rack his brain, eager to help the police so that they might overlook the two Mexicans working for him without green cards. But Dave would just be another dead end for Lenny, the big ox, tripping on the way up the bridge, obviously terrified before his jump. She wished he didn't have such a gentle face, that he hadn't tried so hard to hide his fear, that he hadn't been so trusting when he handed her his gun. Ah, well . . .

By now Lenny would know she did it. Learned her name and what she looked like and put two and two together: that his gun was responsible for Matt being dead. She felt sorry for him, working on Saturday when he should have been having fun with his daughter, dragging her along to a murder scene instead of playing with her in a sandbox. But he would be angry and come after Li-Jung. Relentlessly. She had to stay focused—destroy the letter and get out of the city.

She was so lost in thought that she almost missed the post-man, who wasn't a man at all but an overweight lady who pushed the mail cart with such disdain that Li-Jung would probably be doing her a favor by setting it on fire.

The woman struggled up the steps with the bundle of mail for number 386, the cart parked on the sidewalk. Maybe she was used to working behind the counter, but because it was a Saturday, she was filling in. The mail lady entered the foyer, and the door closed behind her.

Li-Jung made sure the top to the bottle was open as she crossed the street. She stopped by the cart and doused it with the lighter fluid. First the left side, then the right. The smell filled the air. She was about to light the match when she saw the letter. It was obvious. The envelope with her mother's name in Chinese characters right above the return address. She reached in and took it. It was partially soaked with fluid. She put it in her pocket. She stood up and looked around. No one had seen.

She turned and walked away, back to the Strand, joyous that it had worked out. Behind her, no cops, no sirens, no screaming mail person.

She got to the bookshop and handed her number to the clerk. He bent down for her suitcase and stayed bent much too long before coming up from behind the counter.

"Um . . . it's gone," he said.

"What?"

"Um . . . it's not here. Whatever it was. Look."

He placed another ratty square of cardboard on the counter next to hers. They both said 47, only the 7 on hers looked like a real 7 but on the other one it looked more like a 1 that had a little line added to it to make it look like a 7.

Someone had swiped her suitcase.

"I just got on," the guy behind the counter said. "So it must have happened before. I'm really sorry."

In the slot for number 41 they found only a newspaper.

"I'll call the manager," the young man said. His hair was cut real short, and he had the kind of glasses that Dennis the Menace's father wore. Another small-town kid lost in the city.

Like her. He smiled, trying to make the best of it. "Then I guess we should call the police."

"No. It's OK," she said. "It wasn't anything important."

"But . . ."

She left before the guy could finish.

And it truly wouldn't have been anything important, except Li-Jung had put her money in the suitcase. Twelve-hundred dollars in twenties for the train ticket and money she would need to get started in Boston. So now she had no way of getting out of town and no place to stay. She felt her knees buckle, and she had to lean against a lamppost to keep from falling over. Someone asked her if she was all right and she nodded and straightened herself up and managed to walk the three blocks to Union Square park where she collapsed on a bench. She tried to clear her head, to focus only on the sounds of the birds, the wind in the trees above her. She stayed like that for several minutes. When she opened her eyes, there was a young guy sitting on the other end of the bench reading a book. He looked up and smiled. She smiled back.

Hey, I'm a young good-looking girl in New York. How hard could it be for me to get a few hundred dollars?

Besides, she thought, in her backpack she still had the gun.

Bliss was alone in the apartment, sitting at the kitchen table holding the bullet he had dug out of the mattress. The bullet that had been fired from his gun. He almost had to laugh. The Big Jump had only served to screw everything up. It was like he had bungeed back into a different life; when they pulled him up through the hole, he'd taken the blackness of the water with him.

The door opened and Bliss jumped.

"Easy, partner."

It was Ward. Bliss had called him earlier.

"It's over, partner," Bliss said.

"Not yet. The boy, Matt, is gonna be all right. I just radioed the hospital."

"Still . . ."

"Still nothing," Ward said, angry now. "It's another case. That's all. We look for clues. We find her. We cut her a deal and get back your piece, or we shoot her."

"Ward."

"I'm serious. She had a gun, she tried to use it, we took her down. Why wouldn't they believe us?"

"She's just a kid."

"She stole your piece. She tried to pop a guy in the head. She's like Ben Gay on your nuts. Look, they killed Bambi's mother who, as far as I'm concerned, had a lot more going for her than this girl."

"It doesn't make any sense."

"Hey, 'Louie Louie' was number one on the charts for how long? And no one to this day knows what the fuck they were singing about."

"What about this?" Bliss pointed to the bullet.

"It's nothing. A chimera. A snowflake on the windshield." Ward pocketed the bit of metal. "Gone. Took a Houdini." He clapped his hands enthusiastically. "Now, let's get moving here! Get some prints, phone records, names of friends, place of birth, to lead us to a Chinese girl whose arm we can twist around her back until tears squirt out of her eyes like juice from a lemon."

"I looked."

"You looked, but *I* didn't look. Because I have the hand. The magic hand with the hole in it. Step aside."

Bliss went downstairs and took Cori to lunch. They brought back a slice of pizza for the policewoman. Then trudged back up the five flights through the sour-smelling hall to the girl's apartment.

Ward was holding an apron. He pushed it toward Bliss's face.

"Smell."

Bliss smelled, then wrenched his head away in disgust.

"You know what it is?" Ward asked, a glint in his eye.

"Fish. Or something."

"Shrimp! It's shrimp! I should know. All the times I've made my famous gumbo. And look!"

He showed Bliss where the name of the uniform cleaning service was printed on the apron.

"We call them, get the list of who they service—caterers, you said—start calling asking for Li-Jung. . . . Two, three hours tops."

Bliss nodded approval. His partner was good. Cheered a bit, he sat on the couch to collect his thoughts. Ward sat next to him. They stayed that way for several minutes. Together they managed somehow to do their job, to solve crimes, catch criminals and bring them to justice while still maintaining some level of sanity. As long as Bliss held tightly to his Dixie cup and knew that Ward was on the other end of the string, he was all right.

Ward lit a cigarette and took a deep drag.

"You shouldn't have given her your gun," he said.

"Well, partner, maybe it was some kind of subconscious message—giving up my gun, meaning I really want to give it *all* up. If it was a play, that's what the audience would think. That my character's coming to the end of the line, and he needs to retire. When Rachel gets famous, I'll take care of the kids, help them with their homework, pick out their dresses for the prom, be a shoulder for them to cry on when their hearts get broken."

"If you quit the force," Ward said, "what's Rachel going to use for her routines?"

"She's clever. She'll think of something."

"Partner," Ward said, "you're the best cop I've ever worked with, the best cop I know. You're just in a slump. You need to push through it, get back in gear."

Bliss couldn't bear to tell him that trying to do just that was what got him into this mess in the first place.

DeWayne sat in his cab outside the Dunkin' Donuts. It was humid. His cab stank. He could barely swallow. He took a sip of his coffee, then nibbled his cruller. A woman bent down and spoke through the open passenger window.

"You free?" she asked.

DeWayne looked up and stared at her earnest face through a haze of weariness that glazed his eyes. He finished chewing and slowly swallowed.

"Excuse me, but are you *free?*" she asked again.

DeWayne cleared his throat. "Lady," he said, "right now I'm about the *least* free son of a bitch in the entire United fucking States of America."

Chapter 19

It was four o'clock when he finally got back home.

"I can't believe you took Cori to a crime scene," Rachel said. "This is the kind of thing I *joke* about. Now it's true! How can I go to Hollywood tomorrow with you on this blind mission to make the front page of the *Post?*"

Julia jumped in. "*Cop's Kid Cracks Case!*" she shouted.

"*Case Cracks Cop's Kid!* is more like it," Rachel said.

"You're leaving tomorrow, Mommy?" Cori said, her little voice quivering.

"Yes, sweetie."

"Oh."

Rachel faced her husband. "I just found out this morning. While you were out priming our child for Prozac."

"That's exciting," Bliss said.

"Yes, it is. It's very exciting. That's why I'm a little on edge. I'm sorry."

"I'll ask Ward to help out with the kids."

"He's worse than you are."

"He's mellowed since he's been shot."

Rachel started working herself up again. "So Ward gets a hole in his hand and now he's a new man? Why? Because he can get a job in a restaurant working as a strainer? Because it's easy for him to cheat at peek-a-boo? Because now he has a place to keep a spare bullet?"

She stopped. Bliss could almost see her brain on overdrive, looking for the punch lines, the zingers.

"Aren't you going to write these down?" he asked her.

"I'll remember. Anyway, Ward can't change. He's eternal. Like the pyramids. He's a walking epiphany. Ward is Ward."

"It's all right with us, Mom, if he comes over," Julia said.

"Sure. Because he'll make chocolate malteds for dinner and he'll . . . he'll . . ."

It was Cori's sweet voice that stopped her—*punchlinus interruptus.*

"Mommy, I don't *want* you to go away for a whole week."

"But, honey, I need to talk with Clint," she said, her voice getting sweet, losing its edge. "He has some writers he wants me to meet, honey."

"But for a whole *week*?" Cori was working her over pretty well.

"Well, sweetie, me and the writers, we have to brainstorm—"

"Brainstorm?"

"To come up with some possible story lines."

"Story lines?"

"Yes, sweetie. That what the writer does when—"

"Mom, can I go, too?" Cori asked, really putting the screws to Rachel now. "I like stories. You could read them to me."

"Um, actually no, Cori, because . . . Cori, stop now . . . please . . . because . . . Cori, come on now, honey. This is a *business* trip. It wouldn't be any fun. If I go back another time—honey, look at me—if I go back again—sweetie, please—then I promise . . . I *promise* you can come along. OK?"

"OK," Cori said, sniffling now. "But Julia's not going with you this time, is she?"

"No. Julia's staying here, too." Rachel flashed her husband a look as if to say, Don't you *dare* enjoy any of this because if you had taken Cori for ice cream instead of visiting dead bodies, she wouldn't be in such a fragile *place* right now.

"I don't want to go, anyway," Julia said. "Bunch of big phonies out there."

Bliss smiled. It seemed Julia had some of his genes in her after all.

Then his beeper went off.

"Maybe it's the morgue calling," Rachel said. "One of the corpses has come back to life and wants to tell you who shot him."

"*Dead Man Reveals Killer!*" Julia shouted like a newsboy.

It wasn't the morgue. It was Constance—at last. Bliss called her. She apologized for taking so long. If he came over now, she said, she would answer any questions he had for her. He put his hand over the receiver.

"It's someone with info about the Roderick case," he said, giving his wife a plaintive look.

"So go," Rachel said. "You need to talk to a witness, *go*! It's not like you're off bowling with the guys. You're solving murders. Aiding justice. Doing noble deeds."

So my husband gets a call—a woman being held at gunpoint—and he looks at me like I'm supposed to give him permission. If I say no—bang! the woman's dead. If I say, "It's OK, honey, you go out and do your police work," she's saved. Now, I ask you, is that fair? I mean, did Mrs. Ness have to give Eliot permission to go after Capone?

He took down the address Constance recited, a loft in Soho. It would take him forty-five minutes, he told her. She'd have tea ready.

"I'd better go."

"Maybe you want to take Cori with you again."

"I told you, she sat outside on the stoop the whole time. A woman uniform kept her company."

"What'd they do, clean her gun together?"

He started putting on his shoes.

"Her name was Sharon," Cori announced. "She was nice. She said she wanted to be a great detective someday, like my daddy."

Man, he was getting some strong backup. His kids were really coming through. As if they actually admired and loved him.

"Here, Dad." It was Julia, handing him a sheet of paper. "It's your part in the Bas Mitzvah ceremony, the prayer for opening the ark. I had the rabbi write it out in English for you."

"I still don't understand why I don't get a part," Rachel said.

"You will. Only this is the special part for the father."

"Why can't the father *and* the mother do it?"

"I don't know," Julia said. "The rabbi just told me to give it to my dad."

"Oh," Rachel said.

Even the rabbi was on his side tonight.

The young man on the bench introduced himself. His name was Jason Altree. He, too, had just come from the Strand and proudly displayed his most recent purchase, a new translation of *The Magic Mountain*. Li-Jung had never heard of it and thought maybe it might have something to do with Disneyland, though the cover looked kind of serious and why would something about Disneyland need to be translated.

They started talking—first about books, which she couldn't quite follow, then about New York. He bought her a lemonade from one of the carts in Union Square, smiling warmly as he watched her drink it. He asked if she wanted to go for a walk, and they headed downtown.

"Let's see Mark Twain's house," he said, excited as a kid in a playground. When they got there, he stood in front of the building for several minutes like it was some kind of shrine. Then he led her a few blocks away to Patchin Place, a neat little courtyard that didn't feel like New York at all. He said the poet E. E. Cummings had lived there.

It was after four o'clock. He suggested that they walk down to Chinatown for an early dinner. She said okay. He seemed like a nice guy, and maybe if she stuck around for a little while she could figure out how to get her bus fare to Boston from him without having to shove the gun in his face.

"You okay with this?" he asked. He'd been talking to her, and she hadn't responded.

"Yeah. It's great," she said.

"I mean, maybe you need to go or something," Jason said. "That's okay if you do."

"No. Chinese food would be fun. I haven't been to Chinatown for a while."

He still hadn't touched her, hadn't slipped his arm into hers as they crossed the street, hadn't even casually let his hand brush hers. He just talked with great animation—about the neighborhoods they walked in, about "real New Yorkers" he'd met, about the best place for this and the best place for that, even about some graffiti, a figure on a wall half covered by weeds and trash that he said was by some now-famous artist who was always counting in his head and the number on the bottom of the figure was the number he was at when he finished drawing it.

"If this were on a canvas," he said, "instead of the side of a building, it would be worth thousands of dollars." He laughed.

Li-Jung smiled, too, but she was really thinking about what she would say when she asked him for money. Rent, perhaps. Or tuition. But why did she need cash? Maybe a story was in order—owing money to someone, like what happened to a girl in her class, coming to school one morning with two black eyes because she hadn't paid Joey Collins the 58 dollars she owed him for the crack he sold her. It had all come out in the local paper, how Joey was arrested because the girl told the cops and how Joey's older brother busted up the girl's father's car with a baseball bat and hung their cat from a tree, but no one could ever prove it for sure. Li-Jung could tell Jason she owed someone money and he was threatening her. She needed two hundred dollars. Now. Tomorrow. She couldn't go back to her apartment or anything until she paid him. Otherwise he would hurt her. The story sounded good, especially if she added some tears. If it didn't work, she'd wait until he had all his clothes off, then she'd take out the gun and make something happen.

Martin brought the teapot to the breakfast table and poured himself and his wife a cup of Earl Grey tea.

"Constance killed James so he couldn't be with me," Promise said. "I know it."

He fit the cozy over the teapot and sat down across from his wife.

"I made lemon cake this morning," Martin said. "Do you want a slice?"

"Just because we're sisters," she said, ignoring the offer, "why do we have to be so alike? So entwined. I once heard about a game fishermen play on their boats, returning with the day's catch. They tie fish hooks to each end of a piece of line about ten feet long and bait the hooks. Then they toss the line off the back of the boat and watch as two gulls come along and grab the fish and swallow them. The hooks get lodged in the gulls' stomachs, and now the birds are tied together. They try to fly away, but they wind up dragging each other down into the sea and drown while the fishermen laugh."

"Your tea is getting cold."

"I see that, Martin."

"It's Earl Grey."

She picked up her cup. It was at least a century old, the set a wedding present from Promise's parents. The cup made a lovely, delicate sound when you placed it in its saucer.

She brought the teacup to her lips, took a sip, then threw it at the wall. The cup shattered into small pieces, and the tea made a large brown stain.

"I hate tea," she said. "Why haven't you once just taken me, Martin?" she shouted at him. "Just thrown me down on the rug and screwed me, ripped off my clothes and humped me like an animal! Why, Martin?!"

He stirred his cup, watching the sugar cube slowly dissolve.

"Just once! Can you hear me, Martin?!"

He looked at her, locked in her desperation. He knew that this was just the beginning of much loud, ugly abuse she would pile on him until he was gone.

"My lover takes me like that."

"That's what lovers are for, Promise."

"He wants us to hide in the Metropolitan Museum until after closing so we can copulate on the Temple of Dendur. Are you listening Martin?!"

Her little fists were clenched tight. He smiled inside, getting pleasure from her pain. Knowing he had worked things out, that his plan was already being carried out.

"You touch me like a curator!" she said. "You hold my breasts like you're looking for a clue to date them! You poke my vagina the same way you test the turkey to see if its done! Poke, poke, poke!"

He was thinking now about the last dozen golf balls he had

hit the other day. He had to remember to turn his right hand over a bit more on his grip.

"What do *you* do for passion, Martin? I've often wondered, lying in bed at night after having been with him, been consumed by him. Can it be the scones? I ask. Is that how Martin gets off? Getting hard as you slip on the oven mitts, climaxing as you pull out the baking pan?"

He sipped his tea. If he had felt it was worth it, he would have told her that his passion was for things to stay exactly the way they were; the little routines that made up his life were just fine. His golf, his cigars, his pilgrimages around town for special spices, fresh berries, aged cheeses, fine wines, scallops in their shell with the soft orange of their roe nestled like a sunrise beside them. Tiffany on Monday afternoons at two. Cassandra on Wednesdays at three. But now Promise was causing too much upset. Rumblings to the oven where the delicate soufflé of his life was carefully rising. He would do whatever was necessary to protect himself. Promise unfulfilled was becoming volatile, unhinged. Tomorrow, if all went according to plan, evidence would be discovered, and the detectives would once again be knocking at their door. It wasn't happening a moment too soon. The bitch was losing control.

Chapter 20

Bliss took Broadway downtown. The most famous street in the world. Angling through the city, it created the only triangles in Manhattan north of Greenwich Village: Needle Park, Times Square, Herald Square, the Flatiron Building, Union Square, all shaped by Broadway's curious, wanton course.

Bliss had the sheet with his Bas Mitzvah lines on the passenger seat, glancing at them whenever he was stopped at a light. The congregation rises, it said. Then two lines in Hebrew, translated phonetically, announcing the opening of the ark. It was comforting to have a part written out. He practiced the prayer on the light, seeing if he could make it turn green.

It was intermission on Broadway; theatergoers lingered under the marquees, schmoozing about the first act. A few splintered off, looking for a pay phone to call the sitter, perhaps, or a quick beer before the second act; some maybe heading to the car to get back to Jersey, the husband, dragged to the play by his wife, had had enough. *If we leave now, we'll beat the traffic. Your friends already told you how it ends, anyway.*

He drove past the new, sanitized Forty-second Street, Mickey and Bugs where once were Beaver and Snatch. In high school he used to go to the movies there. Not the X-rated films but to the theaters that played a first-run feature and two B movies for a buck and a quarter. Bliss would find a seat far away from everyone else, watch the movie with one eye, the audience with the other, wary of anyone moving closer to him, of whispered invitations to go to the bathroom, like in *Midnight Cowboy*.

He saw *Walking Tall* there, lots of Charles Bronson and Lee Marvin. He saw *Point Blank* at least twice. In it, Lee Marvin pulls a big heist, and then his partners double-cross him, take the loot, and leave him to die. But he doesn't die because he's Lee Marvin. He comes back to find them and get his revenge. In one scene he surprises his former partner while the guy's fornicating, grabs him by his hard-on and throws him off the penthouse roof like he's pitching horseshoes. Bliss could imagine his father doing the same kind of vile, baroque gesture, then telling the story that night at dinner, relishing all the sordid details. His mother would shrink down in her chair, mortified as her husband described the pain he so enjoyed inflicting. Lenny would watch his mother transform like some kind of time-lapse nature film, her skin getting paler, her hair whiter, a new network of lines surging across her face. Her body was a map that charted the course of her husband's sins.

Monty Bliss loved Lee Marvin. *Greatest fucking actor who ever lived*, he'd said on more than one occasion.

The movie theaters were gone now. Demolished or sanitized. He remembered fondly the jokey titles of the X-rated films blazoned on the marquees: *Bob and Ted and Daryl and Alex*, *Organ Trail*, *Adam and Yves*, *A Hard Man Is Good to Find*, *Pumping Irene*. Some people had memories of fishing as a kid, their dads putting worms on the hook, catching seven sunnies in an hour, a four-pound catfish. Not Lenny Bliss. He had the titles of porn films in permanent residence in the destitute S.R.O. of his brain.

So where did they go, the dirty old men, the sordid onanists now that their domain on Forty-second Street had been all cleaned up, fallen to Visigoth raiders with M.B.A.s. Back then, at least, they were all in one place. Now they were scattered about the city, looking for a quiet spot to sit with their overcoats in their laps. Or maybe they were all bungee jumping off a bridge. Or they found religion. *All rise, please, for the opening of the ark*.

He practiced his prayer again, partly because he didn't want to screw up and partly because he didn't want to think about Constance and how she would look when she answered the door. He was afraid he'd let her beauty sway him, that the allure of her distress would lead him astray.

His father hadn't had such problems. Monty Bliss had shared a whore with a couple of other cops, setting her up in an apartment. Co-op pussy. Pudenda time-share. It was one of the last bits of advice his father had given him before moving down to Florida. *Kept me out of trouble for eighteen years*, he told his son.

But Bliss knew he couldn't handle that kind of arrangement. After the first week, he'd start feeling sorry for the girl, wanting to save her, like Holden Caulfield. He'd buy out his partners, convince the girl to finish college, help with her tuition. Even hit up his father-in-law up for another loan. *You see, Anton, I have this special friend who needs a couple of grand to finish cosmetology school. I know you're already paying for my kids' tuition, but what can I do? I'm not the fancy lawyer you wanted your daughter to marry. I'm just a poor flatfoot trying to make an honest dollar and keep from succumbing to the wiles of tantalizing women.*

He forced himself to focus on the case. One actor dead, one freaking out from flashbacks, one making a confession, the another one recording it. Then there was the pair of mysterious sisters. No one was surprised that this kid was dead, but no one made sense as the killer. He needed a motive, some reason that did make sense. They'd found no evidence of drugs, no suspicious characters, no vendettas. It all added up to a whole lot of nothing. He could wait for the deus ex machina to descend in the last act and solve everything, but this was avant-garde theater, so he was on his own.

Bliss felt that he was losing control of the investigation, allowing himself to get caught in their play. He needed to reassert himself. When he saw Constance, he'd get right to the point and ask her if she killed James. And if she said she didn't do it, then he'd ask her if she knew who the fuck did.

As it often happened in Chinatown, Li-Jung and Jason were seated at a large round table where a family of five were already eating, talking to each other excitedly in Chinese. As the pair joined them, Li-Jung overheard the son tell his parents that his older sister had a crush on her English teacher. The sister shouted back that he was an idiot and had no more brains than the scallops they were eating. The father shook his finger and the mother laughed and Li-Jung laughed along with her. Then she caught Jason looking at her in a way that she had only seen in the movies. Embarrassed, she quickly turned away and was relieved when the waiter came.

She spoke to him in Chinese, ordering a whole steamed sea bass with black bean sauce, twice cooked pork, and some chow fun noodles.

"Is he bringing menus?" Jason asked.

"I just ordered," she said.

"I've always wanted to do that," he said.

Li-Jung nodded, but her attention was focused on the family, envy swelling inside her. The mother returned her gaze and smiled, perhaps imagining her own daughter someday going on a date. Li-Jung smiled back. The son then announced that one of his sister's friends had gotten a tattoo and that set them all off again.

"What are they talking about?" Jason asked in a whisper.

"Family stuff," she said. "Just family stuff."

Li-Jung hoped Jason was like most Westerners, unable to decipher the mysterious ways of the East. Maybe then he wouldn't see just how sad she was.

The day had gotten away from DeWayne. Here it was, after 4 P.M., and he still hadn't picked up his kids' presents. What kind of father was he? He'd been hoping to get a fare to take him near one of the big department stores, but all day he seemed to be going up one side of Manhattan and down the other, stuck on the FDR or the West Side Highway, and he'd just been jammed up for almost an hour by the South Street Seaport with three French tourists who failed to tip him. But now he finally had a chance to turn on his OFF DUTY light and head to a toy store.

He pulled up in front of Toys 'Я Us in Union Square and was about to get out when the back door opened and two kids climbed in. A fancy woman's head appeared at the passenger-side window.

"Could you open the trunk?" she said, obviously already a little peeved at him. "I have a lot of bags."

DeWayne lowered the window. "I'm off duty."

"But you stopped. And my kids are in the back."

"You have to take us," the older boy barked at him. "It's the law. You have to take us wherever we want to go." He crossed his arms and sat there, indomitable.

DeWayne popped the trunk.

"Could you help me put them *in?*" the woman griped, rolling her eyes in disgust.

DeWayne got out of the cab and met her at the trunk.

"That's not greasy, is it?" she asked, pointing to the spare tire.

The flap of carpet that covered it had slipped off. DeWayne pulled it back in place.

"That's better," she said.

DeWayne put her bags of toys in the trunk and closed it up. The woman joined her kids in the back seat and gave him an address in the upper Seventies.

After a few blocks, DeWayne decided to risk asking them for advice.

"I've gotta get my kids a couple of presents, and I'm not sure what to buy them," he said, angling his head so they could hear him through the partition.

"How old are they?" the woman asked, sounding a little put out.

"Six and ten. The six-year-old's a girl."

"What about the other one?" the older son asked, clearly enjoying being a smart-ass.

"Stop it, Jake," she said, though not firmly, clearly enjoying being the mother of a smart-ass.

"I like action figures," her younger son piped in. "But a girl probably won't."

"How can you say that, Max?" his mother asked, trying to sound appalled. "Girls can like action figures."

"They play with dolls. Like Barbie. Yech."

Then the older boy spoke, and with authority. "When *I* was ten, I liked the more complex Lego sets, but they might be too advanced for your kids."

"I'm sure the people in the toy store will assist you," the woman said, her disdain intimating that she wished to put an end to the conversation. "They're very helpful."

They rode the rest of the way in silence.

When they arrived at their building, the doorman rushed out to open their door. The woman walked around to DeWayne's window to pay him. She handed him a twenty-dollar bill.

"I should be charging *you* for the advice," the woman said, clearly only half joking.

"So keep it," DeWayne said and handed her back the money. Then, without opening the trunk so she could get her packages, he drove away. The woman screamed, and the older boy shouted, *Hey, asshole!* DeWayne had no intention of stopping. Their doorman gave a half-hearted chase but soon gave up—a display of chivalry that, if remembered, might get him a bigger tip come Christmas time.

DeWayne headed east toward the Queensboro Bridge and home. He figured among the three bags there would be something his kids would like. The woman had looked like she had good taste.

Chapter 21

Bliss knocked, the door opened, and there was Constance, barefoot in jeans and a white T-shirt, under which her breasts did a languorous hustle, instantly activating an ancient memory buried deep in his spinal cord, urging him, out of obligation to the species, to consider that moment as a prime one to procreate.

"Come in," she said, in the kind of voice that could make you forget the names of your kids, then closed the door behind him. Her loft was large, with high ceilings, sparsely furnished to show off an obscene amount of empty space. The subtlest way to display your wealth in Manhattan is to have an apartment filled with empty space. The walls and floors were painted white and were offset by richly colored Kilim rugs. He took the herbal tea she offered and sat in a soft leather couch. She sat across from him, sipping her tea and glancing at him intermittently over her cup. She seemed far away. Like most revelations, Bliss thought, this one was not going to be easy.

"You were James's aunt?"

"Promise told you," she said, more a statement than a question.

"I saw her high-school yearbook."

"You *are* a detective."

"I try. She acted, too?"

"That was a while ago. Then she met Martin and just kind of settled for being a wife. She was never very ambitious. She made up for it by spending a lot of money."

"Only the one child?"

She paused. "Yes. James. The one and only child."

"Is that why he came to the Performance Warehouse? Because you were there?"

"He didn't know."

"That you were his aunt?"

"No."

"Odd. How'd you work that out?"

"It was part of the arrangement. What my sister wanted."

"You never had the urge to pinch his cheek, say, 'I knew you when you were just a little pisher.' "

"I didn't know him when. Promise was pretty adept at

keeping me out of his life. Of course, James wasn't around much, what with boarding schools and the trips to Europe that Martin arranged for him."

"Did you have any idea that his life was in danger?" he asked.

"No."

"Can you think of anyone who was angry with James, who might have wanted to kill him?"

"James was troubled," she said. "But he had a gentle soul. He just never got a chance to show it."

"You didn't answer my question."

"I'm sorry," she said. She tucked a few strands of hair into place that had fallen free. "I'm afraid I don't know of anyone who would want to kill him."

Her voice cracked for a moment. Was it genuine anguish, Bliss wondered, or something she'd done once in a play? Maybe she'd break into Lady Macbeth's mad scene and blurt out her confession.

"Why did you leave the theater the other day?" he asked.

"I was grieving."

"You said you didn't know him that well."

"He was my flesh and blood." She set her cup down.

"Were you going to tell him you were related?"

"Yes. Soon."

"Even though it was against the rules?"

"Promise probably sensed it. That's why she killed him."

She reached behind the couch and turned off the lamp. The only light came through the windows, a kind of blue twilight broken only by the flashing red glow of a sign outside. It was getting more noirish by the minute.

Constance got up from her chair and walked slowly across the room, her hips moving in a sybaritic rhythm. She sat down next to him on the couch. She lowered her head and looked at him through her dark, hooded eyes.

"So now you know," she said.

"What?"

"That I think my sister killed him." She made her voice softer and lower, as she had on the answering machine, like Lauren Bacall in *To Have and Have Not*. (Bliss was a sucker for Lauren Bacall. *You know how to whistle don't you?*) He had the feeling he was being pulled into another charade.

"And what does your sister think?"

"That I did it." She casually eased a clip from her hair, letting the hair fall in front of her face, covering one eye. Veronica Lake in *This Gun for Hire*. "What about you, detective? Do *you* think I did it? Do you think I killed James?"

"Yes," he said. He was beginning to think they all did.

She leaned her head on his shoulder.

"I don't believe you," she whispered, her lips full and lustrous. Gloria Grahame in the *Bad and the Beautiful*.

Her hair brushed his cheek. She smelled of magnolias. Then she lifted her head and turned it toward him. Her eyes were closed, but she slowly opened them. Her lips moved imperceptibly, but he knew as clearly as if it were written in Las Vegas neon that she was wanting to be kissed.

"Is Katrina here?" he asked. "Is she videotaping this?"

Her eyes grew wide, shocked, like he'd just shoved a grapefruit in her face. Mae Clarke in *Public Enemy*.

"She told me about the confession," Constance said, pulling away from him, petulant now, biting her lower lip. Mary Astor in *The Maltese Falcon: You've got to believe me, Sam*.

"It was quite a show Algernon put on," Bliss said. "Someone should have been there to review it."

"I'm not the same as they are," she said.

She sighed and stroked him gently on the cheek with the tips of her fingers. Then she moved closer on the couch. Pretend or not, her effect on him was quite real. He turned to her and her lips found his and he shuddered with the contact, so charged were they with a kind of holiness. This was probably

Bliss's true religion, his personal altar. *All rise, please for the opening of the ark*.

But then the Bas Mitzvah prayer came into his head and his daughter's face and then his other daughter and then his wife and he summoned up his bungee courage and retreated from his newfound rapture.

He stood up, took a few steps away from the couch. Rachel had better do the same thing, he thought, when one of those Hollywood types comes on to her.

"You didn't have to do that to convince me to find James's killer," he said.

"What if I don't want you to?"

"Then," Bliss said, "I'll have to assume it was you."

She curled up her legs, stretched an arm along the back of the sofa. "You're not being very nice," she purred.

"Where were you when James was murdered?" he asked.

"I was here. Alone. I always seem to be here alone."

"Don't you care that your nephew is dead? You treat this like it was some kind of performance. All of you. His step-father is pretending to be broken up, but he's a lousy actor. And his mother doesn't seem to care, either."

"Oh, she cares, all right."

"How would you know?"

"Because I am James's mother."

Once she saw his apartment, Li-Jung realized that Jason was just as broke as she was. It was a tiny studio full of books and little else. A futon on the floor. Not even a fancy stereo. Now she wished she had stayed at the table in the Chinese restaurant when he paid the check instead of going to the bathroom. She could have seen if his wallet held only a few grimy singles, if he had counted out the tip with the last change in his pocket. She could have ditched him right there. On the other hand, where would she have spent the night?

He immediately began showing off his books, pulling out one volume after another, like she was supposed to know what he was talking about. Still, he had a cute smile, and he'd get this dreamy look as he held certain books in his hands, like they were something precious.

"You'll like these," he said, showing her a slim volume. "The *Cold Mountain Poems*. You know them?"

She told him she knew "Stopping by the Woods . . ." by Robert Frost and "Shall I compare thee . . ." from Shakespeare.

"Come and sit down," he said, wanting her to join him on the couch.

So here it was, the poems leading into the first caress; then it would be kissing and tongues and business as usual. It was the least she could do, she thought. If he was going to help her.

He read in the same serious tone as her twelfth-grade English teacher, droning on, his eyes wide, as if he were casting a spell. A car horn honked outside, and for a second Li-Jung thought it was Clyde coming by to pick her up, but then she remembered where she was.

"I guess you don't like these much," he said.

"The last one," she said quickly. "Read that one again."

He grinned like his face was going to break while he riffled the pages and found the poem. He read it more naturally this time, and it really sounded quite mysterious and beautiful.

Once at Cold Mountain, troubles cease—
No more tangled, hung-up mind.
I idly scribble poems on the rock cliff
Taking whatever comes, like a drifting boat

"I like that one," she said.

"I thought you would," he said.

She figured that this would be a good time to hit him up for the money—while he was so enthralled.

Instead of the drug story, she told him that she needed the money for the rent. That she couldn't go back to her apartment until she paid for the rest of the month. In cash. Her roommates were vicious.

"God, I wish I could help," he said. "I'd lend you two hundred dollars in a second if I had it. Even more. But I'm just living hand to mouth these days, working as little as possible to have enough time to write."

"Oh."

"I was supposed to go to work this evening, but I wanted to stay with you. I'll probably be fired."

So she'd screwed up after all. She hoped he wouldn't kick her out.

"You need a place to stay tonight?" he asked, as if on cue.

She nodded.

"You're welcome to crash here."

"OK," she said. "Thanks."

He read more poetry while she stared out the window, wondering how she was going to escape New York. The gun was her only choice, she thought. It had gotten her into this mess, it would get her out of it.

Bliss was having a little trouble understanding.

"So you're really James's mother."

"Yes."

"And Promise is his aunt."

"Right."

"You mind explaining this?"

"I traded."

"Is that something you do in Minnesota?"

"I was pregnant without a husband. I was about to go to New York to start my career. I didn't want to be saddled with a child. I was going to get rid of it, but Promise had another idea. She and I went away to Europe together. Promise came home with a baby and three million dollars, my share of the inheritance."

"Everything you owned?"

"No. I still had my trust fund and some stocks. Anyway, money didn't mean much to me back then. I had my art."

"And why would Promise want to raise your kid?"

"The money, I guess. I mean, we were both well off, but the two shares together allow her to live quite comfortably. You've seen her apartment."

"Just the money?"

"I suppose she also wanted everything that I had."

"That's about the most intense case of sibling rivalry I've ever heard of."

"To tell you the truth, Lenny, we didn't think about it. It was just the next in a long series of small steps we'd taken together." She shrugged. "Things happen slow enough, you don't notice."

"You've thought a lot about this."

"It's all I do."

"And how does Martin fit into the picture?"

"Her trophy husband? He comes from a long line of blue-bloods, but his father pissed away the family fortune. Martin added a certain comfort to Promise's life, if not a lot of passion. But mainly he took care of James. In his own way, Martin cared for him very much. He kept him from getting kicked out of every boarding school he ever went to. That and Martin's tart Tatin were his principal assets."

"But it still troubles me, Constance. Your son is dead and you're barely upset."

She gracefully bent forward and held her head in her hands, her thick hair falling forward, shrouding her face.

"I don't know how I feel, Lenny," she said, her voice perfectly controlled. "Literally. I'm not trying to be cute. I'm hopeless when it comes to that kind of thing."

"Like mourning?"

"Like pain, rapture, despair, excitement—all the big ones. For myself, on my own, I'm bereft. I'm desolate, like one of those empty billboards—'*Your Message Here.*' On stage, in character, a full spectrum of feeling is at my fingertips. Every nuance of passion. When the lights are on me, I'm all tears, cries of pathos and pain, joyous songs of exaltation. On my own, I'm a mess. It's not an easy thing to live with.

"I walked into the theater that morning and found my son dead. Lying center stage. My son is dead, I said to myself, and I thought about how many times I had seen bodies fallen there, on that stage, lying as if they were dead, on that very spot. Myself, spread-eagled in only a G-string as Little Miss Muffet, trying desperately not to move my stomach as I breathed while Wolf the spider hovered over me hanging by a gym-class rope singing lieder by Mahler. My son is dead, I said to myself, even as we circled around him that morning and chanted in Navajo and Katrina quoted Rilke. My son is dead, I said, as I sat in the theater and waited for the tears, holding my head in my hands, shaking as if I were sobbing, but no sobs came. When I played the part of Job's wife, I cursed and wailed and mud-stained tears streaked down my cheeks in a steady stream—like a faucet, I cried six nights a week plus a ten-thirty show on Saturdays. Great heaves of grief and pain on cue. The audience couldn't bear to look at me, there was such a torrent. My son is dead, I said, as I sat dry-eyed, ducts barren, waiting for Algernon to give me words to express my sorrow, for Katrina to show me where to stand, when to clutch my breast, when to sink to my knees because the weight of the loss was more than I could bear. And then I thought. Was he even my son? Am I really his mother if he never knew it? Mothers are not supposed to be mysteries. My poor dead son. I wanted to tell him so many times, Detective. To step out of the shadows. You have to believe me. I thought of the ways, wrote the scene in my head hundreds of times. What I would say. What he would say. The hug. Our kiss. The bond we never had now blossoming for the first time. Taking root. Finding sustenance. Finding solace. Finding, hopefully, something very much like love."

"That was a beautiful speech," he said. "Did Algernon write it for you?"

She was suddenly cold, calculating. Barbara Stanwyck in *Double Indemnity*.

"Am I a suspect, Detective?"

"Not at the moment," he said.

"Then I'm going to have to ask you to leave."

He looked for his fedora, so he could pull the brim down low over his eyes; his overcoat, so he could push up the collar to protect himself from the ominous rain that was surely falling, as it always did when the solitary detective left the femme fatale, no longer sure of right and wrong, no longer sure what he was searching for, wanting to be back in her arms but knowing it was the most dangerous thing he could do.

Jason asked Li-Jung if she was tired, and when she said yes, he suggested they go to bed. He took a sleeping bag out of the closet and unrolled it on the floor. He said she could have the futon. The sheets were clean. He offered her first use of the bathroom and a fresh T-shirt to sleep in.

Once in the bathroom, she locked the door and took the gun out of her backpack. She placed it on the sink and stared at it. It was turning into something evil, like something out of one of the sick horror movies she was always being dragged to see. One of those dolls that came to life. Chuckie, with its demented grin, laughing at her from the porcelain. *You thought you could beat me, but you were wrong! Heh-heh-heh.*

Or the albatross from that poem she'd read in high school, *The Ancient Mariner*—hey, another poem she knew! Hanging around his neck. Water, water everywhere.

She washed her face and, since she was without a brush, rubbed her teeth with some toothpaste.

She looked in the mirror at her face. Talk about your albatrosses! Though she probably would have been less noticeable in school with a dead bird around her neck than being about the only Chinese person most of them had ever seen. She and Christine Han, whose parents owned a laundry in town. The restaurant and the laundry. If it had been in a movie, no one would have believed it. They avoided each other in school, for to become friends would have confirmed their freakishness.

But in New York she was suddenly attractive. What made her different at home was alluring here. Even a stud like Matt, who the waitresses all lusted after, had wanted *her*, found *her* desirable. Someone once actually thought she was a model—stopped her on the street and said, 'Hey, aren't you that model?' and then mentioned a name that she didn't recognize. Only a few weeks before she had been in Iowa, being rammed in the front seat of a Ram, ridden bareback in the payload of a Bronco, jimmied in the back of a Jimmy—and now she was being mistaken for a model.

She didn't have any money or clean clothes or any idea how to get them. She was wanted for murder and for stealing a policeman's gun. She had no home and was about to have a sleep-over with a total stranger, hoping he wasn't a secret psycho. It seemed like every albatross in the kingdom wanted to make a home around her frail little neck. But tonight she wasn't going to think about it. She was going to get some rest. She changed into Jason's T-shirt and walked into his room. She suddenly felt very shy. Giggling, she jumped into his bed and pulled the covers up to her chin.

The sheets smelled fresh, the pillow was soft.

"Is this Cold Mountain?" she asked. "Am I there yet?"

"When you arrive," Jason said, smiling, "you won't have to ask." He turned toward the bathroom. "I'm going to wash up."

She wondered if he would try something. Poetry or not, he had to try something eventually. Ellis Issel used to read her poems from greeting cards as his version of foreplay. He'd turn off the truck radio and pull out the card, folded into quarters, from his jeans pocket and read it to her. One time he'd written his own.

> *Roses are red,*
> *Violets are green,*

Here Ellis gave her a knowing nod, that his variation was a discovery worthy of Einstein.

> *You are the nicest girl*
> *I've ever seen.*

He didn't say "prettiest" or "sweetest" but, nevertheless, nice to him she was.

She wondered if Jason would try something soon. Offer her a massage, linger by the futon before getting into his sleeping bag, maybe reach out to shake hands good night and then hold hers a little too long. She hoped he didn't. It was weird. Here was someone who genuinely liked her, who was kind and gentle, and she *didn't* want to have sex with him. She wanted to wait. It was like one of the ironies in the poems he had read.

Jason came out of the bathroom after only a few seconds. "I guess you left this in there," he said.

She looked up to see that he was holding the gun.

Rachel was asleep when Bliss got back. Her bags were packed and stood at the end of the bed like the two dogs guarding the gates of hell. On the way home Bliss had had the idea of checking to make sure she was leaving her diaphragm in New York. Now he found the case in the bathroom, opened it and saw it there, happy as a clam. Why hadn't she put it in, so they could make love before she left? What was *that* about?

He slipped into the bed beside her. She had grabbed all the pillows, and he had to wrestle one loose. She stirred.

"Did she confess?" she asked.

"I don't think so," he said.

"Did she put out?"

"Cute."

He rubbed her back.

"Oh." She yawned. "I'll do you later, okay?" she said. "In the shower. In the morning. Good night."

"Okay. I'll hold you to it."

"I *know* where it is," she said. "I've held it before."

Even in her sleep, she was still giving him zingers.

It took a few tears and some fast thinking to get Jason to accept the gun. She was holding it for someone else, she said. She hated it; that's why she'd left it out, because she didn't *want* it anymore. He sat on the edge of the bed while she talked to him, then she started stroking his arm and then pulled him down next to her. He murmured a protest, saying she didn't have to, that he understood, that they didn't really know each other yet, but soon he was under the spell of her caresses, and there was no more resistance. He came quickly—nervous, he said, from being with someone new, but Li-Jung sensed that she was too much for him. It saddened her that she couldn't make love like a kid anymore. She was glad when he took her in his arms and snuggled up. That part was nice, made her feel less ferocious.

He fell asleep, and the gentle rhythm of his breathing soothed her. She closed her eyes and allowed herself to drift away, embracing the sleep she so sorely needed. Besides, there was nothing more she could do that night.

Martin sat alone in his library and sipped an Armagnac. He looked at his Pollock. He'd bought it at auction when they were first married, as a kind of test, to see if he really did have access to the potato fortune. He'd raised his finger at 1.2 million, and the hammer came down. He wrote a check for it the next day in a plush private room in the upstairs of the auction house. The secretary brought him coffee, and when he asked if they happened to have any biscotti, she happily went across the street to get some. Then he wrote out the words—one million, five hundred thousand, including the commission. The check didn't bounce, and the painting was delivered a week later.

He still wasn't sure how he felt about it, why instead of something less volatile, like an Impressionist landscape or a Lautrec drawing, he had fixated on this abstract phantasmagoria of splatters and blobs. Sometimes he thought it appealed to him because Pollock made a kind of order out of all that chaos, and order was something Martin could relate to. But there were other times when he felt the painting was a fraud, a hoax, not really art at all, just some kind of charade—the emperor's new clothes. And yet there it was, in all its falsehood, ensconced in the library and revered as something sacred and powerful by all who came before it.

Martin could relate to that, too.

Act V

Chapter 22

Li-Jung got up early and quietly slipped out of bed. Jason opened one eye, but she shushed him back to sleep. She took a shower and decided to keep the shirt he had given her. Even though it was big, tucked in her jeans it looked kind of cute.

She gathered her tank top and the gun and zipped up her bag. Again he stirred as she moved past the bed.

"I'm just going down for coffee," she said. "I'll be back soon."

"Take the keys," he mumbled still not quite awake.

"I'm going to read the paper," she said. "You'll buzz me in later."

She blew him a kiss.

"It was nice last night," she said. "See you soon, Jason."

And before he could say anything else, she opened the door and left. She didn't want to stay any longer. Jason's comfort might make her lose her resolve. She still had to get away before they found her. She couldn't forget that.

She decided that a cab would be her best bet. Shove the gun to the back of the driver's head and make him give her his money. She'd get out of the cab at Grand Central and lose herself in the crowd, then work her way over to Port Authority and take the first bus to Boston. She also promised herself that after she was finished in the cab, she would throw the gun into the first large body of water she saw.

She let a few taxis go by, hoping against hope she might see a woman driver. She knew there were a few of them around, but none drove by that morning. She decided the next cab to stop would be the one.

"Grand Central," she said, getting in the back seat. She was glad to see the partition window was open.

He swung over to the Bowery and started heading uptown. He had greasy hair and long scraggly tufts growing from the back of his neck. A large red pimple was hidden underneath. That's where she would aim the gun. Bull's-eye.

There was a lot of traffic for so early on a Sunday morning. She was afraid someone in another car would see her holding the gun. She needed to get off the Bowery and onto one of the side streets where it would be quieter.

"I need to pick up something at my apartment first, though," she said.

"Where's that?"

He didn't seem too happy.

"Eleventh Street, between First and A," she said. She thought it would be empty there, especially at this time of day. They headed east on Sixth Street, then up Avenue A past Tompkins Square Park. As she'd hoped, the streets were quiet. People were sleeping—in their own beds, in their own homes, all tucked in and cozy.

As they turned onto Eleventh Street, Li-Jung slipped the gun out of her knapsack. She had faced the water, the blackness, and jumped without a second thought. She had faced her tattoo without booze, watching the needle prick her skin without a single flinch. She had faced hands that fondled her, foul breath panting in her face. Now it was time for this, doing what she needed to do to make her escape. And it started now, with this man, this moment. She saw the hole in the bridge leading to the abyss, and once again she jumped.

"Give me your money," she said, pointing the gun through the partition window.

The cabbie glanced in his rearview mirror.

"I haven't got any fucking money," he said, without missing a beat, like she had asked him for a match. "I haven't even got change for a five. I just started."

She wasn't prepared for that. She didn't know what to say next.

"Give it to me!" Even though she was shouting, he still didn't react. He chewed his gum, looked straight ahead, only glancing at her in the mirror, waiting to see what she would do next.

"Nice piece," he said finally. "Where'd you get it?"

She wasn't sure what he meant by "piece."

"The gun," he said, as if reading her mind. She saw his eyes in the rearview mirror. Crinkled, like he was smiling. "Where'd you get it?"

"From a cop," she said.

"You're kidding!"

"No."

Then she felt her determination crumble, and she couldn't do it anymore. She lowered the gun, waiting for him to pull over, to call the police, to point her out and smile as they put the handcuffs on her. But he kept driving.

"This cop, he your old man? Your boyfriend?"

"No."

"So why would he give you his gun?"

That's when she told him about the bridge and the jump and how she took the gun and slipped away and ran back down the walkway without falling once. She didn't tell him she'd used it already, however.

"You know the cop's name?"

"Lenny," she said. "I think he's like a detective. He doesn't wear a uniform."

He let out a whoop.

"If this is true, little girl, then this gun is worth a bundle. You see, he's shittin' bricks right now, this cop, figuring out how to get back his piece, because if one of the brass finds out, he's shit out of luck. So we just have to call him up and tell him we got it and that he's got to fork over two grand or we send his gun to his precinct commander with a little note attached saying just what you told me. We can't ask for much more because cops don't have any money. Unless he was dirty. You think he was dirty?"

"Dirty?"

"On the take. Bribes from bad guys, that kind of thing."

"No. He has a kid."

"Don't matter," the cabbie said. "Actually, the more kids he has, the more likely he's dirty. I should know. Name's Reardon, by the way. DeWayne Reardon. But I don't spell it the regular way, like Duane Allman. You know him?"

"No."

"The Allman Brothers? You heard of them?"

"Yeah."

"You ever listen to *Live at Fillmore East?*"

"No."

"The greatest fucking live rock-and-roll album ever made. Forget *Live at Leeds* and *Get Yer Ya-Yas Out.*" He whipped open the glove compartment and started rummaging through it. She saw that he had a gun, too, and wondered if she shouldn't just jump out of the cab now and run for it. But she didn't. Where would she go? He whooped again when he found the right cassette and then popped it in.

"Well, little girl, this is your lucky day. . . ."

The music blasted—so loud that it rocked her back in the seat. *Woke up this morning / Had them Statesboro blues. . . .* He pulled away from the curb and started driving. "That's Duane, on slide," he shouted, bouncing in his seat to the rhythm. The guitar wailed, the notes bending, crying. "Sounds like the guitar is talking to you, don't it?"

It did. Duane was sending her a message, a cry of warning—only she couldn't make out the words.

"I spell my name capital D, small e, capital W," he shouted.

She sat back in the seat. She pulled her knees up and grasped them tightly. The music was thundering around her.

The singer wailed over the pulsing rhythm, like someone in great pain, someone who'd been locked up in a dungeon somewhere and was begging to be let out. The singer was practically screaming over the band. *Wake up mama / turn your lamp down low....*

He turned the music down a bit. "You have any breakfast, little girl?" he asked her. And because they were at a red light, he turned around and for the first time she saw his face: pale as a ghost, his eyes red, his mouth like a wound, cut in a sinister smirk that wanted to be a smile but had long forgotten how, his eyebrows pressed together like he was being tortured. "Me," he said, "suddenly I'm feeling very hungry. Then we've got to find us a pay phone, little girl, and track down a detective named Lenny."

The light changed and he shot the cab forward. He cranked the music up and was speeding up First Avenue as if he was one of the horsemen late for the Apocalypse.

Wake up mama! Wake up! Please, *please*, wake up! Someone please wake me up!

Bliss was lying in bed. A long rectangle of sunlight coursed across the sheet—his yellow brick road. He was thinking about the woman on Oprah, the one who said he had to find his own inner celebrity. *We all have one, but sometimes it's deep inside us and we have to let it out. Now, everyone close their eyes and take a deep breath and say, "I believe."* The only problem was that Bliss had a strong suspicion his own inner celebrity would turn out to be like Don Knotts. In high school he was voted Boy Most Likely to be Found Dead in a Motel Room. Maybe they were trying to tell him something.

His wife was clearly on her way to finding *her* own inner celebrity, with the first-class ticket to L.A. that Clint had sent her.

"You're really going?" he asked.

"Leave me alone."

What now? he thought.

"What now?" he said.

She was curled up away from him, motionless, lost somewhere at an opening-night party or a concert hall filled with adoring fans, all roaring with laughter, nodding with recognition, rising in unison to applaud her.

"Of course I'm going," she said. "Everything's been leading up to this." She meant her monologues, her routines based on living with her husband the cop. Soon Bliss would be immortalized in the movies. Give his father one more reason to laugh at him. *I saw some guy playing you in a movie the other day. Why didn't you tell me they got some faggot actor to play my son? I never would have gone.* The lady on Oprah said he had to forgive. Forgive himself, forgive those who'd wronged him. He had to put aside his anger and forgive his father for leading him to the edge of the jagged cliff called being a cop and then forgive himself for being trusting enough to have jumped off.

Rachel got up and went directly into the bathroom. Without passing GO, without collecting $200.

"My mother will be here soon to say good-bye," she shouted through the door.

Needless to say, there would be no connubial activity in the shower that morning as advertised.

"If you want to be helpful, make coffee," she called.

Annette Davis, Rachel's mom, was coming to say good-bye to Rachel and, no doubt, get the scoop on Clint. Annette was a gossip hound. She nearly keeled over when she found out she'd missed Goldie when the actress came to see her daughter's show. Rachel's father was probably off playing golf with his developer buddies, planning ways to make high-rise apartment buildings even more profitable. *If we could just get rid of the tenants. They're the ones who screw things up.*

Bliss headed for the kitchen in his boxers scratching his butt and ran into Julia just waking up. He wondered how many years of therapy his daughter would need just to get over her casual, everyday encounters with him—never mind the deeper psychic wounds he instilled through steady contact with his own troubled soul. Maybe Julia's stories would be so entertaining, the therapist would pay *her*. That's how his wife had become a comic—pouring out the vast stock of pain she had accumulated living with him. Now Lenny's angst was muse to a second generation of comediennes. He should feel proud.

He started looking for the coffee and then remembered Rachel kept it in the freezer. Why the freezer? *His* mother didn't keep her coffee in the freezer. No one he knew growing up had kept coffee in the freezer. When did this start?

He put the bag of grinds on the counter but couldn't remember the precise coffee formula that Annette was demanding these days. Half decaf sounded right, but it could have been a more subtle equation. Annette was a stickler. Mix the coffee wrong, and the whole morning could be shot.

As he looked for the coffee filters, Bliss wondered what the fellas in Attica would think if they saw him now, men he'd helped put away for decades, what they would say watching him in his underwear holding the measuring spoon, a look of impending doom as he prepared to face his mother-in-law. Would they laugh at how ridiculous the mighty cop was acting? Would they be angry that a man suffering a coffee crisis had been able to track them down and arrest them? Or would they just hang their heads with remorse because even such a pathetic display of domesticity, the chance to indulge in a moment of intense stupidity in one's own kitchen, was a freedom they didn't have?

He decided he'd go with half decaf and hoped she would ask first. Whatever it was, he'd say yes.

While searching for the filters, he realized how unpre-
pared he was for Rachel to be gone for a week. She had posted
a schedule of the kids' after-school activities, which looked
more daunting than the case board at the precinct. Desert
Storm couldn't have been any more complicated. Rachel's
mother had promised to help out, but seeing as she hadn't so
much as scrambled an egg in the last thirty years, Bliss wasn't
sure how much real assistance she was going to be. They
could always order take-out, he thought.

He gave up looking for the coffee filters and was just wedg-
ing a paper towel into the coffee maker when the phone rang.

It was Cardozo.

Some folks went to church on Sundays for inspiration. Bliss
found faith in a morning call from the morgue. Cardozo chose
an interesting topic for his sermon that day: reflecting on
James Roderick and the cause of his premature death.

"I don't think he was murdered," Cardozo said.

Bliss sensed Cardozo was expecting a response. He didn't
have one.

"Lenny, you there?"

"Yeah, I'm here," Bliss said. "Whattaya mean, you don't
think he was murdered?"

"I mean that the kid had a severe aneurysm. He had a little bottle of champagne in his head. The cork popped, and
the celebration started—only it was a little too soon."

"How come I didn't know this a couple of days ago?"

"Because we were busy. Because it's the weekend. Because
we were excavating under his fingernails since we *know* how
much you guys like fingernail archeology—fibers, skin, hair,
dirt from Transylvania—it's like a hot fudge sundae for a
homicide cop, right? And because there were definite signs of
strangulation, like the red bruises on his neck. So we put the
kid on the back burner for a day or two since we had a few
unexpected guests drop in. But the main reason you didn't

find out, Lenny, is because he was a twenty-three-year-old kid and twenty-three-year-old kids very rarely just up and die unless someone kills them. Is that reason enough? Or do you want more, Lenny?"

"That's enough."

"Because I might also point out that there wasn't anyone who *didn't* think he was murdered. Sometimes the cops say something, like 'I don't think he was murdered.' Or the family says something along the lines of 'There's no way our kid could have been murdered.' But this time, silence. Like it was expected."

"I hear you, Cardozo."

"You hear me, but are you *listening*. If you were listening, you'd be thankful."

"I'm thankful," Bliss said. "Now give me something to work with."

"My conjecture, should you decide to accept it, is that James engaged in rough sex with another man. When it was over, he got dressed and was about to tie his shoes when he keeled over, his crown fell off, he whacked his head, convulsed, and then died. Like all conjectures, this one will self-destruct in five seconds. Good luck, Lenny."

"You don't think we should be looking for the other guy?"

"We should all be so lucky to have sex like that, but it's highly doubtful it killed him. The kid was living a short life, that's all. He was a walking haiku. He had a time bomb tucked away in his brain. He just ran out of ticks. Hey, listen to this, Audrey just came up with another rhyme. 'I see London, I see France, I found semen traces on her underpants.' How do you think that would look on a cocktail napkin? With a snazzy little cartoon next to it?"

Martin noticed a grass stain on his four iron and wiped it off. As arranged, it was the one club he had brought with him to the driving range that morning. He'd been having trouble lately hitting his long irons. Teeing up another ball, he swung. The ball sliced badly.

"You're breaking your wrists just a tad too soon," said the man at the tee next to him, who sent each ball lofting on a sublime arc, landing well beyond the 200-yard marker, his swing fluid and effortless. Martin watched with awe, then returned to his ball and sought to emulate the ease of his neighbor's swing. Once again his ball skidded along, colliding with several other balls and scattering them like frightened birds. Martin sighed. He needed another lesson. Then he smiled when he thought how easy that would be, now that his schedule had been cleared up.

The man hit another long drive, then placed his club on the mat and leaned against it. He wiped his forehead.

"Hot," he said.

"Yes."

He turned and gazed at the Manhattan skyline visible in the distance beyond the end of the range, glimmering in the morning sun.

"The garbage has been taken out," he said.

"That's good," Martin replied.

"You done with that paper, by any chance?" the man asked, nodding at the newspaper that sat beside Martin's bucket of golf balls.

"In fact, I am."

Martin handed him the carefully folded copy of the *Post*. The man held it firmly closed, as if there were something quite valuable inside—say a thick wad of hundreds—without seeming in the least bit unnatural.

"Why don't you finish up my bucket?" the man suggested. "I've got to get home."

"Thanks," Martin said.

The man walked away, leaving not just the unhit balls but his golf bag as well. Martin bent down and unzipped the pocket usually reserved for extra balls. He smiled at seeing the dull metal of its contents. Then he zipped up the bag and decided to hit the rest of the bucket the man had left. Martin suddenly found himself in a wonderful groove, the ball rocketing out into sky, soaring as if it would never come down.

Chapter 23

Li-Jung wondered why she wasn't running away. At a red light she could have jumped out, just shoved the door open and bolted. He'd never catch her. But the light changed and then another light changed and she was still in the cab, letting DeWayne take her wherever he wanted them to go.

If she *really* sensed danger, that DeWayne was taking her to some alley to slit her throat, wouldn't she bolt? Didn't some instinct automatically kick in, some uncontrollable surge of fear that sent you fleeing when you sensed death was close? She hoped so.

But where would she go? Jump out at the light and then what? Look for another cab to hold up? DeWayne had at least promised her half the proceeds from the gun sale. And though he looked scary, he seemed too weak to be a serious threat. So she decided to sit there and see how things played out. After all, she still had the gun.

Anyway, they were now getting on the Queensboro Bridge, so it was too late to think about escaping. As far as she knew, no matter how desperate your situation, Queens was not a place you wanted to be lost in.

DeWayne announced that he had decided not to stop for breakfast. He also decided he wasn't going to use a pay phone. "What the fuck," he said. "I don't care if Lenny knows

where I live. He'll just be happy to get his piece back. Maybe
I'll have him clean up a little while he's there. Make that part
of the bargain. Twenty-five hundred bucks *and* he has to
wash the dishes and mop my floor. Yeah. That's a good idea.
The man's stupid enough to lose his gun, he deserves it."

"I thought you said we'd ask for two thousand," she said.

"I did a lot of dumb things in my eight years on the force,
but I never did anything as dumb as losing my service weapon.
We need to teach him a lesson. Another five hundred bucks
seems reasonable. Don't you think?"

"I guess."

"And since we're splitting it fifty-fifty, there'll be more for
each of us. Right, partner?"

That's right. They were partners. At least she wasn't alone.

She thought about how the worst moments in her life
always came in cars or trucks—guys driving her places
she didn't want to go—but maybe that was the trade-off she
made for at least going somewhere.

DeWayne turned off the music. "Do you think it smells
back there?" he asked.

There *was* the faint odor of something foul, but she decided
not to risk upsetting him. She shook her head.

"You know what really got me pissed, little girl? Not getting kicked off the force, not the divorce, not losing everything I had—my house, my kids, my car. No, what *really*
pissed me off was I never got to decide about any of it. Not
really. The money, it just found its way into my pocket. It
wasn't like I *decided* to be a jerk, it just *happened*. And eighty-
five thousand dollars later I had nothing to show for it. That
was the lousy part. Like it was someone else's life I was leading. You ever feel like that?"

"Lots," she said.

"I guess we're a lot alike, we two," he said.

"I guess so," Li-Jung said. She shuddered at the thought.

"We're soul mates. Whattaya say we ask for three thousand?"

"Okay," she said.

"I have a good feeling about this, little girl. That it was fate we should meet. That our destinies are, like, you know, linked."

The coffee was looking like a rusty leak when the doorbell rang. Bliss still wasn't dressed and called Julia to let Grandma in. In the bedroom he found Rachel staring wistfully in the mirror.

"Your mother's here," he said.

She was scrutinizing her face, the face that would be in Hollywood soon, and thinking . . . what? That she still had it? That someone in L.A. might find her desirable, someone with a little class, who drove with the top down, who knew the names of the sushi? Clint was married, but maybe one of his friends was free, one of those beach guys, a hang-gliding daredevil of indeterminate age who made her feel young, vivacious, carefree, who didn't hear the voices of the wounded and dying in his sleep. But could Mr. L.A. take a punch in the stomach like Bliss? Not a stunt punch with sound effects dubbed in later, but a *real* punch. Then again, maybe it didn't matter. Real, pretend—it was Hollywood, after all.

"You look beautiful," he said. Rachel had an indestructible beauty that even the quandaries of living with Lenny Bliss couldn't diminish. "Watch out they don't cast you in a movie."

She didn't answer. Maybe she was already lying on the sand wrapped in Burt Lancaster's arms, the Pacific surf washing over them. She would go to California and discover her inner and outer celebrities at the same time. Then she'd never come back. Bliss and the kids would have to read about her in *People. The Enquirer* would inform Julia and Cori if they were about to have a baby brother.

The phone rang. He picked it up. It was Constance. He had to come immediately. She was at Wolf's apartment. He was lying on the floor. There was a gun beside him. He was dead. He'd put a bullet in his head.

Lenny said he'd be there as soon as he could.

"I have to go," he told Rachel.

"My mother's here."

"There's been another homicide."

"How is it every time my mother comes over a new corpse shows up? Coincidence? I don't think so. I think you're in cahoots with the criminal element. You order murders like some people order Chinese."

"But I only knew your mother was coming a few minutes ago."

"Then you're better at it than I thought. Who's dead this time?"

"Another member of the theater company."

"Man, they couldn't *buy* this kind of publicity," she said. "You'll see, their next show will sell out in minutes."

It was then that Lenny realized she couldn't leave him. George to her Gracie, Rachel was dependent on him to be her straight man. He smiled. He felt better.

"What time is your flight again?" he asked her.

"Four o'clock."

"I'll be back."

Later he'd show her just how straight a straight man he was.

Martin stood alone in his kitchen, lord of his counter. The job was done, the evidence in place, everything ready for the final act to begin.

He liked the talking in code. *The garbage has been taken out.* It was as if he were in some kind of spy movie. It was fun. Passing the money in the newspaper, picking up the gun

. . . It sent a tingle through him. Made him feel adventurous. Dangerous. He wondered what Tiffany was up to later. Maybe he could stop by.

He'd picked up some caviar on the way home yesterday, and now he was making some shirred eggs that he would finish off by stirring in a teaspoon of crème fraîche and top with the Beluga. He was just making enough for one. Promise was asleep. He'd make her breakfast later. Maybe.

He smelled something burning. The muffins. He yanked open the oven and pulled them out, their tops black and smoking. He hadn't burned anything in a long time.

He wiped the counter.

He sharpened one of his knives.

He separated the dinner forks from the dessert forks.

He'd burned the muffins! They sat on the counter, charred in their tins. He tried digging them out so that he could clean the pan, but they were stuck.

Fuck it.

He threw out the pan.

Chapter 24

Wolf, America's greatest unknown actor, was lying on the floor of his apartment, his brains and blood leaking from the bullet hole in his head. A gun lay by his hand, an old-fashioned revolver. Music played, some kind of Native American chanting—though it could have been Aztec for all Bliss knew.

Wolf had apparently been sitting cross-legged on a mat, maybe a prayer mat, before he tipped over. A half-burned pel-

let of incense rested on a tiny silver pedestal in front of him;
a bottle of whiskey sat by his feet.

The apartment was dark. Snake skins and raccoon pelts
hung from the ceiling. An entire large bird, maybe a pheas-
ant, hung head down, its wings spread; a string tied to its legs
was looped around a light fixture. Clusters of eagle feathers
were tacked to the wall. Skulls of small animals dotted the
tables, and strange looking pipes and fetishes were lying
around. On his bed was an Indian blanket; a ceremonial
spear of some kind hung on the wall above it. The room was
charged with a palpable energy, like the sanctum of a medicine man.

He found Constance in the kitchen, which was in the back
corner of the loft. She sat in a wooden chair at a Formica
table. Her glass was half filled with whiskey.

"You didn't touch anything, did you?" Bliss asked her.

"Just the whiskey."

"From the bottle near his feet?"

"Yes."

"Anything else?"

"I kissed him on the cheek."

She took out her cellular phone and dialed a number.

"This was on my answering machine," she said. "He must
have called last night, but I didn't check my messages until
this morning. As soon as I heard it, I came over. I guess I came
too late."

She pressed in a code and handed the phone to Bliss.

"It's long," she said. "Wolf often talked into my machine
straight through the night, until the tape ran out. I'd give the
tapes to Algernon, and he'd type them up."

"And that's how Jazz was born," Bliss said.

"I'll get you a drink."

"I can't drink now," he said. "But I could use some water."

She placed a glass in front of him as a beep went off and

he heard Wolf's voice, sounding worn and tired. In the background was the same Indian chanting.

"It's Wolf. I'm bad. I'm sinking fast. I've messed up, Constance. I took something I shouldn't have. I want to apologize. To you especially because I know you'll understand. You'll explain to the others. Please. Let me tell you a story."

Here we go again, Bliss thought.

"I want to tell you about the scariest moment I had in Nam. This is one I didn't use in the play. I've kept it to myself. It happened during a Special Forces mission. The CIA wanted the head of a Cambodian village taken out. I've never known why—something to do with heroin or maybe a personal vendetta. They sent me and one other guy, a kid from Pittsburgh, Dale—father worked in the steel mills, high school football hero, the whole thing. He was wired and looking for action. The plan was for us to be choppered just inside the border, where we'd be met by a special Cambodian unit that would lead us to the village.

"We were dropped off on a small hill in the middle of nowhere. Nothing but jungle as far as we could see. The helicopter pulled out, and as its sound faded in the distance, a profound, stunning silence fell on us. No birds, no insects, no wind. Just intense silence. I thought maybe our hearing was shot from riding in so many choppers. Or maybe the cries of pain, the screams from someone having their leg blown off or looking at their arm lying just out of reach, had caused our ears to shut down. Or just maybe—and this is what I think, Constance—the entire jungle, every plant, animal, and insect, was for those few minutes conspiring against us, purposefully trying to drive us mad. Every living thing in the area somehow knowing that after months of being in the shit, utter stillness would be our most terrifying enemy and the best way for the Land to get its revenge.

"I could feel Dale start to lose it. The silence was shooting bolts of panic through him, and he started screaming, turning around wildly in circles like a mad dog chasing its tail, his rifle out, completely freaked——like at every moment there was someone behind him and he'd whip around to catch them but they'd be gone and then behind him again and he'd turn and turn again, on and on for what seemed like ten minutes, with an unearthly stamina. Then he stopped, pulled out a pistol and put it to his head. The gun, he had told me on the chopper, was one his father used in World War Two, and it was with this gun that Dale Sr. gave him for good luck that he shot himself and collapsed at my feet, staring up at me with a look of wonder on his face, as if to ask, How can silence kill you? But what was really odd was that as soon as the gun went off, birds flew from the trees, the wind began to blow, the insects droned, the monkeys cackled——everything waiting for that morbid cue to start celebrating some horrible victory."

A pause. Bliss looked at Wolf's slumped body and thought what a shame it was that this voice had been silenced, that these monologues would cease.

"I dragged Dale down into the jungle, buried him as best I could, and almost got myself shot by the Cambodians coming back up the hill. They asked where the other one was. I gestured, extending my arm in a slow, sorrowful arc, trying to take in the entire majesty and terror of the landscape. They seemed to understand. The other one had been sucked in by the jungle. I felt sure they'd seen it before——the jungle reaching out and grabbing a person, thick ancient roots dragging them under the soft sod. And you know, my dearest Constance, I have often thought that with that one gesture, I discovered I was an actor."

"I wanted you to hear this, my dear Constance, so you'll understand my remorse about James. Another boy I didn't take care of, I couldn't save. Who——"

There was a click.

Wolf's spirit, hovering above his body, dancing on cellular wavelengths, spoke his last words and then vanished.

"The tape ran out," Constance said. "So his last story never really ended. Fitting, don't you think?"

"Yes."

"I wish you could have met him when he wasn't so freaked out," she said. "When he wasn't completely stuck in the past."

"But that was the source of his monologues. His past."

"There was more to Wolf than his stories. He knew about everything. He was one of those people you encounter once in your life if you're lucky. He was truly touched with genius."

Bliss wasn't happy, either. He liked Wolf. He didn't want to see him dead.

"That must be the gun," Constance said. "Lying by the body. The one the boy in the story shot himself with."

"Probably."

"We used it as a prop in the Vietnam play. *Wolf's War*."

"Pretty nasty prop."

"I guess he was looking for some kind of retribution."

"You mean, killing himself with the boy's gun."

"Yes."

"Except this pistol hasn't been fired in a long time."

Her astonishment seemed genuine enough, but Bliss wasn't trusting his instincts in the truth department lately—a disconcerting side effect of his exposure to the Performance Warehouse. Bliss and the truth used to be tight, at least when it came to other people telling it.

"Seems like the pistol was just a prop in *this* play, too," Bliss said.

"But he was shot."

"Yes. At close range from behind. Either he didn't hear the person coming or he knew them well. You have a key to his apartment?"

"What are you suggesting?"

Bliss didn't think he was suggesting anything. But maybe he was.

"I found you in here. I just assumed you had a key. You've been close for so long."

"I do have a key."

"You see, the truth isn't so hard, once you get used to it. Please don't touch anything."

He went into the bathroom to check a few things. Bathrooms revealed a lot about a person. And even if there were no revelations, at least he wouldn't be bothered. He also wanted to let her sit for a while. Sitting was helpful if someone was trying to hide something. The more they thought, the harder they tried to cover it up. Bliss needed any edge he could get to determine if and when Constance was telling the truth.

Wolf's bathroom was the bathroom of a monk. The medicine cabinet was as bare as Mother Hubbard's cupboard. Instead of toothpaste, peroxide and baking soda sat on the sink. The guy definitely had moxie. There wasn't even the standard Right Guard, just a wooden box with the words DEODORANT STONE. A candle and a loofah sponge rested on the edge of the tub.

Bliss closed the toilet seat and sat on the lid and thought. With the gun at Wolf's feet, it seemed that he'd been thinking about doing himself in, perhaps trying to copy the young soldier in his story. Maybe as some kind of penance. But whether he planned to kill himself or not would forever remain part of Wolf's unfinished story. Someone else had definitely shot him, and not with the antique pistol.

It could have been Constance. She could have tossed the murder weapon somewhere, tossed it down the trash chute, in a garbage can behind the building, then returned to the apartment. Bliss would have an officer check the alley out back, the trash bins downstairs. But why would she then call the police? Guilt? To confuse him more?

When he emerged from the bathroom, Constance was sitting on the bed, her fallen colleague at her feet.

"You have anything you want to tell me?" he asked.

"His first name was Gerald," she said. "The kids in the neighborhood called him Jerry. It's hard to imagine him as a Jerry. He got 'Wolf' in Nam, shortened from Lone Wolf."

Bliss looked at the headdresses and spears on the wall.

"Wolf said being in the theater was like being a Native American, that there was a war against us, too," Constance explained, fingering the feathers on the headdress. "Only our enemy wasn't the cavalry or the Indian fighters but the basic dumbness of America. Like the Indians, we've been relegated to the outskirts of society, barren reservations. For us, it's the depths of lower Manhattan. Except now that the area's authenticity has been discovered, our place of exile has become prime real estate, and we can barely afford the rent. And instead of subverting us with firewater, Hollywood and its promise of wealth became the liquor that has gotten the theater warriors drunk, destroying our traditions, making us weak and stupid. He told this to each new member of the company, to let them know what we were about. Then he'd show them this."

She opened her hand in which she cradled a rectangular metal tag. It was brass, about three inches long, etched with the words BUREAU OF INDIAN AFFAIRS. Below that it said CORPSE NUMBER, next to which was a blank space where someone could take a metal stamp and bang in a number. At the end of the tag was a hole for a leather thong to tie it around an Indian's toe.

"The government killed so many, it was worth their while to have these made up—a dog tag for a dead Indian."

Bliss called the precinct to let them know about Wolf. Then, like an eel to the Sargasso, he came back to Constance. She put her hand on his arm and looked into his eyes.

"You called the police?" she asked.

"We're already here," he replied.

"Yes," she said. "That's true."

She leaned closer to him and rested her head on his shoulder.

"It's been a rough few days," she said.

"Your son, now your friend."

"Yes. You shouldn't get too close to me," she said. "Something might happen to you."

Something *was* happening to him, what usually happened when incredibly beautiful women let their hair rub against his cheek, let their hands fall casually on his thigh.

"You don't really think I did it, do you?" she said, her voice a soft whisper now. "I mean, in your heart of hearts?"

Officer Bliss…

That's Detective *Bliss.*

Whatever… if you could please tell the court how long after you arrived at the apartment did you phone in the report of Wolf's death?

About twenty minutes.

"Do you have a lover, detective?"

"I have my wife."

And during that time, Detective, did you not take advantage of Miss Bennet?

Hardly, she—

Crudely pawing at her, ignoring both your duties as a police officer and any sense of common decency?

She kissed me first.

Of course.

"Your wife, is she your lover?"

"She's my wife."

And did you or did you not then unbutton her blouse, Detec-

tive, *bringing your lips into a tactile relationship with her breasts when you should have been looking for evidence?*

Objection, Your Honor!

Overruled. Continue council, I want to hear more about the breasts.

After which, Officer—

That's Detective.

Not for long. Did you or did you not reach under her skirt in an adolescent attempt to engage in digital contact with her pudenda, at which point she pulled away in horror?

She didn't pull away. I did.

"What's wrong?"

"I shouldn't be doing this with a suspect."

"So I *am* a suspect?"

"Yes."

I find that hard to believe. And wasn't it at this point that you used the N word?

What N word?

Nookie.

I've never said "nookie" in my life. Hey, what kind of court-room is this, anyway?

"I just want you to hold me. That's all. Do not begrudge me that."

"I don't know."

"He was one of my oldest friends. Please."

Why, if you had strong suspicions that she murdered Wolf, weren't you interrogating her?

She said she wanted me to hold her. "Please hold me," she said.

"I need you to save me."

"I don't know that I can save anyone," he said.

You expect the court to believe that Constance Bennet wanted you?

Hey, I bungee jumped off the Brooklyn Bridge.

Yes, your honor, it is *pathetic. I have to laugh, too. And as to why you were shamelessly letting this woman manipulate you into a compromising position, the obvious answer is that you are an idiot!*

Objection! Conjecture!

Overruled. He is an idiot. A horny, misguided, existentially bankrupt, and completely de-Zened idiot. It's a miracle he's as good a cop as he is.

The doorbell rang. Bliss got up to open it. Cardozo entered in his usual moribund manner, followed by his minions.

Constance retreated to the kitchen as the medical examiner got to work.

"Jesus Christ, Lenny," Cardozo said, "two actors in one week. You trying to get a part in the next play or something? Hey, whattaya think of this one? 'Jack be nimble, Jack be quick, but Jack left blood on the candlestick.' That Audrey, I'm tellin' ya'."

Cardozo moved into the room and addressed the body. He stood by Wolf's feet, scratching his chin, considering the corpse like he was lining up a birdie putt.

"Either this guy overmeditated," Cardozo said, "or he shot himself. Given the fact that there's a rather large pistol near his hand, I'm going to go out on a limb here and say self-inflicted gunshot wound to the head."

"Except that pistol hasn't been fired," Bliss said.

"Picky, picky," the medical examiner responded.

Cardozo slipped on his rubber gloves and began gently probing for other wounds or anything else out of the ordinary.

"And what's this, I wonder?" Cardozo said, holding an earring he had apparently found under Wolf's body. "Pierced. Noting the paucity of holes on the lobes of the deceased, I posit that this earring did not belong to the corpse. Besides, the color doesn't go with his eyes. Though I guess it doesn't matter much if they're closed."

Cardozo handed the earring to Bliss, then leaned close to his ear and whispered, "Psssst, I think it's a clue, big guy."

The earring had two interlocking hoops, one silver, one gold. He went into the kitchen and showed it to Constance.

"You recognize this?" he asked her.

She stared at it for as moment.

"Yes," she finally said. "It belongs to Promise."

"How do you know?"

"Because I gave them to her."

They both took a moment to let this sink in.

"I guess that means my sister was here," she said.

"It would seem so."

Ward had the police sketch of Li-Jung and was taking it around the neighborhood, seeing if anyone recognized her, knew anything, had her phone number, was holding on to a long rope, one end of which was tied around her waist. He decided to walk west from her apartment. Farther east were only decrepit buildings and those futuristic liquor stores where you walk into a womb of bulletproof glass and shout out your order.

So far, zip. The dry cleaners, nothing. The cheese shop, nothing. Six pizza parlors, the video store, used record store, junk shop, nipple-piercing emporium—ixnay. Looking at the drawing, she was just another Oriental girl—Korean, Chinese, Vietnamese, Thai. All the same. *Sorry, can't help you, Officer.* The art-supply store, the pool hall, the supermarkets, the wine store, about eighteen cappuccino bars. Nothing.

He was starting to worry that the girl was gone. Disappeared into Chinatown—or even farther, into the great abyss beyond the Hudson. Just gone. He held out his hand as he walked, listening to it, waiting for a throb, a jolt, some kind of sign to flutter through the hole. Suddenly it moved sharply, pulling to the right like a divining rod. Drawn to what? Ward looked that way, saw a black kid in a sweatshirt. It was him.

The boy from the grocery store. He was alive, after all. And next to him, was another just like him.

"Whattaya you pointing at?" the young man wanted to know. "You puttin' some kind of spell on me? Some voodoo shit?"

Ward's hand was throbbing, like someone was flossing the hole in his palm with barbed wire. The young man stared for a moment, then walked away, obviously deciding Ward was crazy.

Maybe the kid was right.

Suddenly woozy, Ward had to sit down. He found a seat at a restaurant with an outdoor café. Ward rested, not accustomed to feeling weak or confused. He didn't want this hole in his hand anymore, reminding him of the bullet that had come just inches from slamming into his kidney, his groin, his spinal cord.

The other diners were staring at him. He didn't care. His hand hurt. He looked down and saw he was clenching it so tightly, the knuckles had turned pale. He released his fist and watched a trickle of blood begin seeping through the bandage. He saw someone walking his way, puffing up his chest. Probably the manager. A young waiter trailed behind him.

"Everything OK?" the manager asked, trying to sound tough, but probably hoping this wasn't going to be another New York scene, another showdown with a crazy man who wanted to sit all afternoon, drinking coffee, scaring away the customers. "We have a four-dollar minimum at the outdoor tables this time of day."

"Yeah," Ward said, pulling himself together, "everything's OK. I'm a police officer. I'm looking for this girl." He held out the picture.

"Oh, that's Li-Jung," the young waiter said, eyes lighting up with excitement. "I *know* her." Then, as if realizing maybe he shouldn't have said anything, he asked, "Is she in trouble or something?"

"I need to talk to her," Ward said. "You know where I can find her?"

"I just met her yesterday," the waiter replied.

"So that's where you were, Jason," the manager said. "She spend the night?"

The waiter blushed. Ward liked that. If the kid knew how to blush, he knew how to tell the truth.

"Listen," Ward said to the manager, "I'm going to talk to Jason here for the next little while. So I want you to cut him some slack."

"That's all I do."

"And you can bring me four dollars' worth of a hamburger with some sautéed onions."

Jason took off his apron and sat across from Ward. "It's about the gun, isn't it?" Jason asked.

"Yeah, Jason, it's about the gun."

Then Ward put his hand on the table. He knew it would happen. He knew that if he believed, the hand would lead him to the right spot.

DeWayne's apartment was deep into Queens. Since crossing the bridge, they had driven past warehouses and factories and then hit a long stretch of car-repair places, one after another, with homemade signs painted on stacks of tires, marking their shops like sinister totem poles.

"Here we are, little girl," DeWayne said.

They had turned onto a street of decrepit wooden houses. Pieces of cardboard were taped up where windows should have been and metal bars covered front doors. Bottles and cans and broken glass littered the sidewalk, and for some reason several busted baby carriages rested along the curb. Then a homeless man shuffled by with all his belongings piled up in one of these carriages, and she understood why they were there.

"Well, little girl," DeWayne said, pulling the cab up in

front of one the shithole houses, "this is my home. Wanna come upstairs? I've got homemade cookies, fresh from the oven."

Li-Jung had been in New York long enough to know that when it was easy to find a parking spot, you were in a really bad neighborhood. The street reminded her of the mobile homes clustered on the outskirts of her town back in Iowa, everything covered in a layer of dirt and grease, garbage and broken cars in front, dogs so thin you could count their ribs straining at their leashes and barking in your face, no doubt begging you in dog talk to please shoot them and put them out of their misery.

DeWayne removed the taxi meter and the radio. He opened the glove compartment and took out his gun and the tapes. He put everything inside a brown paper shopping bag and tucked it under his arm. Then he locked up the cab.

Opening the metal gate that served as a front door, he led her up the three flights of steps to his apartment. A huge padlock hung on his door, but DeWayne just pushed the door open. He made a gracious bow and gestured that she should enter.

"After you, mademoiselle."

As she passed, he yanked the pack with the gun in it off her back, nearly wrenching her shoulder out of its socket as he did. He pushed her inside and slammed the door.

She was a getting more nervous now.

"Sorry," he said. "I thought it'd be better if I held on to the gun."

He fished it out and stuffed it in his belt and tossed her the pack. He dropped the keys on the kitchen counter, then thought better of it and put them in his pocket. He held on to the paper bag.

"Have a seat," he said, gesturing toward the couch. A yellowed pillow and crumpled blanket suggested it was also his bed. A pair of underwear was draped over the back like a lazy cat. She didn't want to sit on this couch. She didn't want to stay in this house. But the door seemed miles away, and what was outside gave her no comfort. So she brushed aside a half-eaten slice of pizza and several beer cans and sat down, leaning forward to make sure that she stayed clear of the rank briefs behind her head.

"Sorry," DeWayne said. "It's the maid's day off."

The sink was filled with dishes, the floor littered with newspapers, brown bags, empty Chinese take-out containers. The room smelled like rotting food and dirty socks. There were boxes everywhere, as if DeWayne had never unpacked. Her partner was really starting to frighten her.

"So did Lenny *say* he was a detective, or did you just assume he was?"

"I'm not sure," she said.

DeWayne positioned himself in front of his refrigerator like he was getting ready to wrestle it. Taking a deep breath, he wrenched opened the door, quickly grabbed a beer, and slammed it shut. He exhaled and popped the beer.

"Drink, partner?" he asked, extending the can to her.

"No, thanks," she said. At which point the odor of rot washed over her like a wave. DeWayne conjured up smells like a magician produced doves. Her nose involuntarily wrinkled.

"It's bad," he said. "I know."

He was pacing in front of her, drinking as he walked. She watched his bony Adam's apple bob up and down.

"So you're not sure he's a detective," he said.

"No."

"So what *are* you sure of?"

"I—I saw him at this apartment where a murder took place."

"How'd you happen to be in the vicinity of a homicide?"

She didn't know what to say. DeWayne helped her out.

"Just a coincidence, right?"

"Yes." She nodded, maybe too enthusiastically.

DeWayne set the down the beer, pulled Lenny's gun from his belt, and sniffed the barrel. Then he checked the clip.

"This has been fired recently, hasn't it?"

DeWayne was looking at her differently now—maybe thinking she was someone to reckon with. She wasn't so sure that was a good thing.

"You think he works Homicide, right?"

"I guess so."

"Lenny in Homicide . . . That shouldn't be too hard."

He picked up the phone book and looked up some numbers. He dialed, then held out the receiver. She got up and took it from him.

"Ask for Lenny," he told her. "Say you have some information about a recent case. They want to know which one, say, 'The black kid that was shot.' They've always got one of those working."

She asked for Lenny. She said she had some information. The woman on the other end said Lenny wasn't there but she'd connect her with Lenny's partner. She covered the receiver and relayed this to DeWayne.

"Give it to me," he said, grabbing the phone out of her hand.

"Listen," he said, "You Lenny's partner? . . . Well, I got a message for Lenny. . . . Never mind who this is; get a pencil and copy it down exactly. Word for word. You tell him . . . um . . . tell him Mr. Gunn called. And because you're a cop, I'll spell it for you. G-U-N-N. His *old friend* Mr. Gunn—underline 'old friend'—who he hasn't seen for a while. Underline 'hasn't seen.' And if Lenny wants to see Mr. Gunn as much as Mr. Gunn wants to see Lenny, tell him to call me."

DeWayne gave his number and hung up. He smiled his

crooked slit of a smile that looked like someone had glued his lips shut and he was trying to pull them apart.

"Pretty clever, huh, partner? You get it? 'Mr. Gunn.' Made that up right on the spot."

She nodded but apparently without enough enthusiasm.

"What, you got a better idea?!" DeWayne shouted. "You got some other *plan of attack*? Because I'm willing to listen, little girl, if you think you got a better idea than someone who was a *cop* for eight years, who *knows* a thing or two about this kind of shit!" He shook his finger at her. "Fifteen hundred bucks you're making off this deal without doing diddly squat, so don't go criticizing *me*!"

He walked away from her, picked up his beer, and plopped down on the couch where she'd been sitting.

"This is fun, huh?"

Li-Jung nodded, trying to show some enthusiasm. It didn't seem to matter.

"Feel it? The rush?" He closed his eyes and leaned back on the couch. "It's been too long." Then he opened his eyes. "I wonder if that was the right guy," he said. He took another swig from the can. "Anyway, how many homicide detectives with a pansy name like Lenny could there be?"

Chapter 25

Bliss was alone in the kitchen with Constance. Cardozo and the lab boys were still hard at work, the photographer getting pictures of the corpse. Katrina would probably love to get her hands on those, he thought, make some slides and project them during one of their shows.

"I have to ask you, did you kill Wolf?"

"Why would I?"

"You thought he murdered your son. You wanted revenge."

"Like Lady MacDuff."

"Whatever."

"It was Promise's earring."

"That doesn't answer my question."

"They found it under the body."

"There are plenty of ways it could have gotten there. You have a key."

"That's true."

"You could have slipped it under the body after you shot him."

"But that would take courage."

"Is this your way of saying you didn't kill him?"

"It's my way of saying that I needed you to hold me, with great tenderness, and then maybe, just maybe, I could have felt something—for Wolf, for James, for myself."

Just then the front door opened and Katrina rushed in, video camera pressed to her face. A cord led leashlike back to Algernon, who was talking intently into the microphone. Katrina panned the room.

"Wolf's here," Algernon said, closing his eyes, thrusting one hand high above his head. "I feel him—his spirit, waiting for us to ease his soul, to send him to the next world in peace."

Algernon shoved the mike in Cardozo's face.

"Did you hear it, on his lips, the name of his killer?"

For once Cardozo was momentarily at a loss for words.

"Bliss!" he then shouted, "Get these people out of here!"

A uniformed cop went to grab Algernon, but he darted away and started chanting, lurching around the room in spastic jumps like he had swallowed a bone and was frantically trying to dislodge it. Bliss assumed this was Algernon's pathetic attempt at some kind of ritual Native American dance. The detective got up from the kitchen table. As he did, his beeper went off. Katrina darted the camera at him, as if she had radar.

"Call them back!" she shouted, a director swirling in her creative frenzy. "Where's the phone? It's reality. It's why we're here. Maybe it's a witness."

"The killer's been caught!" Algernon shouted. "He's going to confess!"

"We'll wait while you call," Katrina said, keeping the camera pointed at Bliss. "It's part of the story."

"It's the *truth!*" Algernon shouted, keeping the mike in Bliss's face.

Bliss quickly checked the number. It was Artie at the precinct. What did *he* want. Whatever it was would have to wait.

"Get back!" Bliss shouted. "Get the fuck away! You're contaminating the crime scene."

"*Contaminating the crime scene,*" Algernon said gleefully. "Lenny, I *love* the way you talk!"

"Fuck off!" he shouted. He was losing control and they were capturing it on tape. He'd be on *Entertainment Tonight* or, worse, *Cops.*

They moved into the hall, Algernon keeping up a steady monologue, his face contorted with passion.

"Wolf is here yet not here. He is still here. He is still . . . here. He cannot still hear, yet he can be here, still. He *is* here still. Here/hear. Still/still. Here stillness. *Hear* stillness. The stillness of Wolf, here. His hereness. His highness. Wolf."

Then Katrina turned the camera on herself, holding it at arm's length.

"There are tears to be shed," she said into the lens. "There is also skin to be shed. And fear. And love. There is much love to be shed."

Then she turned the camera toward Constance, who had emerged from the kitchen and was moving toward them as if drawn by a giant magnet.

"Of all of us, he loved you most, Constance," Katrina said. "You must be the one to find his spirit, Constance. On his lips. His last words still on his lips. Take them, Constance."

Constance stood up. Her face had changed, transformed into a mask of pain and sorrow, like she had stepped out of Picasso's *Guernica*.

"Please . . ." Bliss said. Katrina whipped the camera at him. Algernon aimed the mike at his face like a ray gun. "It's evidence," Bliss said. "You can't disturb it."

"Yes, it *is* evidence," Algernon said, "but not for what you think."

"You'll hear his last words," Katrina said. "The name of the murderer."

Bliss ripped the mike out of Algernon's hand and raised it up as if to strike him. Algernon crouched down, covered his head and cowered in fear. Bliss lowered his arm.

"I just wanted to see you afraid, Algy," he said. "Just for a moment, I wanted to see real fear in your eyes."

Bliss disconnected the mike from the cord and shoved it in his pocket.

"Lenny . . ." It was Constance, calling to him, her voice barely above a whisper.

He turned to her, as did Katrina and Algernon, the three of them waiting for her to speak.

"What is it?" Bliss asked.

"I can't do this anymore," Constance said. She reached out to Bliss, her eyes filled with what Bliss took to be genuine sorrow. "Take me home. Please, Lenny. Just take me home."

Katrina lowered the camera. Algernon sank to the floor. The show was over. Constance's pain had brought up the houselights.

Bliss led her down the steps and out into the afternoon light.

"You see, you did save me," she said. "Thank you." She kissed him gently on the cheek and walked away.

Bliss was proud of her, though he wouldn't have minded if she'd just touched Wolf's lips quickly before she left, contacting his spirit, capturing the name of his killer. That would have been nice to hear. Then Bliss might have a better clue as to who it was. Though the earring found by Wolf's body— Promise's earring—which was tucked away neatly in a plastic bag in his pocket, gave Bliss a glimmer of an idea.

After beeping his partner, Artie waited for Bliss to call him back. The phone didn't ring. Typical. Artie was disappointed with Bliss. He clearly wasn't interested in working with Artie. All he talked about was Ward. And even when Bliss *didn't* talk about Ward, Artie knew he was thinking about him. Artie felt like going to the lieutenant to complain.

Artie had been working hard. He had tracked down the caterer Li-Jung worked for and spoke to a dishwasher who remembered Li-Jung saying her parents owned a restaurant. That seemed *important.* It definitely had some of the essential requirements of being a *clue.* But was he consulted about the situation? No. Was he asked what he had uncovered? No. Bliss just ignored him, bullying him out of the way. Artie wanted to talk to the lieutenant about that, too.

And now Bliss didn't even call him back. Mr. Veteran Detective didn't seem to think Artie knew what he was doing. But Artie had set up the garment center sting operation *himself. He* had been in charge. The store he had as a front was perfect. Artie ran it like it was legit. He'd had *regular customers,* for Christ's sake. Ladies who came in every week, wanting his advice on the latest styles. Was it *his* fault they didn't catch anybody?

Fucking Garment Center Task Force. He might as well
have been wearing the dresses himself for all the good it did
his career. He was supposed to have been dealing with the
mob. Wise guys, tough guys, shoot-outs on Delancey Street,
shouting, *Freeze, motherfucker, drop those garments! Release
those hangers!* And when it was done, the mayor was going to
thank him personally. Instead, he ate kishka and blintzes for
six weeks, gaining weight as he stood by the changing room,
counseling some old lady about whether the color of a dress
went with her hair, whether or not it made her look "hippy."
After the second week, he put a lock on the changing room
altogether, letting them take the shit home to try on.

Now this odd phone call. From Mr. Gunn. It sounded suspicious. It sounded like Lenny was involved in some kind of
a situation. A situation that if Artie could sort it out, reaching
out to this Mr. Gunn on Bliss's behalf, then maybe things
might be a little different between them. Maybe then Bliss
might have a little more respect for the person sitting across
the front seat of the car from him, however temporary that
arrangement might be.

Artie dialed the number he'd written down on the pink
message pad, just to see what would happen.

"I wanna speak to a Mr. Gunn," Artie said, using his gruff
Brooklyn voice, the one he'd perfected at the store.

"That's me," the man said.

"It's Lenny. Whattaya want?"

"Didn't you figure it out?"

"Can't say I did."

"Shit, you're even dumber than I thought. How'd you get
to be detective?"

"Like I said, whattaya want?"

"I got your gun. You want it back, it's three grand. Cash.
You can bring it to my place by this afternoon. Otherwise I let
your lieutenant know you lost it. And *how* you lost it. I'll give

you two hours exactly. I gotta see my kids this afternoon. Bring the three grand and a roll of wrapping paper, you get your piece back."

"Wrapping paper?"

"Yeah. For the kids' presents. One roll of pink, and one of blue."

Then he gave Artie the address and hung up. A street in Queens. Two hours. He had to follow through now. It was close enough to lunch for him to go out there on his own time. Do his partner a favor. And at the same time, show him just what kind of cop he was.

He checked his piece, slipped it back in his holster, put on his sports jacket, and headed out the door. Maybe now Lenny would see what Artie Barsamian was made of. Maybe Artie would find out, too.

"It's lookin' real good, partner," DeWayne said, hanging up the phone. "*Very* good. *Three* thousand I asked for. You heard, right? He didn't say boo. Probably letting him off the hook too easy." He took another swig of beer. "He knows he's up shit's creek. It's lookin' good."

"What's the wrapping paper for?" she asked.

"Presents for my kids," he said.

"Oh. Um . . . DeWayne, what about breakfast? I'm pretty hungry."

"I got mine," he said, referring to the beer. "Check the fridge if you're hungry. Have whatever you want. Just watch out when you open it. Could be some new life form sprang up in there." He laughed like one of those professional wrestlers and plopped down on the couch.

She found some Italian bread on the counter, the outside of which was rock hard, but the center was still kind of soft. A jar of peanut butter was sitting there, but it was laced with suspicious flecks of red that might have been jelly or jam, but she didn't want to risk it. She dug out some of the soft bread and ate that. She resisted going into the fridge.

There was a poster of a blond woman on the wall with major hair.

"Farrah," DeWayne said. "Fucking Farrah."

And then she saw DeWayne looking at her, the look that she knew from across the front seat of the pickup—when it was time to pull off the highway, to head down the dirt road to the edge of the lake. The look that gathered quiet and darkness around it, headlights off, music off. No distractions.

"How old are you anyway, little girl?" DeWayne said, taking another drink.

Maybe he'd pass out. Because it was morning and he hadn't eaten much, maybe he'd pass out right there on the couch. Then she could sneak away. Being lost in Queens had to be better than being in this disgusting toilet of an apartment with an obvious psycho. He took another swig from the bottle, but she knew he wasn't going to pass out yet. They never passed out until after they got what they wanted.

"I asked you how old you were," he said, sounding angry now. That was bad. Angry was bad.

"Twenty," she said.

"Take off your shirt," he said.

She did what she was told. She didn't want him to get any angrier. Her arms broke out with goose bumps, and she shivered slightly. It could get really ugly when they got angry.

"You call those tits? Jesus. Twenty years old you should have more tits than that. Those are like monkey tits."

That was good. Calling her names. Maybe now he didn't want her.

"Now throw your shirt over here," he ordered.

She did what she was told. He shoved it under one of the cushions.

"This will keep you from trying to run away," he said.

But he still had that look. She could run for it, but the couch was between her and the door. And besides, she remembered how Clyde could be drunk in the bar, but when it came time for a fight, he was suddenly steady and could punch someone in the face like a machine without stopping until the bartender hit him on the head with a bat.

"Come on over here, baby," he said.

As she got on her knees, she thought about Jason, his apartment full of books, the way he had stroked her cheek and held her and apologized for his lovemaking. She'd go back there, she decided. She'd forget about Boston and go back there and ask him to help her, to hide her. She'd cook for him, clean his place. She'd do whatever she had to so she could stay there and let him comfort her.

DeWayne shuddered when he was done and collapsed back on the couch.

"Wake me up when the son of a bitch gets here," he said. He didn't bother pulling up his pants. He brought out the gun from between the cushions and put it on his lap, where he cradled it gently like it was some kind of stuffed animal.

Li-Jung didn't move, staying as still as a little rabbit, hoping for him to nod off. His head finally fell off to the side and his mouth opened, but still she didn't move for another five minutes, during which time she planned her route to the door. She'd follow the rug, being careful not to knock into the beer cans or the floor lamp that was already tipped over. Her own shirt was inaccessible, but in the corner by the door was a heap of clothes. Maybe there was one in there. Shirt or not, she'd grab something on the way out and use it to cover herself as best she could. Maybe the homeless guy had an extra shirt in his baby carriage. She wanted to get to Jason's, to take a long bath and lie in his bed and sleep and sleep.

The monster DeWayne wasn't moving. It was time. Like on the bridge. No holding back. Her size was her asset now as she crept silently as a tiger across the room and picked up some clothing in the corner in one quick motion and opened the door just far enough to let her thin frame slip out. She skipped down the steps like she had wings and was out the door in an instant, careful not to let the metal frame with the bars bang back.

The homeless man looked up at her and smiled as he watched her put on what luckily turned out to be a short-sleeved shirt. It wasn't a mean smile. It was almost as if he knew she had escaped something bad and he was happy for her. She buttoned the buttons as she ran down the street, wanting to get a few blocks away before looking for a pay phone to call Jason. Then she had to find a subway heading back into the city.

She didn't care about the gun. She was done with the gun. She had caved in to her anger, and in return the gun had given her one moment, one flash of power, and then it turned her into something she couldn't recognize as herself.

DeWayne and the gun belonged together. Maybe somehow the gun would find a way of sending a bullet deep into his heart.

DeWayne was almost going to say something when she'd found his uniform as she was sneaking out the door. She was cagey, that one. She'd been around. The tattoo on her shoulder told him that. He'd watched her with his eyes open just a slit as he pretended to be asleep. Christ, she crouched there completely motionless forever. He had to admire her perseverance. At one point he wanted to shout at her to go already, but he stuck it out, playing his part of the sleeping body. He had barely heard her as she moved. She'd make one hell of a cat burglar.

He felt good. She'd made him feel good. But he had wanted her to leave without a shirt, give the bums on the street a little show, give Henry something to think about when he did his business behind the dumpster—though with those tits he wasn't sure if Henry would have been able to tell if she was a boy or a girl. To Henry, it probably didn't matter.

She deserved the humiliation for being dumb enough to believe that he'd split the money with her, for thinking he had the strength to go after her if she'd decided to make a break for the door and run down the stairs. He'd once chased a guy fleeing the scene after smashing his car into a street-light. Puerto Rican kid. They're supposed to be fast. Had sneakers on, too. DeWayne was running in his work shoes, but he caught him, took him down. That was when he was younger, when he worked a fifty hour week and could still spend the weekend helping out the guy installing his pool, saving a couple hundred bucks. That was back when he was wrestling with the kids on the living room floor, playing paintball with the guys, touch football in Corona Park while his family watched, cheering him on. All gone. His stamina, his determination—all gone.

But he was still sly. No judge, no I.A. probe, could take that away from him.

He'd played it right. Scaring her, acting jumpy, out of control. He'd had no intention of sharing the money, so why have her around when Lenny showed up? Besides, DeWayne was doing her a favor. The girl had her whole life in front of her, whereas DeWayne wasn't sure just what he had left.

He would wait until the bell rang and Lenny came with the cash. Then DeWayne would get the presents from the trunk and figure out a way to wrap them up. He took the safety off the gun just in case. He didn't want Lenny to think he could surprise him, catching him with his pants down, which they were. He'd pull them up later. Or maybe he'd have Lenny do *that* for him, too.

Li-Jung found a phone and called Jason. Her heart sank when she got his machine. But there was a message on it for her to call him at work. She dug out another quarter, dialed the number, and waited while someone at the restaurant found him.

"Hi," he said, excited to hear from her. "It's good you called. There's news. I spoke to a detective, a friend of Lenny's, the one you took the gun from. He said the boy isn't dead. Matt isn't dead. He said you'd know what that meant. Li-Jung? Are you there?"

Matt wasn't dead, meaning she wasn't a murderer!

"I'm here."

But now Jason knew. What would he think of her?

"That's great," she said.

"He also said he just needs the gun back and everything will be okay."

"I don't have it."

"Do you know where it is?"

"Yes."

"Hold on," Jason said. There was silence for a moment, then he came back. "Listen, the detective, he wants you to come here. Right now. He says if you do, he can make things all right."

"I don't think so," she said. She was afraid of meeting the police. She didn't know what to do. She was tired. She felt lost. She didn't want to be so alone.

Then she took a big step toward emerging from the darkness she'd been in for so many years. A greater jump than the one off the bridge.

"Jason, I need you," she said. "I need your help." She'd never asked for help before, wasn't sure until she heard them that the words would come out of her mouth. "Jason, what should I do?"

"I trust him," Jason said. "He says he's your only hope to put this behind you, and I believe him."

"Then I'll be there."

At the subway station she realized she'd spent her last quarter on the phone call. She pulled back the turnstile halfway and slipped through it and found a train to Manhattan. It wasn't until she was sitting down that she caught a glimpse of the tag on the front of her shirt. REARDON, D. W. it said. N.Y.P.D.

Unlike DeWayne, she wore the shirt with pride.

Chapter 26

Bliss was just getting out of the car to pay another visit to the Rodericks when he remembered he had to call Artie at the precinct. The receptionist said he'd gone out. Didn't say where. Probably combing the hillside for clues.

He hung up and took a moment to plan his strategy. Constance could have murdered Wolf. She had the key to let herself in. But how would she have gotten the earring? Promise also could have done it. She looked enough like her sister that Wolf, in his shaken condition, could easily have mistaken her for Constance and let her in. Their motivations: revenge for James's death. It was possible.

Then there was Martin, flitting about on the sidelines. What did he have to gain from Wolf's death? Nothing—unless Promise was convicted. Then he'd probably have free run of the estate. Martin was an odd bird. Mincing and prim. Bliss could see him being the type to get his rocks off dressing up in a tutu and hanging from a noose tied to the chandelier in the living room. But was he a murderer? Bliss felt he was deeply involved, but he still wasn't sure how. Being dependent on his wife's fortune probably had something to do with it. Martin was a *schlimazel*, the kind of a guy you wanted to bully—break his science experiment, push him over the shrubs and into the mud, stick a gun in his mouth and threaten to blow his brains out unless he told you what you wanted to know. That kind of thing.

Bliss gave his name to the doorman and waited as he called up.

Martin was gushing anxiety.

The doorman said the detective was on his way up. He was back because Wolf had been found dead, and if everything had gone according to plan, they'd found the earring—and perhaps already knew the ballistics results.

Martin had prepared his props for the show. The suitcase was packed, with the gun now tucked away inside. Now he needed to work on his performance when he met the detective in the front hall. Should he act eager? Concerned? Nonchalant? He stood on the Italian tiles, his arms fluttering with excitement.

He took a deep breath.

He centered a lamp on the table in the hallway.

He opened the front closet and straightened the sleeves on his overcoats, making sure they weren't being crushed.

He took out his handkerchief, licked the corner, and wiped away a smudge on the mirror by the elevator door. He returned the handkerchief to his pocket, took it out again, folded it so that the damp spot was in the center, then returned it to his pocket.

He watched the dial on top of the elevator approach his floor.

He got a sudden urge to go into the kitchen, to put on his chef's hat. He dashed away just before the elevator arrived.

The elevator doors opened on an empty foyer.

"I'll be out in a moment," Bliss heard from the kitchen. And sure enough, a moment later as advertised, Roderick emerged, dressed in an apron and one of those chef's hats that Bliss knew had a special name but didn't know what it was. Surely Martin would.

"A toque." Martin informed him when asked, adopting his usual effete tone. "It's French, like most of the essential things in cooking."

"Right," Bliss said. "*Oui.*"

Bliss watched as Martin approached the hall table.

He picked a bit of wax off a candle.

He straightened the wick.

He pulled a drooping flower off a plant.

Bliss wanted to put him in handcuffs to keep him from *potchkying* around so much. He smelled something in the oven.

"What are you making today?" Bliss asked.

"A crème brûlée. Do you like it?"

"I'm not too big on brûlées in general," Bliss said, "but if I am forced to have one, I always go for the crèmes. They're the best of the brûlées, if you ask me."

"Yes. Well, unfortunately it won't be ready for a little while."

"I got time."

"What brings you here, Detective?"

"You know Wolf, the actor from the Performance Warehouse?"

"Yes."

"The same Wolf who was probably the last person to see your stepson alive?"

"Yes, what about him?"

"Well," Bliss said, "Wolf got dead."

"Wolf's dead?"

"Yeah, Wolf's dead."

Martin seemed to ponder this for a moment, without any particular expression. He definitely wasn't giving Bliss much to go on. Then again, no one was.

"I'd better go check the brûlée," Martin said.

"Nothing worse than overdone brûlée is what I always say."

He followed Martin into the kitchen.

Bliss watched him open the oven and bend to look inside. It was one of those fancy stainless-steel jobs, like they have in restaurants. Bliss had a flash. He should get Martin to baby-sit for his kids while Rachel was away. He could do all the cooking, cleaning, straightening up. Of course, if he was a murderer, Bliss might want to keep him away from the kids.

"Do you think it was the same person who killed James?" Martin asked, sounding earnest.

"Definitely not," the detective said. "Because James wasn't murdered."

"What?!" Martin said.

This time, Martin actually sounded surprised. Hey, finally someone was showing some emotion.

"Then how did he die?"

"Some kind of aneurysm in his brain."

"You're serious?"

"I'm always serious."

"So I guess that means Wolf didn't kill him?" Martin asked.

"Did you think he had?"

"We weren't sure. We didn't know what to think."

"You sure think about your cooking, though," Bliss said. "Your stepson's death hasn't affected you there."

"Cooking soothes me, Detective," Martin said.

Bliss wondered what it would take to get this guy rattled. Break one of his wooden spoons? Nick the blade of his paring knife? Leave the refrigerator open?

"This is how you tell if it's done," Martin said. "You tap the pan ever so lightly, to see if the center seems loose. If you're in doubt, you use a toothpick. If it comes out clean, you know it's ready."

Bliss watched Martin deftly perform the maneuver, pulling out the toothpick and examining it closely, with deep concern, as if checking the thermometer of a feverish child.

"Another few minutes," Martin said, gently closing the oven door.

Bliss moved closer to him, crowding him just a little.

"And what about you, Martin?"

"What do you mean?"

"I mean," Bliss said, his voice grave, "that if I stick this toothpick in you, does it come out just as clean?"

Martin froze, for a moment his eyes fluttering in his head, like a cornered rat. Then he composed himself.

"Would you like some coffee, Detective?" he asked.

"You didn't answer my question."

"You didn't answer *mine*."

"Black, please." Bliss bet *Martin* knew where the filters were kept.

Bliss watched him with fascination as Martin swooped around the kitchen.

He poured spring water into the tea kettle and put it on the stove.

He wiped a knife and put it in the knife block; then took it out, wiped it again, put it back.

He sponged off the counter.

He opened the fridge, looked inside, saw that the vegetable drawer was ajar, pushed it in, closed the fridge. The guy straightened up more stuff in five minutes than Bliss did in a month.

"Is your wife here?" Bliss asked.

"She's due back any moment."

"Then I'll wait," he said. "I think it's a good idea for the three of us to have a little talk."

Chapter 27

Jason held Li-Jung's hand as they sat together at the restaurant and she described DeWayne's house to Detective Ward.

"Sounds disgusting," Jason said, comforting her. How nice that felt.

"Never mind the decor," the detective said, clearly impatient, "how do I get there?"

She described the route she had taken to the subway in reverse.

"How will I know which house it is?" he asked.

"He parked the taxi right in front. He lives on the third floor. The stairway smells like pee."

"And you're sure he has the gun?"

"He was holding it on his lap when I left. He was passed out," she explained.

"Then why didn't you take it?" he asked. Scolding her, like she'd done something wrong running away from such a deranged human being. What he meant was, *Why didn't you take the gun and make my life easier?* But hey, she didn't *ask* Lenny to give her the gun on the bridge. He just *handed* it to her.

"I didn't want to wake him up," she said.

"Right," he said. "Let sleeping dogs lie."

The detective gently rubbed his bandaged hand, his brow creased in pain. She noticed the gauze was stained with a circle of blood.

"You're sure it was him. DeWayne Reardon."

"That's who he said it was."

He was staring at her breasts. Then she realized it was the name on the shirt.

"He's scary," she said.

"I know," the detective replied. "He's a fuck-up. He's a cancer in the testicles." He took a deep breath, like someone getting ready to dive into very cold water, then focused on her with a grim stare. "The way this works is you have to go away. Tonight. Tomorrow morning the latest. You go away and you never come back. Move to another state. As far away as possible. You hear about settlements on Mars, you sign up for the first shuttle. You change your name. That's *very* important. You grow your hair. You keep a low profile. Forever. The boy you shot, Matt, his parents aren't sure they really want to find you. They aren't certain they want this to go to trial. It's a lot of exposure. A big ordeal. They're thinking this whole episode could be a kind of wake-up call for Matt. That maybe now he'll get his life together. He'll spend the summer in the Hamptons, dating rich girls from families they know. But they could change their minds, and that could mean trouble for everyone. For Lenny, for you, for me, for your boyfriend. If one of us goes down, we all go down. That's why you have to go away and never come back. Never set foot in New York. And if I ever see you, if I ever *hear* about you, I'll track you down. And since I can't take you into custody without incriminating me and my partner, I'll take it upon myself to shoot you both and bury you in a place where no one will ever find your bodies. Is that clear?"

"We'll go to my parents in Michigan," Jason said decisively.

"Michigan sounds great," the detective said. "Get packing."

"Good luck," Jason said.

Li-Jung liked the way he was trying to sound like he was one of the guys.

"Oh, um, listen," she said, "he has another gun, too. In a grocery bag."

"Thanks."

"And tell Lenny when you see him there that I'm sorry," she said.

"See him where?"

"At DeWayne's."

"He's there?"

"DeWayne spoke to him on the phone. Just before I split. It sounded like Lenny was on his way over."

"Shit!" Ward said.

He left without saying good-bye.

Martin was doing his best to hold it together, but the detective was unnerving him.

"How about I stick in the toothpick this time?" the detective said.

He was clearly trying to keep Martin off balance. Not let him get comfortable or collect his thoughts. But Martin had to trust that everything was in order, that the scene would unfold the way he planned. He didn't want to improvise, especially when the detective made him so jumpy.

"I just push it in?" the detective asked, holding the toothpick above the brûlée.

"No!" Martin shouted. "In the middle! And watch your knuckles! You're pressing down!"

Christ, he was sounding like nervous wreck. Up until now he'd been cool and collected. He needed to calm down.

"I'm sorry, Detective," Martin heard himself say. "It's because of James. This was his favorite dessert."

"He liked your brûlée?"

Obnoxious prick. "He said I made it better than anyone else."

"Yes, I can see how that would be disconcerting," Bliss said.

Martin felt himself sweating. He wiped his forehead. "The heat from the oven," he said. He hoped it made sense.

"So what do you think?" The detective held up the toothpick. "It came out clean. Is it ready?"

"Yes," Martin said. He reached into the oven, carefully pulled out the dessert, and placed it on the counter.

"You mind if I use your phone?" the detective asked. Without waiting for an answer, he grabbed the telephone and started dialing.

DeWayne sat on the couch and waited. He hadn't moved since the girl left. Hadn't pulled up his pants. Any pleasure she had given him had already vanished. He finished his beer and threw the empty can on the carpet.

DeWayne knew things were closing in. It wasn't like the danger he felt on the job, not knowing who was around the next corner, what psycho hid behind a door he had to open.

This danger wasn't coming from the outside. It was more about doors inside him closing. Doors without handles. Doors that couldn't be opened again.

He could have done a good deed, helped Lenny out, delivered his gun and the girl, too. He would have been one of the good guys again. He would have had a story to tell Antoinette and his kids to make them proud.

But no.

Like everything else, all the drug money he had taken, he just did it. He didn't think about what would happen.

Why didn't he think things through? Sometimes he felt

like he was just a character in a story, and he was watching himself do all this stuff that brought ruin on his own head. Was everyone's life like that? Li-Jung, the girl—at least she'd tried to stick him up, take some initiative. And then she got out when she could. DeWayne never seemed to know when the right time was to get out. But he could feel that time was coming. It was coming very soon.

Artie turned off the engine. He didn't like what he saw. The building was falling apart—door barely on its hinges, windows broken, trash and debris everywhere. Random pieces of the garbage had organized itself into something resembling a human being that was now shuffling its way toward the car.

"Hungry," the garbage said, somehow knowing how to speak. The garbage then started rubbing the side of Artie's car with a filthy piece of cloth, leaving black streaks in its wake.

"Here," Artie said, quickly getting some money from his pocket.

An arm made of discarded rags raised up, and something like a hand with gnarled and twisted fingers opened partially. Artie placed a dollar on it. The hand stayed put. Artie added the few nickels he found in the console between the seats. The hand closed, and the arm sank down to the side of what might have been the body.

"You know who lives here?" Artie asked.

The garbage-man looked at the house, then back at Artie.

"You don't want to go in there," he said, lips barely parting. "You don't want to have no truck with that man." Then he silently turned and shuffled back the way he came.

Artie got out of the car. The third floor was where he had to get to. He walked up the front steps and checked the name on the bell marked THREE. It said GONZALES. But the guy on the phone hadn't sounded Hispanic. The metal gate was open. He went inside.

He took his gun out of his holster, held it behind his thigh
pointing down, trying to stay casual, not wanting to scare
anyone, just wanting to find out what was up with Mr. Gunn.

Inside it smelled of piss. Who lived in places like this?
His mother would have a heart attack if she saw such filth.
His mother, from good Armenian stock, hated dirt.

He crept silently up the first two flights. No one appeared
on the stairs. The hallway was getting darker the farther up
he went—the fixtures were broken, and the light from the
street was the only light there was. Artie stood to the side
of the door on three, his back against the wall. He had his
gun in his right hand, the safety off. He knocked. A voice
answered.

"Lenny, that you?"

The voice sounded cheery, like a party was about to start
and Artie was the first guest to arrive.

"Yeah. It's me. Lenny."

"Good. Come on in."

He held his gun down behind his leg again. He wasn't sure
what he was going to encounter. He figured he'd wing it, get
the lay of the land, talk the guy into giving him Lenny's gun.
Artie was sure "Mr. Gunn," whoever he was, would come
around eventually. After all, you didn't fuck around with
cops, and Artie was a cop. He took a deep breath, pivoted from
the wall, faced the door, and opened it.

The room Artie was looking into was filthier than the
street. Trash strewn everywhere. The man he presumed was
Mr. Gunn sat on the couch, his pants down by his knees like
he was sitting on the toilet.

"I see you got yourself another piece," the man said.

"Yeah," Artie said. He had to remember he was playing
the part of Lenny.

"Still, you want to have your gun back. It's the one that's
got your name attached to the serial number."

"That's right."

"It's the one you're responsible for."

"Fuckin'-A," Artie said. "So give it to me."

"You bring the money, Lenny?"

Artie wasn't exactly prepared for this.

"I didn't have enough time to get it. I'll have to owe it to you."

The man on the couch licked his lips.

"You'll *owe* it to me?"

"Yeah. That's right."

"Ordinarily, Lenny, I'd say yes, but you see, I'm dying. I've got this incurable disease. It's a rare disease called my whole life is turned to shit don't give a rat's ass what the fuck happens to me anymore. It's terminal, Lenny. No one recovers from this one. Worse than the Big C. So I really do need the money now."

Artie instinctively brought his gun up and pointed it at the man. "I promise I'll pay you the money when I can," he said.

"Did you say you *promise?*"

Artie was thinking this wasn't going as well as he would have liked.

"That's right. I promise. Now, may I please have the gun."

"Did you really say *please?*"

"Yes."

He knew he should have been more clever. This was like one of those stories where you have to say something to the wizard guarding the bridge—you have to say the right thing, outsmart him. He says stuff and you have to be wiser and then you get to cross to the other side. But Artie was feeling like he was saying everything wrong. He wondered what the wizard would do now.

"Give me the fucking gun!" Artie shouted, but as soon as the words were off his lips, he knew they were wrong. He felt like the man was looking through him, that Artie was the one with his pants down.

"All right," the man said. "You win, Lenny. I'll give you the gun. But you promise to pay me later?"

"Yeah."

"Say it."

"What?"

"That you promise."

"I promise."

"Cross your heart?"

"Just get the gun."

"Cross your heart."

"No."

"Fine. I just have to go get it," the man said. "But let me pull my trousers up first."

Then a sound—a pop—and the bullet tore through Artie's shoulder, twisting him around, his own gun flying out of his hand, and he fell back into the hall as warm blood started soaking into his jacket. A searing pain was surging through one side of his body, but as he lay writhing on the floor, all he could think was how his mother would have a heart attack if she knew he was going to die in such a filthy hallway.

DeWayne was pleased by the way he'd shot Lenny through his fly. His plan to keep the gun in the bagging crotch of his pants had worked perfectly. Slip the nuzzle right through the open zipper and fire at will. Fitting that the prissy detective should get caught by someone else with their pants down.

It was the first thing DeWayne had done in a long time that actually worked out, and he took a strange satisfaction in it. He figured it wouldn't last long.

He pulled up his trousers and walked out into the hall to look at the wounded imbecile, now lying in a small pool of blood. In his years as a cop he'd seen the damage done by others, strange signatures left by men on the bodies of their enemies, but this was the first person he'd actually shot. DeWayne waited to see if he felt anything special, any remorse, but he knew he was way beyond that. Instead, he got down to business.

"You tell anyone you were coming?" he asked. He could see that Lenny was in big-time pain, maybe even going to pass out. He tapped him in the ribs with the toe of his shoe to get his attention. "Anyone know you came out here?"

"No."

Figures. Wouldn't want to say where he was going; then he might have to explain *why* he was going there.

DeWayne bent over and started foraging for the cash Lenny had held back from him, the three thousand bucks, fully expecting to find it the way he had so many times before, putting his hand on the stash as if by magic. But this time the cupboard was bare. He turned the wounded man over and, ignoring his cries of pain, roughly searched his pockets again, his hands now smeared with blood. He found a wallet and opened it up and couldn't believe the name on the license— not Lenny but some guy named Arthur Barsamian. He found the guy's shield. The same thing. Who the fuck was Arthur Barsamian and why was he doing all these horrible things to DeWayne Reardon? What had DeWayne ever done to him? And why hadn't he brought the money and the wrapping paper like he said he would?

Bliss was on the phone talking to his wife while Martin was at the sink washing dishes.

"So you're telling me you can't get back in time to say good-bye," she said.

"It's a complicated case."

"*You're* a complicated case."

"So you've said."

"Who's going to watch the kids this afternoon?" she asked. "I leave for the airport in an hour."

"I thought your mother was staying."

"She's going to an opening at the Whitney later."

Still, he should be there to put Rachel's bags in the taxi, to kiss and hold her before she left for the land of *Baywatch*. He wanted to tell her he felt bad about it, but the words didn't come out.

"What do you propose we should we do?" she said.

"Can't Julia watch Cori for a little while?"

Martin had left the crème brûlée on the counter to cool. Bliss found a spoon and tasted it. The guy could definitely cook.

"Cori's a little scared right now. She had to wait at a crime scene while Daddy played This Little Piggy with a set of dead toes. So the answer is no, I don't think Julia can watch her."

"Shit. I'm sorry."

"I know it's not all your fault, but she's deeply worried— about you, about me, about what's in her closet and under her bed. Not purple monsters but real men with evil faces who want to hurt me, you, Julia, everyone she knows. She needs an adult here, and I have to go to California soon. So what should we do?"

Bliss heard the front door to the apartment open.

"Ask your mother to stay for a little while. An hour. Two at the most. I think things are winding up here."

"Fine. I'll ask her. Hold on a second."

While he waited, he dug a huge divot out of the brûlée and shoved it into his mouth. Rachel returned to the phone.

"She's says she'll do it if you agree to a divorce."

He tried to swallow and laugh at the same time, but he had taken in too much brûlée.

"She's a real kidder isn't she," Rachel added.

His mouth was too full to talk, and he could only manage a few choked grunts.

"Are you being strangled, Lenny? Does the killer have his hands around your throat? Let me speak to him. Right now! Put him on."

Now he *was* laughing.

"Hold the phone to his ear."

She was making it worse. It would be coming out of his nose soon.

"Hello . . . Mr. Bad Guy, that's my husband you're throttling. He may be a putz, but I'm not ready for him to die."

He snorted and splattered Martin's counter with a shower of what Bliss suspected was now more crème than brûlée.

He gasped and caught his breath.

"You're funny," he said. "Did you know that?"

"Yes," she said.

"And thanks for not wanting me dead yet."

"Don't mention it."

"Say hi to Clint."

"Sure. Bye."

"Bye."

He put down the phone and steeled himself to deal with Martin Roderick, the man he was beginning to feel sure was responsible for putting at least some of those bad men in his daughter's closet.

Promise walked into the kitchen.

"Well, this is a cozy picture," she said. "More domestic bliss than I've seen around here in a while—no pun intended." She turned to him. "You have something on your chin."

Bliss wiped off some brûlée.

"Couldn't stay away from Martin's cooking, Detective? Maybe you should move in." She took off her sunglasses. "If you want, you can have my spot."

Chapter 28

Ward saw the taxi and behind it another car with NYPD plates. Maybe that was DeWayne's car, but it didn't make sense that he would still have police tags. Maybe he had some friends over. Ward hoped they wouldn't start any trouble. He didn't like those boys. Dirty cops. He wasn't going to put up with any shit. He wanted his partner's gun, and he was going to get it.

He walked up the front steps and silently entered the hallway. It smelled as bad as the girl had said it would. He heard something coming from up the stairs—a low moaning. He took out his piece and moved up the stairs two at a time.

He peeked around the top landing and saw a man down, bleeding badly. Ward swung out into the hall, gun pointing at the man's head.

"You Reardon?" he asked.

The man was in serious pain. He tried to speak, but nothing came out. Ward caught a glimpse of what apparently was the guy's shield lying by his feet.

"Reardon in there?"

The cop's eyes came alive for a moment. Ward took that as a yes. Ward took out his cell phone, called in for an ambulance, then inched along the wall to the edge of the door. He wanted to help the wounded man, but he was lying directly in the doorway. Ward had to apprehend DeWayne first. Immobilize him, possibly by shooting him in the head.

He looked at the wounded man. He was barely breathing, his eyes were closed. It was going to be touch and go for him.

Ward had two ways he could play it: barge in and shoot

first, ask questions later. Or try to talk to him. The guy on the floor had lost too much blood. Ward took that as his cue to enter.

He moved into the room quickly, crouching low, gun out. He saw DeWayne. He was facing the fridge, his back to the door. He was casually holding the gun at his side, for the moment pointed at the floor.

Bliss suggested they go into the study. On the way, he filled Promise in about how James died.

"So my sister didn't kill him," she said.

"No."

"I'm relieved, and at the same time disappointed. Killing James would have meant that she was still jealous of me, that she coveted everything I had."

"But you never really *had* James, did you?" Bliss asked.

"That's true. Say, you're *more* than just a detective, aren't you Mr. Bliss."

"So they tell me."

Promise sat on the couch, Martin in his chair. Bliss moved to a space between them.

"I might as well cut to the chase," he said.

"If James wasn't murdered, what more do we have to talk about?" Promise asked.

"Wolf."

"The one who was molesting James? The one who had his hands around James's throat? Why do we have to talk about him?"

"He's dead."

"Good," she said. "One down, three to go."

It was going better than Martin could possibly have imagined. He couldn't have written her a better line. She had practically incriminated herself already. A chill ran through him as the detective reached into his pocket and pulled out a glas-

sine envelope. There was something shiny inside. Something
metal and round. The moment of truth had arrived. All his
planning, coming down to this moment. He forced himself to
keep a straight face. He forced himself to resist telling her
how well his plan was going.

That was the only problem. He couldn't gloat.

Bliss casually angled himself so that his back was toward
Martin. Then he held out the earring, the one he had just
bought on the street for three dollars. The other one, the earring found by Wolf's body, he kept in his pocket. He was playing a hunch, hoping Martin would get cute.

"What about this earring, Mrs. Roderick?" Bliss asked.

"I've never seen it before," Promise said.

"Are you sure? Look at it closely." He held it so that his
back completely blocked Martin view.

"Absolutely," she said. "I've never owned a piece of jewelry
like that."

No one spoke. Bliss's hunch didn't seem to be panning out.

Then Martin saved the day.

"Darling, isn't that one of the earrings that . . . Oh dear."

Martin put his hand over his mouth.

"What were you about to say, Mr. Roderick?" the detective
asked him.

"Nothing."

"But you started to say something, as if perhaps you recognized the earring."

Martin looked helplessly at Promise, pretending he *didn't*
want to incriminate her. Pretending he'd let something slip
out that he shouldn't have. He was sorry, he told her with his
eyes. *Who's the actor now?* he thought.

"Go ahead, Martin," Promise said. "Say what you were
going to say."

"No, I—"

"Say it, please."

"I—I just thought it was one of the earrings your sister gave you."

"You're sure, Mr. Roderick?" the detective asked him.

"If you look on the back you'll see they came from Tiffany's." Then he turned to Promise. "Honey, I'm so sorry," he said, his face awash with worry and remorse.

"These aren't from Tiffany's. These are junk," she jeered. "They're cheap shit, like you buy on the street."

"What?"

"Yeah, I don't see anything saying they're from Tiffany's, Mr. Roderick," the detective said.

Martin's hands sprang to life. He forced them back in his lap. None of this was in the script.

"Look again," he said, trying to keep his voice steady. "I'm sure it's there."

"No. I'm quite certain," the detective said, like he was gloating. "Do you see any marks, Mrs. Roderick?"

"No. I'm telling you, they're junk." Then Promise stared at her husband, her eyes narrow, charged with suspicion. "Why did you think these were the earrings my sister gave me, Martin? Why?"

He sprang from the chair and grabbed the earring out of Bliss's hand, jabbing the post into his finger as he did. It *was* a cheap piece of shit. Not the evidence his man was supposed to have left under Wolf's body. Martin was hit with a wave of panic. What had happened? Fear rose up in his throat.

He burst out of the room and ran down the hall. He returned moments later, gasping for breath, and practically threw the suitcase at the detective's feet.

"Her bag. Look! I found it in the closet. Packed. And *look!*" He unzipped the outside pocket. "Here! Her passport. She was about to take off. To run away. To flee the scene of the crime. She must have planned it all."

"Is that true, Mrs. Roderick?"

"No," she said.

Martin could tell that the detective believed her. How could that be? How could he believe *her*?!

"The travel agent called! This morning! She's flying to St. Croix! One ticket! Open ended! She was never coming back!"

"Martin . . ." she said, like he was her dog and he'd just peed where he wasn't supposed to.

He tore open the zipper.

"Here," he said, holding the gun for the detective to see. "In her bag! The gun that shot Wolf! It's evidence! *Look*, why don't you?!"

The detective was on him in a flash, twisting the gun from his hand and practically breaking his wrist. A searing pain shot through his arm. Then he was off his feet and landing facedown on the rug, the detective on top of him. He gasped for breath. The detective now had his knee leaning on his neck, ramming his cheek into the rough broadloom.

Then all was still, except for the detective panting above him. Then he heard her voice, a jagged knife cutting through him to his heart.

"Oh, Martin."

He felt the detective rise.

Martin was in tremendous discomfort. He didn't want to get up. He curled up on his side, pulling his knees to his chest.

He would call his man tonight! That's what he would do. Have him take care of Promise once and for all. *Take out the garbage*—meaning take out Promise.

"Mr. Roderick . . ."

It's what he should have done right from the start.

"Mr. Roderick . . ."

The cop, too. Mr. Clever Detective. Take out *his* garbage, too.

"*Martin!*"

His wife's voice snapped him out of it.

"Yes?"

"Martin, the detective has something to tell you," his wife said, her voice cool and collected, barely containing her sense of victory. "And if I'm not mistaken, I think it involves finding yourself a good lawyer."

"Drop the gun, DeWayne," Ward said.

But DeWayne didn't drop the gun. He didn't turn around. He just stood there, his back to Ward, holding the gun at his side. He didn't seem to hear.

"And get your other hand where I can see it."

DeWayne didn't do that either.

"You Lenny?" he asked.

"I'm Lenny's partner."

"So who's that other guy—Barsamian?"

So that was Artie in the hall. How'd he wind up here?

"That's Lenny's other partner."

"What'd they have a sale?"

"Drop the gun, DeWayne."

"I think Lenny needed two partners because he was such a fuck-up."

Ward needed to work it through: DeWayne standing there, Artie dying, Lenny's gun . . . Something had to happen right now.

"I'm trying to figure out how to salvage something from all this," Ward said.

"Sometimes you just got to go with your gut," DeWayne said. "You know. Like, what the fuck."

"Yeah. What the fuck, DeWayne."

DeWayne wasn't moving. Not doing anything. Then he gave a deep sigh, shoulders rising, then sagging. As if resigned to some kind of decision. Then he raised his hand, the one not holding the gun. His pants fell down.

"I'm going to make this easy for you," DeWayne finally said.

"You're doing the right thing, DeWayne," Ward said, still pointing his gun directly at DeWayne's head.

"That's a laugh. Me, doing the right thing." He sucked in deeply. "Tell Antoinette, the kids . . ."

Artie was gasping louder now.

"You gotta do it quick, DeWayne."

"The railing. Tell her I never fixed the railing. Tell her I got presents for the kids in the trunk of the cab. The keys are on the table—if you can find them. And also, tell her I'm sorry."

"Do it, DeWayne!"

"Yeah. I gotta do it. Yeah. I'm going to turn around now and I'm going to bring up the gun and . . . ahh, what the fuck, you'll figure out the rest."

DeWayne turned slowly and raised the gun slowly, moving it in no particular direction, just raising it, almost in some kind of supplication.

Ward shot him once. The bullet went into his head, jerking it back and slightly to the left. He collapsed in a heap. Just crumpled silently. And that was the end of DeWayne Reardon, Ward thought, at least as we knew him here on earth.

Sirens.

"Hang on, Artie!" he shouted as he took Bliss's gun from DeWayne's hand and stuffed it in his pocket.

"Keep breathing!"

Ward checked the wall by the doorframe, shoulder height, and found the slug. The one from Bliss's gun that had gone through Artie. He took out his pocketknife, using his teeth to open the blade, and very carefully pried out the slug from the plaster. He put it in the pocket with Bliss's gun. From his other pocket he pulled out a cloth. Like a magician, he thought. In the cloth was the slug he'd sucked out of his hand. He pressed it into the hole. It fit well enough. The paper bag was on the couch. The girl was as good as her word. In the bag he found DeWayne's gun and a cassette of *Live at Fillmore East.* He held the gun with a T-shirt he found stuffed in the couch, so he wouldn't get his prints on it, and left it by DeWayne's hand. He put the Allman Brothers tape in his pocket.

No one was going to look into this too closely. Ward had DeWayne to thank for that. De-ranged DeWayne. More of his erratic, self-destructive behavior. Now he was trying to shake down a cop. Pretending he had his gun. It was an act of such desperation by a former New York City police officer that no one would want it revealed. Artie could easily be persuaded to not say anything. Only Ward knew that DeWayne had done the right thing in the end. He'd try to remember to tell the wife about the presents in the trunk.

He moved beside Artie and knelt by his head. Damn, he'd lost a lot of blood. But he was still breathing as the paramedics tore around the stairwell and emerged into the hall and set down their boxes and got to work.

"Hold on, Artie," Ward said, holding his hand. "Please."

The paramedics were hooking up an IV to Artie.

"How's he look?" Ward asked.

"He'll make it," one of them said. "What about that guy?" he asked, referring to DeWayne.

"He's at peace," Ward said.

Act VI

Chapter 29

Bliss had spent most of the past twenty-four hours in the hospital with Artie until he was sure his partner was out of the woods. Ward and Malikha took turns watching his kids. When he spoke to Julia on the phone, she said he could take his time coming home.

Bliss was taking it hard. The consequences of his foolishness had escalated beyond anything he had imagined. He wanted someone to blame. And he wanted someone to forgive him.

Ward tried.

"He had no business going there," Ward said, his voice a whisper as they stood in the corner of the hospital room, watching the tubes attached to Artie lifting gently with every breath.

"But he *did* go there. For me."

"To *impress* you."

"Same thing."

"Pride goeth before the fall."

"Still, it's because of me he got shot."

Artie's mother sat next to her son, holding his hand while he rested. She wore a look of such maternal beneficence that Bliss felt there was no way she would allow her son to die. But so much else had gone wrong in the past few days, he knew he couldn't count on the will of one mother alone to rescue him.

"He's going to be a better person because of this," Ward said. "You'll see."

"Better how?"

"Hey, Lenny . . ."

It was Artie, his eyes half open, a kind of timid smile on his face.

"Hey, partner," Bliss said.

"I guess I fucked up," Artie said.

"Artie, don't curse," his mother scolded.

"Sorry, Mom."

"You did fine, Artie," Bliss said, but his words sounded hollow. "DeWayne was crazy. No one has a chance against someone like that."

"Ward did," Artie said. "Ward had more than a chance. Ward took him down."

"Ward's like Shane," Bliss said, "like the man who shot Liberty Valance. He's the stuff of legends."

"Still . . ." Artie said. Then he closed his eyes and drifted off. His mother shushed Bliss and edged him away.

"Let him sleep," she said, her voice tired but firm. "Let my boy rest," she said. "You've done enough."

More than enough, Bliss thought.

But maybe Ward was right. Maybe Artie had lost some of his innocence along with his blood. Left it back in the hallway of DeWayne's apartment. In a couple of months they'd find out.

Ward took him by the elbow and led him into the hall. He waited for Artie's door to shut before he spoke.

"We've got to return to normal, partner," Ward said. "We each took a little detour. Now we'll get back to doing what we do best."

He held out his hand and slowly opened it to reveal a bullet.

"It's the one I took from DeWayne's wall, that went through Artie's shoulder. The one from your gun."

Bliss stared at it like it was a specter from his past, a child he'd abandoned, now standing in front of him, wanting justice, wanting reparations. He felt weary.

"Keep it for me," Bliss said. "Tuck it away somewhere."

"Sure, partner."

Bliss turned back to Artie and watched the gentle rise and fall of his chest—each breath, Bliss hoped, one degree closer to recovery. Bliss quietly whispered his prayer, the one for opening the ark. It was the only prayer he knew.

The kids were in the park with Malikha, and he was home alone when Rachel finally called.

"You'll never guess where I am," she said.

"Swimming naked with Warren Beatty," he said.

"Close," Rachel replied. "Just kidding. Actually I'm on a jungle gym. Can you believe it?"

She sounded younger.

"It's the newest kind of workout in L.A. Clint's people got me a session with him."

"*Him?*"

"Roberto. It's incredible that I'm even here. There's a *huge* waiting list. It's not like a workout. It's like play. Like you're a kid again. Playing. Goofing around. Only Roberto has it all figured out so you also get a really serious workout. You do the seesaw, the monkey bars, climb up the pole—"

"Whose pole?"

"—Chin-ups, even a trapeze bar. Right now I'm talking on the cellular and sitting on the swing."

Then she laughed and he heard her say, *Wait, not so high!*

"You know who I saw on my way out? Susan Anspach."

"Who's she?" he asked.

"An actress."

"Did you tell your mother? She'll be excited."

"You know, they may be a lot of things out here in L.A., but one thing they're *not* is sarcastic."

"So how will you fit in?"

She chose to ignore the question.

"How are the kids?"

"Great. Ward and Malikha have been watching them."
Silence. "Rachel?"

Silence.

"Rachel, it's okay."

"Good. That's, um . . . good."

"How are the story conferences?"

"Fine. Except all Clint wants is to hear about your exploits."

"Sorry."

"And which jazz guys you like. I told him Stan Kenton. Was that okay?"

"I hope he knew you were kidding."

Then she was laughing again. "This is fun!"

He couldn't tell if she was speaking to him or Roberto.

"Will you call later so the kids can talk to you?" he asked.

"I have meetings all afternoon. But I'll definitely call before they go to sleep."

"By the way, nothing funny has happened. You haven't missed anything good."

"Okay. Listen, I've gotta go now."

"Say hi to Clint."

"Um . . . sure. Bye."

"Bye."

He was worried. It didn't have anything to do with Roberto. She had just as low a tolerance for insouciance as he did. But it was the laughter that ate him up, the fact that she was having fun. Fun he couldn't compete with. People enjoying life in any kind of obvious way—like smiling, like looking contented. His strengths were irony, despondency, getting an extra pickle with his sandwich. Bliss didn't know from fun. Once that door opened up and the wanton sunshine started to peek through, it was very hard to get it shut again. They'd Jacuzzi Rachel until she was blithe and content and he'd never be with her again.

So maybe Bliss had to find fun—make it part of his inner

celebrity, the journey he had to take. He'd start by taking the kids out for pizza—which he'd planned on doing anyway, whether fun was involved or not, since there was no one around to cook dinner.

Chapter 30

STRANGE DOINGS AT PERFORMANCE WAREHOUSE

It started out as an ordinary evening in the theater—that is, if any evening at the Performance Warehouse could be considered ordinary—when one of the audience members unexpectedly walked onto the stage. At first the rest of the audience thought it was part of their current show *James and/or Macbeth*, a fragmented retelling of the death of James Roderick, a former member of the theater. But soon the audience realized that even for the surrealist-influenced Performance Warehouse, this was out of the ordinary.

The unanticipated guest on stage turned out to be Lenny Bliss, the New York City police detective who handled the Roderick case. He emerged from the shadows and cava-lierly strode onto the stage. The cast was moving in a cir-cle around the prone body of the actor playing the deceased James, who lay inside the chalk outline that the program notes indicate was the original one the police drew when the body was first discovered.

Curiously, the detective didn't say anything. He stood next to the cast, arms crossed, slowly shaking his head and making a soft "tsk-tsk" sound, reminiscent of a parent coming home to find that his child had broken something precious and irreplaceable.

As the actors became aware of this staunch figure, they gradually stopped chanting. One by one they hung their heads in what seemed to be collective shame, and the performance stopped.

After a few minutes the houselights came up, and an announcement was made that the show was cancelled for that evening, and we would be getting our money back. At which point the silent detective walked off the stage and out into the street.

Life imitating art? Art imitating life? Let the postmodernist theater critics sort that out. As for this reviewer, I chose not to ask for my money to be refunded, as the events that transpired that night were about the most interesting I'd seen in the theater in quite a long time.

Bliss was up on the *bima*, standing next to the rabbi, looking out over the pews in the synagogue. It was Bas Mitzvah rehearsal, and even though he only had to pretend to open the ark, Bliss had become overwhelmed by a surge of feelings running recklessly through him.

"Did you forget your line, Dad?" Julia asked him.

She looked so grown up, so much not a kid anymore, standing by the podium. Even her babyish petulance had evolved into a more advanced and mature species of disappointment reminiscent of her mother.

"No, honey," he said. "I'm just . . . it's just that . . ."

The rabbi came to his rescue.

"Your father's wrestling with a number of big emotions right now," he explained to Julia in a solemn, rabbinical way. "This is just as big a day for him as it is for you. In many ways, even bigger."

"Yeah," Julia said. "He's got to pay for it."

"Julia," the rabbi said with Talmudic seriousness, "sarcasm is not appropriate for a Bas Mitzvah."

"I have one last day. I'm trying to cram in as much as I can."

Bliss sensed that was his cue—time for him to jump. He cleared his throat and in a loud, clear voice announced to the empty seats that the ark was about to open and his daughter was about to become an adult. And with his words, he prayed that he, Lenny Bliss, her father, would discover how to be a mature, wise, and responsible person—or at least be able to do a better impersonation of someone who was.

"There's one," Jason said. He bent down and brushed aside a few oak leaves to reveal a large morel. Cone shaped, nut brown, and crinkly, it looked somehow prehistoric. Li-Jung's father had had a bag of dried black mushrooms that he kept locked up in a drawer in the restaurant. He soaked them for a few hours until they puffed up and softened. Two very thin slices, and *only* two, would go in each bowl of wonton soup.

"Mushrooms have no roots," Jason said. "Did you know that?"

No roots.

"Like me," she said.

She watched him gently lift the mushroom from the soft dirt, then held out the basket and he added it to the collection. This one made eight, and it was by far the largest.

"Not bad," he said. "These sell for sixty dollars a pound in New York."

"But we can't go back to New York," she said. "Or at least I can't."

"Sorry," he said.

He reached out his hand and she took it. She wasn't sure if she was liking him more because she had to or because she was falling in love with him. For the moment she was content not to know.

"You want to keep going?"

"Sure."

The woods seemed especially comforting that afternoon. Part of it was being away from the city, from the craziness of the past few days. And part of it was that this time the forest was not her enemy, the dark and dangerous site of a perpetual deflowering. Instead she was discovering treasures. The woods giving her something back, as if repaying an old debt. The trees were just beginning to bud, and there were no leaves to disrupt the sun. She could see the tiny sprouts of ferns pushing their way through the fallen branches and rotting leaves. Was it her imagination, or was there rebirth all around her?

Jason stopped and pulled her to him and kissed her. He was becoming somewhat bolder, though in a cute way. But for the moment there was no sex. They were staying with Jason's parents, who seemed very nice and hadn't asked too many questions about how she and Jason had met. They were sleeping in separate rooms. His parents wanted it that way. Actually, she did, too. So she could get to know him. A kind of courtship.

She was staying in Jason's older sister's room. It was the room she'd always wanted as a kid. There was a dresser with trophies and lots of team photos. The desk had a turquoise typewriter sitting on it with a model of the Statue of Liberty beside it. The bookcase was packed with books, from Dr. Seuss to *Siddhartha*. There was shag carpeting on the floor and a Grateful Dead psychedelic skull poster on one of the walls.

But what Li-Jung was especially drawn to was the bed. A single bed, with an old-fashioned wooden headboard. It was tucked in the corner and covered with a white chenille spread like grandmothers are supposed to have, patterned with those little knobby things. And against the wall was a pile of stuffed animals—bears and tigers and a funny looking monkey and a grinning raccoon that looked like it had just ransacked the garbage. That first night she had lain down on the bed and covered herself with the animals, arking herself and imagining that she floated above the flood that she hoped would swallow up and drown all the troubles and fears she'd ever suffered through in her life. She hugged the bears and tigers and closed her eyes and waited for the waters to rise and for her past to become a blur, a distant memory—a landscape covered by the rain-drenched sea that would soon become the stuff of legend and then, one day, be forgotten and disappear forever.